Healing Forces

A LAKE HARMONY NOVEL

TANJA WALTRIP

ACKNOWLEDGEMENTS

Healing Forces, the fifth book of my Lake Harmony, weaves threads of harmony and balance into the fabric of each narrative. My holistic belief practice has been the gentle whisper guiding me toward authenticity and connection. It has infused these pages with a deeper understanding of love's power to heal and transform. With a heart full of gratitude and love, I offer this story to honor the magic of romance, the power of belief, and the warmth of community. I would also like to thank my readers for being a part of this beautiful journey.

DEDICATION

To my dear friends Brian Michael Myers & Jon Grant,

Your vulnerability and honesty have been the cornerstone of Jax's evolution, guiding him through the darkest of times towards the light of healing and self-discovery. In honoring your struggles and triumphs, we celebrate the transformative power of resilience and the boundless capacity of the human spirit to rise above adversity.

With deepest gratitude and admiration, this book is dedicated to you both. May your stories continue to ripple through the world, igniting sparks of courage and healing in all who encounter them.

With love and appreciation,

Tanja

Contents

ACKNOWLEDGEMENTS 3
DEDICATION 3
Chapter One.. 9
Chapter Two... 13
Chapter Three 19
Chapter Four 23
Chapter Five... 31
Chapter Six 35
Chapter Seven 43
Chapter Eight 51
Chapter Nine 59
Chapter Ten 63
Chapter Eleven 67
Chapter Twelve 75
Chapter Thirteen 79
Chapter Fourteen 83
Chapter Fifteen 91
Chapter Sixteen 95
Chapter Seventeen 101
Chapter Eighteen 105
Chapter Nineteen 111
Chapter Twenty.. 119
Chapter Twenty-One 123
Chapter Twenty-Two 127
Chapter Twenty-Three 133
Chapter Twenty-Four 139
Chapter Twenty-Five 147
Chapter Twenty-Six 151
Chapter Twenty-Seven... 157
Chapter Twenty-Eight.. 161
Chapter Twenty-Nine 167
Chapter Thirty 173
Chapter Thirty-One... 181
Chapter Thirty-Two... 187
Chapter Thirty-Three 193
Chapter Thirty-Four.. 199

Chapter Thirty-Five 203
Chapter Thirty-Six 211
Chapter Thirty-Seven 215
Chapter Thirty-Eight...221
Chapter Thirty-Nine..225
Chapter Forty 229
Chapter Forty-One..233
Chapter Forty-Two 237
Chapter Forty-Three 245
Chapter Forty-Four 251
Chapter Forty-Five 257
Chapter Forty-Six...263
Chapter Forty-Seven...267
Chapter Forty-Eight..271
Chapter Forty-Nine 275
Chapter Fifty 281
Epilogue...285
About the Author 291

Chapter One

Stella

"I did it! I really did it!" I sing to myself as I throw my hands up in the air and dance a silly jig before I take a deep exhale.

I walk through my wellness studio, stop, and sit on the beautiful window bench that runs along the front of the shop and curl my legs underneath me. I know I'm the youngest of five, and it doesn't help that I was potentially an oops baby, but I feel like my family has never taken me seriously. I get that I've lived a floaty life and, instead of taking the traditional road to college, I left home to travel and find my own way. My family refers to me and my way of living as a gypsy or hippie. I'm okay with that because I know they love me and have allowed me to follow the universe when it was pulling me to yet another opportunity.

I've worked in various jobs including waitressing, being a nanny, dog walking, and always following my heart and eventually ending up in Sedona. That's where it all finally came together, and I learned to catch my breath and listen. In Sedona, I learned from a holistic healer how to finally focus on my own beliefs and why I need the energy that I do in my life to feel complete.

I landed in Sedona about four years ago when I was heading home from living in California for a bit. As soon as I found myself among the amazing red rock formations, I began feeling a new energy pull. I had to stop to find my grounding. I know, hippy-dippy woo-woo stuff, but it was as if I could finally take a deep enough breath and relax. I've learned from my wandering ways to listen to my heart and let the universe guide me. It took me straight into Sedona and to the doorstep of the woman who helped me heal my soul and find my purpose, Tillie.

Matilda, who goes by Tillie, is a holistic intuitive who works with energy healing and meditation. She taught me how to relax and clear my energy blocks, restore my balance, and protect myself. The lessons I learned allow me to now share my knowledge with others, helping them find their balance using the power of their mind to create a relaxed and focused state.

All of those lessons bring me to this moment. I'm sitting in my wellness studio, Mint and Sage, which will teach that knowledge to others through yoga, meditation, and my natural essential oil products. The shop is done and ready for our soft opening this weekend. My family and friends have given me their time and strength to get this place open and ready. It's beautiful, and I'm proud of what I've accomplished.

"Hey sweets, I was wondering where you ran off to," Griffin says as he walks into the studio. Griffin is my best friend and shares the apartment above the studio with me. He also works for our friend Hillary at her catering business. Hillary also happens to be married to my oldest brother, and sheriff of Lake Harmony, Garrett.

"Hey Griff, I was just sitting here taking a moment to appreciate what we've accomplished." He sits down next to me, puts his arm around me, and drags me in closer.

"I think you've got that wrong Stella. This is all you, honey. This studio is your dream come true and your accomplishment alone."

I smile at him, "I couldn't have gotten it finished without everyone's help though, Griff, and you and I both know that."

He taps me on the nose, "Maybe, but I also know that the vision of this," he gestures around the room, "is all you, Stella. We only helped make sure your vision became a reality. The studio, the classes, the products, the customers…that's all YOU, honey. Please take the kudos you are being given because you deserve all of it and more!"

I hug him and rest my head against his shoulder. "It is pretty awesome, isn't it?"

"It's fucking awesome, and I am so proud of you!"

We both sit a little longer and take it all in. "I still can't believe I finally have my own studio. I feel like I've finally accomplished something on my own. Something that my family can be proud of me for. I hated feeling like I never measured up to my sisters and brothers. At least now I feel like I'm right there with them. I have my own business, and I got here without their financial help. I did it myself."

"You sure did, and they know that. I know they tease you all the time but that's because you're the little sister." Griffin continues, "And maybe you didn't follow a map, but you still found your destination. You've always lived your life by your own rules. Hell, I've tried to follow your example because, when I look at my bestie and see how she's blooming, even with some of the teasing, I know if you can do it, maybe I can too."

"Griff, you are amazing, and don't ever feel less than, okay? You know how much I love you, and my family loves you. Even if you flirt shamelessly with my brothers and their friends, they'd do anything for you. You, my flirty friend, have some amazing people that would do just about anything you need. You're stuck with them now, so stop it. Plus, my parents have adopted you so no matter what life throws your way you will never be alone. We don't have to be blood-related to love you. We are your family."

"Have I thanked you for saving me and believing in me?" He asks.

"Hmm, not today, but you don't ever have to thank me for loving you. You're my bestie. I know you miss your family, but if they can't love and support who you are, then they don't deserve you."

"Love you, Stella bug."

"Love you too, Griffin."

"Tomorrow is the big day, and this place looks amazing. I think Mint and Sage is going to be a huge success! Are you ready to head up, and eat a big bowl of ice cream before we go watch some housewives be ridiculous?"

"That sounds amazing! Dibs on the Oreo ice cream!" I say.

Chapter Two

Jax

I'm stretched out on the couch relaxing. I've been memorizing lines for the last two days and have two weeks before I start filming. This role is a drama where I play a young father. Scary, right? Maybe I should go home before we start and see if Bree will let me watch baby Jameson for a bit. Then again, what the hell do I know about babies? Fake it until you make it, they say. Good thing I'm an actor and the kids in this film aren't babies.

My phone buzzes and I see it's Sophie's calling. Sophie is my best friend, also an actor, and Hollywood's current It Girl who had to deal with a stalker, so I hid her in my hometown where she fell in love with a local. Thankfully, he's from a great family and I know him from all of us growing up together.

"Hey, you! I miss you so much. I can't believe you went to Lake Harmony and fell in love and left me to die here alone in LA."

"Hello, Jax. I see you are still in the guilt-throwing stage," Sophie laughs. "I did not leave you to die. I came here, fell in love with an amazing man, and didn't leave. You're the reason I'm here."

"I know, but I'd rather make you feel guilty than make myself feel bad. I'm lonely. I miss my best friend."

"You're ridiculous, and nothing says you need to stay in LA. Come and move back here with me in Lake Harmony. You already have the lot and house going up next door."

"I'm not sure I'm ready for that yet," I tell her. "I'll be a bachelor forever I if come home now. I'll move eventually. That's why we have our best-friend houses being built next to each other on the lake, but I still want to have a home base here in LA. It wouldn't be so bad if the guys weren't touring still."

"When is this tour over for Brick Row?" Sophie asks.

"They're heading home this week for the fourth of July on a family break but then head back out on the road to close out the Brick Row tour for eight more weeks. Mattie wants to be home when his kiddos start school."

"I can't believe they're both going to be in school already. I remember when his youngest was born, and now she's going into kindergarten. Did you hear that he called Bree to find out what types of books and learning materials he should have to make sure his school was providing the right curriculum?"

"Yeah, Bree called and told me. She thinks it's hilarious that Mattie, the famous rock band drummer, constantly calls her or Noah for their opinions."

"I agree with Mattie. It's nice having two doctors as good friends. I'm so happy here, Jax. Your friends, who are now my good friends, make it feel like home. I don't have to worry about WHY people want to be my friend here."

"Sophie, you're a Hollywood actress who is loved by pretty much everyone in America, but I agree. When I come home to Lake Harmony, they treat me like a nobody. Not an actor from LA that was just listed in the Hottest Men of Hollywood magazine article."

"Rob, Time! How long did it take?" Sophie yells.

"About five minutes. You win," Rob, her boyfriend, yells back to her while I am on the phone hearing this commotion.

"Um…what the hell is going on?" I ask. Sophie is laughing, and I can hear her talking to Rob and not to me, "HELLO?? No worries. I'll just sit here and talk to myself while you have a conversation with Rob. No, I don't have anything better to do than listen to your side conversation. I could be relaxing or running my lines but no…."

"Sorry, Jax. Rob came to bring me ice cream and a kiss. He sends his hello," Sophie says.

"That's nice but what was all the yelling about time?"

"We had a bet going on how long it would take for you to talk about your new Hottest Man status, and I won! So, he brought me a kiss and my winning ice cream."

"Thanks, I think…but what if he won?"

"You don't want to know but it also involved ice cream."

"Gotcha. Hey, I didn't nominate myself for that. I can't help it that my charming good looks are so great they put me on a list."

"You are too much. I love you and I do think you're charming and handsome. We're just teasing, but you're going to get harassed when you come here. Hillary said the guys were posing with your smolder pose at poker last week," Sophie laughs.

"Oh god, that is humiliating."

"Yep. She was cracking up because they were all looking in the mirror trying to match your pose, and she was supposed to pick the best guy."

"Garrett won, right? I mean she is married to the guy."

"Of course, but Rob was a close second. Anyway, go back to this week. Are you hanging with the band while they are home for the fourth or going somewhere else?" she asks.

"You know I hate being out and about on holidays. Too many idiots out there drinking and being stupid. I told Mattie I'd come over to his place. It's going to be just their families and the kids. We're having a cookout and watching the kids in the pool. Then I'll head home because I have just about a week after that before I head to Seattle for the movie," I tell her.

"Are you ready for this one? I think it will be a good change for you to be in a family drama. It'll be fun watching you play a dad to little kids."

"Yeah, I was thinking about that earlier. I don't have a lot of experience with little kids, so it will be interesting. I'm just hoping their parents aren't crazy stage parents. I heard that can be a nightmare."

"You'll have to keep me posted. I'm heading over to the house this week. I can do a walkthrough of your place and send you a video if you aren't free to do the walkthrough with me. I love all the big walls of windows you have on your place.”

“I’d love that,” I say. “I can’t wait to see the view off the back of the house overlooking the lake. It’s going to be awesome.”

“Same. Rob has been working with Scott and Paul to make sure the outdoor spaces are just as good as the inside of the house. Rob thought it was ridiculous that you wanted a gate to open between our backyards with a path.”

“I don’t care what that mean guy has to say. He already gets to keep you, so when I am in Lake Harmony, I want to be able to walk over to your house without going all the way up to the road.”

“Jax?”

“Yeah?”

“I feel the same. That gate doesn’t even have to have a door as long as there is a path and opening. Love you, buddy.”

“Love you too, Soph. What are you two doing for the fourth? It’s a pretty big deal there in Lake Harmony. Parade, vendors, fireworks…you going to enjoy all of that?”

“Yes, and I can’t wait. Mom and Dad, Ollie and Chloe are all coming down to stay for the holiday. Mom likes it here and has enjoyed getting to know Rob’s family.”

“The Stones are good people, and you are a lucky girl. I’m happy you’re so happy.”

“Thanks. You’ll find your girl. I think you’ll find her when you least expect it. Just like me,” Sophie says with confidence.

“Should I get a stalker?” I ask her jokingly.

“No, never say that,” she gasps. “Man, that was a horrible experience for me, but you don’t need a crisis like that to find someone to love. I think for you to find it, you must be open to it.”

“I’m wide open.”

“Keep your eyes open, Jax. You are too amazing and HOT to not find someone to love you.”

“I am the HOTTEST.”

"And with that, I am going to go snuggle my man on the couch. I love you, buddy. Please say hi to the guys for me when you see them. Come home when you can."

"Nite, buddy," I say as I end the call.

Chapter Three

Stella

The studio is open, the sidewalk table in front has some of my products to help bring people inside, and I'm gathering my pamphlets for the studio and class offerings in my hand as someone comes from behind and wraps me in a bear hug.

"I am so damn proud of you, little sister," Garrett whispers.

I take a deep breath and relax before I turn my head and look into my oldest brother's eyes. "Don't you know better as a former special ops guy, and now the sheriff, than to walk up to someone and grab them without announcing yourself? I was ready to use my self-defense and kick you in the balls."

Garrett smiles sheepishly, "Sorry, Stella. I didn't mean for my surprise hug to scare you. Are you good? You still need to try to knock me down?"

"Stop being snarky, Garrett, and thank you for being proud of me. It's nice to hear that I've done something productive in your eyes."

"What are you talking about? You know I'm impressed with you and have told everyone to stop by and check out your shop."

"It's just a change from the usual. That's all. Don't worry about it. I'm heading out in a second for a yoga in the park session. I'm just waiting for Mom to get here. Are you on duty or do you want to walk and talk with me?"

"I'd be happy to escort my awesome little sister to her yoga session. Is Hillary joining you today?" he asks.

"Don't think so," I tell him. "She's got her catering tent open today. As soon as I'm done, I have to head back to the studio and relieve Mom because Griffin is working with Hillary today at the tent. Hey, why do you not know where your wife is?"

"I left early today to help prep and block the streets for the parade. I wasn't sure if she was going to be at the tent today or just Griffin. Mom's coming to watch the store for you?"

"Yes, she offered, and I didn't have anyone else to ask other than Sophie, and she is still getting acclimated to living here and people leaving her alone," I say.

"Gotcha." Garrett says. "Julia is dealing with the vendor tents and parade getting set up. So, that leaves you with Mom….or Dad."

I look at my brother laughing, "Dad! That would have been funny though, huh?"

"I would have paid to see Dad in your shop answering yoga and meditation questions!" He laughs with me.

"How are my favorite kids doing today?" Mom asks.

"Hi Mom," I wave as she walks in. "Thank you for watching the studio. The yoga session is about an hour, then I can head back here. It shouldn't be too bad yet. The parade doesn't start until eleven, and I should be back way before when people start to line the street."

"Honey, don't worry about it," Mom says. "I can manage and brag about you at the same time. Josie is heading in after her stop at Ellen's to grab a drink and muffin. She said she would love to help sell your products and classes. She told her dance troupe to come by and drag their moms in with them."

"Oh, I'll have to thank her and maybe we could do a mom-and-daughter yoga session sometime. Hmm…something fun to think about. Okay, I need to head to the park and get set up. Since this is a soft opening for the studio, I don't expect it to get too crazy."

Mom raises an eyebrow, "Honey, I don't know about that. I hope you're prepared for a lot of interest. I've heard folks talking about your new place, and after Gertie posted her congratulations on Facebook, you know people are curious and will drop in to see what all the fuss is about."

"When did she post something on Facebook?" I ask.

"I think this morning because she saw you taking tables out front and your cute sign with the windchimes."

"Huh, okay. Mom, I need to get to the park, but I'll come right back after. Garrett, do me a favor and pull up Gertie's post while we walk over. I don't have my phone on me."

"You got it. Bye, Mom, see you later," he says.

"Bye, you two. Have a good morning."

"Stella, it's a nice announcement. Here." Garrett hands me his phone to read Gertie's post on the Harmony Hears Facebook page.

UNWIND, REJUVENATE & EMBRACE YOUR INNER ZEN @ MINT & SAGE

Are you tired of the daily hustle and bustle? Do you need a break from the chaos? Well, folks, your oasis of relaxation is finally here! Prepare to stretch, flow, and embrace your inner yogi with Stella Stone at her new wellness studio on Main Street @ Mint & Sage. She offers yoga and meditation classes to help find your inner balance with her carefully curated holistic products. Soft opening today, so stop and check it out!

"Wow!" I give his phone back to him.

"It's perfect! She is proud of you too, kiddo."

I plaster a big smile on my face and put my arm through his. "Come on, I need to get to the park so I can start the yoga class. After that post, I'd better be there to make sure the circus doesn't come through."

"I think Mom was right," Garrett says. "I hope you're prepared for a lot of people. Maybe we should have had Josie do a lemonade stand or something in front of the shop. On second thought, being right there on Main Street, you're going to get a lot of foot traffic. You may want to take your sidewalk sale stuff in during the parade."

I nod, "You're probably right. It'll open the area for the parade watchers. I was thinking I'd lock up during the parade anyway. I have a sign I can hang on the door telling them I'll be back after the parade is over."

"See! You are a very smart business owner already. I'm going to tell you again, since you need to hear it, I am so proud of you and your ability to get things done. I know I've teased you as you wandered the country finding your way, but you've shown me how responsible you are. You push for things that are important to you and that is very admirable, Stella. I love you, kiddo." My big brother hugs me, and I savor the strength in his hug. "Sorry if I made you feel any different before. Love you."

"Love you too. Now, I need to go get my yoga on."

Chapter Four

Jax

The food and drinks are overflowing on the tables, the kids are having a blast in the pool, and the music is beating on the sound system. This is a great day! I'm kicking back and enjoying the day with my good friends from the band Brick Row. They're taking a quick break from their music tour to come home for the fourth of July to be with their families and are allowing me to crash, as always. Mattie, their drummer, is in the pool with his two kids, along with Devin, the lead singer. Each is drinking a beer and has a kid on their shoulders playing chicken to see who can push the other off first. It's hilarious because we all know Mattie's little girl will be the winner. He's done a great job being a dad to his kids and teaching his son to be gentle with his little sister.

Josh, the guitarist, and the only other single guy here, comes to sit next to me. "How are you doing now that Sophie went and fell in love and left you for someone in your hometown? Are you going to join her there soon? I can't imagine you're happy not having your bestie close by."

I shake my head, "Nah, I'm heading to my next film soon and I'll be on set for three months. Once that's done, it'll be close to Christmas, so I'll take a quick break and go home, but then I'll be back here."

"Why are you building that huge house back at home on the lake then? Don't you plan on living in it?" Josh asks.

"Eventually," I say. "Sophie and Rob are building their place with privacy right on the lake, so I wanted to grab the lot next door and build a place too while it was available. Why not? Then I don't have to stay with my parents any time I head home. I can't lose investing money in real estate. Right now, I'm so busy bouncing from one film to the next that I may as well keep LA as my home base."

"I hear ya. But I'd think with her now there, you'd be itchy and wanting to move back too. You hate all the paps chasing after you, and sure, it's easy to find someone to have between the sheets here in LA, but you and I know it's no one of substance. They just want to be photographed on your arm."

"I know, and I hate that, but my hometown is small. It's not like I would find someone there to fall for because I know everyone. Plus, I'm not ready to settle down yet, are you?" I ask.

"Hell no! I may be the only one left, but I love being on tour. I can find someone to keep the bed warm anywhere I want."

"You're a pig, Josh."

"Whatever, but I'm also never lonely. I'm glad you have it worked out, though. Good for you, Jax. If you ever want to be my wingman after the tour wraps up let me know!"

"Will do." I stand up. "I'm going to head out. I'd like to get home before dark and avoid everyone out on the town for the fireworks."

Josh chuckles, "Okay, grandpa. It was great seeing you. I'm serious, though, if you want to hang out when we're back just let me know."

"Thanks, man, I appreciate it."

I walk around the pool saying goodbye to my friends and thanking Mattie's wife for including me. After twenty minutes and with a big plate of food I finally make my way to my car.

Today was a good day. Not as good as I'm sure Sophie's having in Lake Harmony with everyone. That town does know how to throw one hell of a party around the fourth. I text her as I get in the car.

Jax: Thinking of you. Hope you guys are having a blast today. Are you heading to the lake for fireworks?

It doesn't take her long until I see bubbles that she's responding.

Sophie: We are already here. Rob staked out a huge area with caution tape to reserve his spot for the fireworks. Of course, that means the rest of the gang is here. Even Bree with baby Jameson. Noah brought headphones to put on his little ears *laughing emoji* *Picture*

Jax: He's adorable. Sounds fun. Say hi to everyone. We can catch up later.
Sophie: 10-4 buddy. Love you. Happy 4th!!!
Jax: Love you too

I turn on some classic rock and put the car in drive to head home. I had fun today hanging out with the guys and their families. We always have fun, and it's nice to just kick back and relax with good food and friends.

I wind my way down Mattie's road listening to the radio and thinking about my movie and the location. I like being up north a little bit. Getting out of LA is always a nice treat. The LA congestion and air quality can get on my nerves. For this film, we'll be up in Seattle, and the view will be greener and the air a bit cleaner. My leading lady is a friend so that makes it fun. It's not the same as working with Sophie, but at least I know we can hang out and it won't get weird. She's married and has a family, so there won't be any drama or fake stories about us in the magazines. At least, I hope they have more class than to do that to her and her family.

I'm almost home, and as I drive around the corner, a car comes barreling toward me going too fast. They see me and try to adjust and move over out of the middle of the lane but lose control, and I watch as they come directly at me. I quickly swerved to try to get out of their way, but the car clipped the side of my driver's door. Next thing I know, I'm off the road and rolling down the embankment. My Audi crashes through trees and bushes. I hear glass shattering and metal tearing. Then, I come to a hard stop. My airbags are deployed, and I reach up and feel my face and see the blood on my hand as I pull it away. I hear the music still playing on the radio when darkness begins to surround me, and I give in to the pull to just close my eyes.

***

There's a strong antiseptic smell. I hear beeping around me. What the hell is going on? I fight to open my eyes with the bright light above me and see an older lady sitting next to me knitting. What the hell is going on, and why do I feel like shit? She glances over and me, places her knitting on her lap, and gives me a gentle smile.

"Oh, hello young man, it's good to see you waking up. My name is Margaret, and I'm a sitter here at the hospital. You're okay, but you were in quite the accident. I've been sitting here waiting for you to wake up. Let's push the nurse call button now." Margaret slowly gets up, pushes the button, and moves my hair off my face. "How are you feeling?"

"Water? Can you get me some water?" I barely got out a whisper and my throat is on fire. Why do I feel like my entire body is broken and where the fuck am I right now?

"Of course, dear. I have a pitcher here with cold water and a straw. Now, I'll hold it for you because with your injuries I don't think you can manage alone. Here, honey. Take small sips to start. I don't want you to make yourself sick."

The cold water running down my throat is heaven. My voice is scratchy and raw. "Thank you, Margaret. I appreciate your help."

I see a nurse come into the room and smile, "Hello Mr. Turner. It's good to see you awake. How are you feeling?"

I'm starting to remember now that I was heading home from Mattie's and got into an accident. "Like a car ran me off the road and I went four-wheeling in my Audi."

"Sounds about right. How's your pain level? Zero to ten?"

26

"Seven. Maybe eight. How serious are my injuries? My body hurts from top to bottom. Do you happen to have my phone?"

"You were in a car accident last night and have some injuries to your wrists and right knee. The orthopedic doctor who worked on you will be in soon. You knocked your head hard in the accident, and we had to stitch you up a bit but nothing to leave a mark. You have a concussion, and we have to be careful about what we give you for your pain, but I can bring you something now. The police brought in your personal belongings from the accident, and I believe your phone is in there. I can try to find a charger for you since it's probably dead." She looks over at the older woman, "Margaret, can you stay with Mr. Turner for a little longer in case he needs something?"

"Yes, dear. I have nowhere else to be right now."

The nurse walks out of the room, and Margaret looks at me with gentle eyes, "Mr. Turner is there anything else that I can do for you? Do you want some more water? I can just sit here and be quiet too. Whatever you need."

"Thank you, Margaret. I appreciate your help, and I'd love another sip of water." She brings me the cup of water, and I can see her scanning my face. "How bad do I look?" I ask.

She smiles at me with kind eyes, like my grandmother, "Well honey, you have some stitches and bruising on your face, but you're going to be fine. I'm not completely sure of your injuries but you have casts on both your wrists and one on your right leg. I'm sure you're in some pain, so I'm happy to help you with whatever you need. I have a grandson about your age. He's stubborn as a mule, so I imagine you are too. Do you need me to make any calls for you? Do you have a wife or girlfriend who may be worried sick about you? I should probably tell you that your accident was on the television. They've already been talking about you, so it isn't a secret that you're here. The nurse said your family has been calling all night for updates, and they have security outside to avoid unwanted visitors."

"Great. In that case, could you call someone for me right now? I better let them know I'm alive," I say.

"Sure sweetheart. Let me grab the phone, and you can tell me the number to call. I'm happy to step out of the room to give you some privacy."

"Thank you, Margaret. I appreciate you being here helping."

I give her the phone number to my mom and as soon as I say hello to my mom Margaret smiles and walks out of the room and shuts the door. "Hey Mom, before you go crazy on me, I'm fine. Banged up pretty good, but I'll live."

"Oh Jax, we've been a nervous wreck. Sophie's been calling since last night when the news broke. I'm getting on a plane as soon as I can, but I wanted to hear your voice first."

"Wait, what time is it?" I ask her.

"It's almost lunchtime for you, and it's July 5th."

"Jesus, I guess I've been out since the accident. I got hit driving home last night from Mattie's house. It wasn't even dark yet, and I wanted to get home and relax when a car came barreling around the corner and pushed me off the road. I went over the side and crashed the car. I hurt both wrists and my right knee, and I also have a concussion. I haven't seen the doctor yet for details, but you don't need to come out to LA."

"Nonsense," Mom says. "I'm coming and so is Sophie. I don't think you have a clear picture of the whole situation yet and what help you may need when you get home. I won't be able to settle down until I see you for myself. There is nothing you can say to keep me away."

"Okay. Please let Soph know I'm okay and ask her to call my manager. She knows how to get in touch with them. I don't have my cell phone, and I don't have their number handy."

"Don't you worry about a thing, honey. We'll get there as soon as possible and help wherever we can so you can focus on getting better. Thank God you're okay, Jax. I can't even think about how much worse it could have been. I'm sorry we aren't already there to help you."

"Thanks, Mom. I love you and I'll see you guys soon. I'm going to get some rest while I can. The drugs are making me tired." I get off the phone and feel completely exhausted, so I close my eyes and rest.

Chapter Five

Stella

My morning yoga class is full thanks to Gertie's Facebook post and the parade going right past my studio. Today's class is a gentle one that moves through poses slowly and is more of a restorative yoga session. Perfect for those who are feeling the effects of a busy holiday yesterday.

As we close the session, and my participants clean up their yoga mats and head towards the front of the studio, Mrs. Turner comes into the room. "Sorry to interrupt your class, Stella, but I need to grab Sophie."

Sophie turns quickly and walks over to her. "Did you hear an update? Has he called yet?"

"I spoke to Jax right before calling your house and Rob said I could find you here. Since I'm right around the corner I figured it would be faster to come find you. Jax seems relatively okay. I think he is pretty banged up and enjoying the pain meds from his surgeries. He was waiting for the doctor to come in and see him, but the nurse said he had just woken up before he called, which worried me a little bit. I didn't get more information than that because I could hear his energy dropping during our short call. I said we're heading there as soon as possible. We already booked our flights to LA. He asked that you call his manager and let them know he's okay. He didn't have his cell phone and was worried it was lost in the accident. I just know I need to get there and make sure he's okay. I don't think he realizes the situation he's in yet. He said he had just woken up, which means he's been out of it since early last night. Can you call one of the guys from the band and ask them to go now that he's awake?"

Sophie says, "I can call Mattie and ask him or one of them to head over. They've been blowing up my phone since last night, too, waiting for an update. Let me grab my bag. I'll call him right now. Maybe we can get them to do a video call with Jax before we jump on our flight."

"Thank you for going with me, Sophie. I'm so worried about him. He has no clue what it means to have two hands that don't work and a bad leg. This means he can't walk or use crutches. Reality hasn't hit him yet, and I'm afraid of how he's going to feel when it does."

"Oh, crap I didn't even think about that. He's a deadweight with no ability to do much for himself. He is going to flip out. He won't be doing this film next week either, and I bet that hasn't registered with him yet," Sophie says.

Jax's mother nods, "Let's get moving. Call me when you get home and hear something from one of the boys. Mitch and I will swing by and grab you on the way to the airport, so Rob doesn't need to make an extra trip. Get the boys over to the hospital for us in the meantime. See you soon, sweetheart. Let's hurry. I just want to get my eyes on my son."

"He will be okay, Katy. He is too stubborn not to be."

Mrs. Turner heads out in a hurry. I can understand how worried she must be. I look over at Sophie and bite my lip, "Are you okay, Soph? I know Jax is your best friend. Is there anything that I can do for you?"

Sophie turns to me with tears in her eyes and hugs me tight, "I'm so worried about him, Stella. He's there all alone now that I am here. I'm going to stay there as long as he lets me so I can make sure he's situated with his injuries. I don't know how he can even go home if he can't move around."

"He'll be okay. He's a healthy young guy. This sucks for him and for everyone that cares about him, but he'll be okay. Go make that call to the band to get them over there. While you're doing that, I want to grab some things for you to take to him."

She nods at me while wiping the tears off her face. I follow her out of the room and walk to the front of the studio where I keep my products. I want to give her some of my oils for her to take to Jax. Sophie has been my friend long enough to know how to use them.

A small bag in hand, I look through my oils. I grab peppermint oil, which will aid in sore muscles, helichrysum oil, which helps muscle spasms, and a couple of roll-on oils in lavender, sandalwood, and eucalyptus so he has a variety to help him relax, depending on which scent he prefers. I also have some reusable packs filled with barley which can be frozen or heated and used with the oils. With a last look, I grab a Bloodstone. He can use all the help he can get in healing his wounds.

Sophie comes over to me, "Hey, I got a hold of Mattie. He's heading over to the hospital now. He felt so guilty since Jax was heading home from his place, but it was not his fault. Just the jerk that pushed him off the road. I'm going to get ready for when his parents come to pick me up for the airport. I'll call you when I have news to share."

I hand Sophie the bag, "He's going to be okay, and I'm glad you're going with his mom. She's pretty shaken up about it. I grabbed some oils for him and a pack you can give him to heat or freeze. The roll-on oils are for him to use to calm down or to help with sleeping if he has trouble. I also gave you a Bloodstone. Put it in his room or wherever he'll be sleeping. It will promote healing. Every little bit helps right?"

She gives me another huge hug that nearly strangles me, "Thank you, Stella. I appreciate you so much. Thank you for being my friend." She steps back and wipes a tear. "I'll text or call when I have more news. If you can help spread updates on this side with Rob that will help keep the calls coming to him at a minimum. I'm worried about how this is going to play out. His mom and I don't have a return flight booked yet. I need to go, but I will keep you posted. Thank you for all this. I will oil his ass down as soon as I get to him!"

"Be safe Sophie. Stay positive. His energy will feed off to you and yours to him so be aware of that flow and movement. Remember to keep yourself balanced, too. I'm here if you need me."

Chapter Six

Jax

I hear someone say, "You go all out to get some attention these days, huh?" I look toward the door and see Mattie leaning against it with a smirk.

"Fuck you. I'm not the reason I'm lying here in this hospital bed right now."

Mattie walks into the room, sits in the chair next to my bed, leans forward with his elbows on his knees, and looks me over from head to toe. "Seriously though, man, are you okay? You look a bit fucked up."

"The doctor that fixed me up just left the room. You probably walked right past him on your way in."

"So, what's the verdict? Are you going to live?"

"Shut up, Mattie. I'll be just fine…eventually." I look away from him and out the window of my hospital room. "My options are I have to either go into rehab or hire a full-time caretaker until I'm more independent and healed from these injuries." I look back over at my friend waiting for his reaction.

"Jesus. Just the use of the word rehab and the paps are going to slaughter you. What are you thinking? What exactly is wrong with you other than the usual?" Mattie sits back with a shitty smirk across his face, his arms across his chest, and laughs at me.

"Thanks, jackass, I'm hurting here. Have a little mercy, please. Looks like I have a broken knee along with two broken wrists, which means I can't use crutches. I'll be stuck in a wheelchair for at least a month until I can put weight on my leg. As you can see, I have two beautiful casts on each hand. I can't even do my bathroom runs alone."

"You mean you can't even wipe your ass. Jax, my friend, you are in a shit load of hurt right now, aren't you?"

"Yeah. I'm up a creek without the paddle and about to hit some rapids. Fuck man, what the hell am I going to do?

I'm out for at least a month. I'm waiting for my manager to tell me I lost the role in the film I was supposed to start next week. Can't do that if I'm a cripple in a wheelchair and can't even wipe my own ass can I now?"

Mattie gets a serious look on his face. "Fuck, I feel responsible for this. What are you thinking? Or do you want to hear my opinion?"

"You are not responsible. Shut up, but yeah, what would you do?"

"I'd figure out a way to not go to rehab where all eyes would be on me and hire a private nurse or whatever to come to live with me so that I could heal in the privacy of my own home. You just need to find someone you're comfortable with wiping your ass and helping you with basic hygiene. I can't imagine it will be easy to do much of anything with two casted hands."

I lean my head back and close my eyes with a groan, "This fucking sucks, Mattie." I open my eyes and glance over at my good friend. "I think you're right, though. Mom and Sophie should be here later tonight. They can help me set all that up. I just want to go home without all the paps seeing how beat up I am. They just spin everything and make it worse."

"Buddy, don't even pay attention to it. Leave the TV off and focus on healing and getting back on your feet. It's not worth the hassle or energy that they take from us. Get your lawyers to draft NDAs for anyone who is involved in your care outside of friends or family. Maybe you should go home with your mom?" he suggests.

"No way. Mom wouldn't give me room to breathe, and would you want your mother wiping your ass and cleaning your private areas?" I say with alarm.

Laughing, Mattie shakes his head with the same look of fear, "Shit, no. That sounds completely humiliating. What can I do for you right now?"

"I'm starving. Go find a pretty girl to help feed my starving belly. Otherwise, your ugly face is going to need to feed me. Why do they think I can eat Jello or soup right now? I have no damn hands to hold a spoon!"

"If you weren't hurt and so damn miserable, I'd be laughing at you, but it isn't that funny. Maybe in a week or two but not right this moment. Can't you at least push the call button?"

I sigh. "No. It's too hard to grab and hold."

"Come here, Jaxie baby, let Mattie help you eat." He grabs the spoon of Jello and plays airplane with the bite.

"I hate you right now," I grumble at him.

"My kids love this. Be a good boy and eat some Jello so you grow big and strong."

"You're a dick."

"A dick who is feeding your hungry and cranky ass. Eat up, brother. I promise to find a cute nurse to give you a sponge bath when your plate is clean."

"Promise?"

"Eat the damn food, Jax. I'll have some real food delivered to you soon."

***

I tried to rest between getting woken up for pain checks and was completely humiliated by having a nurse assist me in the bathroom. Ugh, my life fucking sucks right now! Mom and Sophie have landed and texted that they are on their way to the hospital. At least the nurse moved my cell phone closer to me and brought me a new charger. It takes me a bit, but I can at least speak-to-text or answer calls on speaker. Thankfully, the staff on this floor put me in a corner room, so I have a little more privacy than usual. I'm here until tomorrow sometime, which gives me time to hire someone to come help me at home and have a bed delivered to the first floor. I can't do stairs, so my office now becomes my bedroom next to a full bathroom downstairs by the pool.

A new nurse comes into the room, "Hey, Mr. Turner. My name is Ted, and I'll be the nurse on staff for you until morning. How's your pain level? We can give you something if you need it now."

"I think I'm okay."

"Alrighty, but can I suggest you take something? It's easier to stay ahead of the pain than to wait until your injuries start throbbing. We can do a mild pain reliever. You're not on anything that strong if you are worried about it. If we give you something now, then we can give you another dose before you sleep and that should help get you to morning without screaming in pain."

"Ted, go ahead and bring the drugs. I'm already dealing with not being able to feed myself or go to the bathroom, so let's go for it. I need to be as calm as possible. My mother is almost here, and she's going to increase my stress level with her worrying."

"You got it. I'll be right back. Can I get you anything else?" He's looking at my current tabletop. "I could probably get you a cup with a lid and straw. You may be able to handle holding that. Want to try?"

"That would be great, thanks." I watch Nurse Ted leave the room. Man, he's a big guy. Is he going to be the one to drag my ass to the toilet later? Ugh. I hear a commotion in the hall before I see it. My mother and a blue-haired Sophie with big glasses walk into my room. Sophie smiles and heads towards me as my mother puts her hands up covering her mouth and tears fill her eyes.

"Hey. It's good to see you guys. Mom, please relax, I'm going to be fine. Don't cry."

"Oh, Jax. Honey, you look terrible," Mom says to me and comes over and kisses me on the head. "The video call didn't show how badly your face was scratched up and bruised. Are you sure you're okay to leave the hospital tomorrow?"

I nod, "Yeah. We just need to line up some care for me at home. I can't do much but sit here. I need someone who can help me get to the bathroom and clean me up, so I don't start having body stank problems. I'm glad you guys are here, though. I'm hoping you can help get me settled before you head home."

"We aren't leaving until you kick us out," Mom replies. "What do you need right now?"

"Mattie was here earlier and helped me with my lunch and to hit the bathroom before he left. I'm not peeing in a pee cup. Gross."

"Honey, it may be worth it for now until you let your body heal a bit. Even your father had to do that with his hernia surgery."

"Jax now isn't the time to be too proud to ask for help. Even the Hottest man in America needs to be open to asking for help," Sophie says to me and winks. "Let's focus on getting you home and set up with a nurse. Does the hospital have a list of where we can start? Have you had anyone give you any information yet?"

"Honestly," I say shaking my head, "I didn't want to even think about it yet. I'm still dealing with the reality of being helpless."

Nurse Ted comes in and smiles, "Well, looks like you have company, so I'll make this quick. Here are those pain pills, and I got you a big cup from the cafeteria with a straw and put it in a rubber koozie, so it won't sweat or get slippery on you. I was told your friend is having dinner brought in tonight, and you won't need to see your hospital options, but do you want to see the dessert options just in case?"

"Thanks, Ted. Sure. Fill me in. My mom and Sophie are going to keep me company for a bit and help me with whatever I need to do to be ready at home. Do you have any information on how to set up care at home that we could have?" He gives me the cup full of cold water and I'm able to grasp it between my two casts.

"We have a paper I can grab you that lists some of the healthcare agencies we recommend and hospital supply companies for any beds, ramps, shower chairs, or anything you need to make your house more handicap friendly."

I grimace at the word handicap. My mother helps me with the cup when I'm done drinking and puts it on the tray next to me. "Thank you, Ted. We would appreciate anything that you can give us to make this situation easier for Jax."

She points at Sophie and herself, "We're here to make sure he gets home and can manage. Until we know that's a possibility we aren't going anywhere."

"Jax, you're one lucky guy. Be glad they're here to help. Once you leave the hospital, it gets a bit tricky to learn how to readjust your way of living around injuries. You'll also feel weaker when you're home, and you'll think you can handle everything like before. I'm here all night so don't hesitate to hit the call button for anything you need big or small, okay? I don't want you to try to do something on your own and hurt yourself more. You have no weight bearing on your leg and the same goes for the two hands. You are going to need some help for a while, so the best advice I can give you is to be willing to ask for it and then accept it. Put your pride on the shelf for a little bit. Healing is your number-one priority right now. I'm here for whatever you need. Okay, man?"

"You better be listening to Ted, dear, because he's right. Sophie and I are going to keep repeating that until you accept this is how things are going to be for a little while."

Ted says, "I'll get the list so you can start making calls now. They should be able to get a bed and supplies to you tomorrow, but the nurse support could take a bit longer depending on how many they staff."

Ted walks out of the room, and I turn to Sophie, "My life sucks right now. Sophie, did you call my manager and get that discussion handled for me? I only ask because they haven't called me back, yet."

"Yeah, I did. Helps that we work with the same person. I let them know I'd be here and give updates as needed and to not bother you right away. They were reaching out to the team doing your film and letting them know that you're out of commission for at least a month if not longer."

"Fuck. I hate that I'm going to lose this film because of all this mess. I was looking forward to working with Laura on this one and doing something a little less Rom-Com. Now I feel like I've let everyone down because I can't be on set in time."

Sophie comes over and sits on the side of my hospital bed, "I know you're upset over it, but if they can't postpone, which you know isn't a big possibility because of cost, and you lose this film, another one will come around. You know Hollywood isn't going to let a little accident stop them from banging down your door, especially with you being on the current Hottest Men of Hollywood list. Let's focus on immediate needs like getting the healing started, getting you safe and at home where you can rest, and leave the rest for now. Stella gave me a bunch of things to help you. They are still in my suitcase but once you're home, I'll get the oils out and give your mental health some boosting. Do you have a bad headache? That shiner you've got looks pretty bad."

"My mental health is fine. What are you talking about?" I say.

"You'll see all the stuff I brought tomorrow. Stella was concerned about your mental health and how that will be affected by your physical injuries. She gave me some oils and a healing stone to put in your room. She's amazing, and her holistic approach and healing forces may help you get back on your feet, so I won't take no from you. You're going to participate in anything we say or else. She gave me all kinds of stuff to make sure you had everything that could help you. So all you have to say is, *Thank you, Sophie and Stella*! I told her I'd rub you down and make you better," Sophie winks at me.

"Thanks? I'm sure Rob won't appreciate you rubbing me down with oil."

My best friend rolls her eyes. "Stop it. You know I've been doing yoga and working with Stella and her products. I'm telling you that you'll be impressed, and her oils will make you feel better. Rob knows you are like a brother to me and my best friend, so he doesn't have a problem at all. If you're worried about it, I can ask your mom to do it.

My mom puts her hand on my face, "Jax, at this point, you need all the healing help you can get so that you gain some independence back in your life. Right son?"

"You're right. I'm just…I'm stuck in a bed and not able to even take myself to the bathroom. I'm trying hard not to lose my shit right now."

Sophie says, "Why don't you and your mom talk? I'll get that info and start making some calls." She gets up off my bed, "I'll get the ball rolling so we can get your house situated for when we take you home tomorrow."

"Thanks, Sophie, I love you."

"Ditto, Jax. I've got you, buddy. Now be good."

Chapter Seven

Stella

I decided to keep the studio closed on Sundays for now. I work every other day as it is, and I need a day for rest. Griffin was probably right about hiring a part-time person to help me out with classes. I'm not ready for that yet, but I'll get there eventually.

Today, I'm heading over to our standing Sunday family dinner. I need to see if Mom needs any help and plan to get there earlier than the rest of them. I'm just finishing my breakfast when my phone rings and see Sophie calling, "Hey friend, how are things in LA with Jax? How are you all managing?"

"Stella, I'm not sure what to do," she says. "I'm hoping you can give me some fresh ideas and calm me down a little bit before I murder my best friend for being an asshole."

"Oh no, what's going on? I thought Jax was being positive about these major changes in his life."

"That lasted about two days. He's already fired the first nurse that we brought in. Something about not appreciating his need for resting and being manhandled."

I giggle, "I don't mean to laugh but WHAT! Explain, please. Is he pulling some sort of Hollywood star bullshit or what exactly is going on there?"

"He is being so mean and obnoxiously rude…his mom is threatening to ground him. The first nurse was this nice former military guy with a medical background. We made it clear that it needed to be someone strong enough to move Jax, who is six foot three and two hundred and fifteen pounds of muscle. This guy was huge and so nice, but he was tired of Jax not wanting to get showered or just wash his damn body. He got frustrated and went all military commander on him and Jax fired him and told him to get out immediately."

"Oh boy. That doesn't sound good."

"Then, we get a new nurse, and he takes one look at her and how pretty she is and asks if she is ready for his sponge bath and gets gross and crude with her. She told him that she didn't care who he was, but he wasn't going to speak to her like that. He then asked if she was a lesbian because she should have been flattered to see him naked. She turned right around and left and said she wouldn't be back. Stella! He has lost his damn mind."

"Hmm, that doesn't sound like his normal behavior. I'd say his injury and loss of independence are starting to get to him. Are any of you ready to deal with the stages of grief? I'd say he's definitely in the angry stage. You and his mom need to take time to look at those stages so you can be prepared for his actions. It may also be beneficial for you to find him some sort of support that's not family or a best friend."

"Stella, his mom and I have talked about that, but he is impossible to deal with right now. We both want to strangle him! Right now, we're waiting for a third nurse to show up, and we asked if it could be someone ready to handle his temper. We're worn out and getting the brunt of his behavior thrown our way."

I can tell Sophie is frustrated. "Jax needs to get his anger out, but my guess is he just doesn't know how. Try not to take the mental punishment he is throwing your way personally but support him. Ignore those outbursts and continue to try to force him to talk. Do something normal like before the accident," I suggest.

"Hmm, that may be a good idea. I'll see if I can get him to do a pizza movie night with me later. That was our normal thing when I still lived in LA. Thanks, girlfriend. You may have just provided another day of life for Jax!"

"You're terrible, Sophie."

"No, terrible is my best friend's crappy attitude."

"True, but let's hope it gets better. Let me know how things go with the new nurse. I wish you lots of luck!"

"I wish I didn't need it, but I will take any good vibes you send our way."

***

"Mom…I'm here," I yell as I walk into my parents' home.

"I'm in the kitchen, Stella bug," Mom yells back.

I head to the kitchen and put my purse on the counter. "Hi, I wanted to come over earlier and check to see if you needed a hand. It's the first time since my soft opening last week and the fourth of July that I even have a moment to decompress and catch my breath."

"Oh, honey, then you should have just stayed home and relaxed a bit longer. You know the girls all start pitching in as they arrive, and it's not usually all on my shoulders to feed whoever shows up on Sundays."

"I know, but maybe I wanted to be selfish and get some alone time with my mom," I say.

Mom stops slicing a tomato and looks at me, "Are you doing okay, sweetheart?"

"Yeah, I am. Just tired. It was the first week that I ran a studio and handled most of the classes. Just trying to keep up with the energy needed to get through my week. I'm sure it will start to balance out once I have a couple weeks under my belt."

"I'm happy to come and handle the front of the studio any time you need me there. All you have to do is ask. Dad would be there for you too."

"Thanks, Mom. I appreciate that. Griffin is pushing me to get another teacher for the yoga classes, so I'm not trying to do too much, but I know it will all flow better soon. I have a part-time helper in front handling class sign-ups and selling products during the day. Right now, at night, I lock up when I have my evening class session in the back. It's working well so far. Everyone knows if I can't come to the door to leave and come back later."

"You do seem to have a solid process, and if it's working for now, don't make any more changes. Like you said, once you have a routine, it should start to settle down some more."

45

"Yes, I think so too. Do you need any help with anything?"

Mom smiles at me, "I'd love it if you could make a pitcher of lemonade. Bree's coming with the baby, and since she's still nursing, she isn't drinking yet. The rest of the kids usually bring their drinks because they all know what they like."

"Who all is coming today?"

"Other than Bree, Julia, Hillary, Sam, Ellen, and their significant others I'm not sure. Oh, Rob will probably show up because Sophie is still out in LA. Have you heard from her?"

"Ah, so everyone. Sophie called me this morning. Jax is being difficult and firing all the nurses. She said they were ready to kill him and that his behavior was bad. I tried to give her some encouragement. She needs to understand he's dealing with a loss of independence and needs her support, even if she'd rather hit him over the head with a hammer."

"Men are babies. I can't imagine it's easy for him to go from being young, strong, and independent to now needing all this extra care. It must be playing with his self-worth a bit, too. I'm glad she has you to lean on through this. She's feeling very guilty right now for living here and not still in LA. Thankfully, Rob is understanding and knows how important their friendship is. Although, he's been at my dinner table since she left."

"I'll have to ask him how he's doing. I didn't even think to check in with him since Sophie left. It's been a busy week."

"He's okay, but I'm sure he wouldn't mind his little sister making sure."

***

Dinner was delicious. Dad and Garrett handled cooking the chicken and burgers on the grill and the girls each brought a side or dessert to share. We're all stuffed and sitting around the table outside.

"Ladies, thank you for a delicious meal," Dad says to us. "You know how much Ruby and I love it when you kids

46

all still come to eat Sunday dinner with us. We know you all have your own lives now, but it's still nice to know we matter."

"Good lord, Dad. It's not like we don't see you all the time. Lake Harmony isn't that big of a town," Rob says.

"Well, lately we see you ALL the time son. Did you forget how to survive alone?"

"The house is too quiet with Sophie in LA. I also don't like to cook for one anymore. Mom doesn't mind that I come over for dinner. Do you, Mom?"

"Nope, not one bit. Have you talked to, Soph? Stella said she was ready to kill Jax. Sounds like he is having a tough time dealing with the accident and his injuries," Mom says.

"Yeah, Soph is trying to keep him from losing his shit completely," Rob replies. "But he found out today that the studio dropped him from the film he was supposed to start next week. He knew it was probably coming, but that just amped up his bad mood this afternoon. Sophie said they sent a new nurse over, and she refuses to listen to him each time he fires her. She said it's been the best part of the day so far. She and his mom have enjoyed watching this new nurse just ignore him and tell him what's going to happen."

Dad laughs, "Yikes, I feel bad for him, but he can't keep taking it out on everyone else. Now, since Mom and I have most of you here, we wanted to have a celebration toast."

Julia smiles, "I love a good toast, Dad. I have one to add if that's okay."

"Of course, but I'm going first. Everyone raise a glass…I'd like to give a big congratulations to our sweet Stella. Mom and I are so proud of you. You've always had a fire within you, a determination to chase your dreams with unwavering passion. You took an idea that made you happy and it grew into a self-made product line and now a studio where you can share your knowledge and health tips with others. Everyone, please raise your glass….To Stella!"

"Congratulations on your success!"

"We love you Stella Bug!"

"Keep pushing and achieving your goals!"

"I am so damn proud of you little sis."

"To the amazing Stella and her studio of love and healing!"

I feel tears streaming down my face, and wipe them away as everyone clinks their glass or beer bottle against my drink. "Thank you, everyone. I appreciate that very much."

Julia puts her arm around me, "Now it's my turn." She turns to look me in the eye, "Ever since you were a little girl you always had your own plan and sense of direction. It wasn't always the same road that we all imagined for you, but there it was right in front of you leading you on a personal journey of discovery. There were times I was so jealous of you and your way of viewing the world. As a little girl, you would sit and observe everything around you. Always watching and learning from your surroundings. Even though we teased, and you may have felt like just our little sister, I think I can say on behalf of your siblings that we are so proud of you and all that you have accomplished. You've never asked for more than to be loved and allowed to find your way. We are simply amazed by you. I love you, Stella."

Everyone shouts again, "To Stella!"

The tears are now falling steadily down my face, and Julia pulls me in for a big hug. "I love you, Stella bug, and never stop chasing your dreams."

"This means the world to me, everyone. Sometimes it's hard being the little sister that always felt in the way because I was so much younger than all of you or watching your lives from a distance. I know that I follow my own path and where life takes me, and I want to say thank you for always giving me the space to wander and find my happiness. It means so much to me that you gave me that space, and I was able to create something amazing for myself with your encouragement and support. It was very important to me to be able to stand on my own two feet and be proud of what I could achieve. I love you guys so much!"

I slowly get passed around the group getting hugs and private praises. The tears continue to fall and my heart is filled with love and acceptance from my family and friends.

Chapter Eight

Jax

My life fucking sucks. It's only been a week since my accident but between Mom and Sophie being here trying to keep me calm and now this third nurse trying to boss me around, I'm a bit over it.

The casts on my wrists are disgusting because every time I try to eat, I spill or stick my hand in the food. I am not a child and don't need to be treated like one for fuck's sake! I do not need to be spoon-fed every time I get hungry. My knee hurts because I keep trying to put weight on it, and I know I'm being an idiot and probably making my healing take even longer. Still, the only thing I can do independently right now is lay here and watch television, and even that I can't do without my stress levels going up.

The accident is public knowledge, and the paps got word that I was dropped from the movie. It doesn't matter to them that the movie had to drop me because I'm injured. They make it sound like I was dropped before the accident due to my person or character. Now all I see and hear from the paps and the stupid entertainment shows is how far America's Leading Hottest Man has fallen. Will I recover? Do producers want to take a risk on me being a hothead and not paying attention? Like the damn accident was my fault. They've even questioned if I was drunk driving! If they could get onto my property to harass me, I would sue the shit out of all of them. I hope they try.

"Chuck! My leg is throbbing. When are you bringing me some pain meds," I yell from my perch on the bed. I see my nurse come around the corner with no expression on her face.

"Mr. Turner, you are not due for more pills for another hour. Where is your pain level from zero to ten?"

"Twenty-five, Chuck. Are you happy now?"

"I'd be happier, Mr. Turner, if you would stop trying to move around on your leg. You have a no-weight-bearing status on that knee for at least two more weeks when physical therapy begins. The only thing you are going to achieve is prolonging that order. Is that what you are trying to do or is there somewhere that I can move you in the wheelchair to avoid you putting pressure on your leg?"

"You're fired, Chuck. Just go, I don't need this attitude from you, and I refuse to be ignored."

"I'm sorry you feel that way, Mr. Turner, but I've been told to ignore your outbursts unless they are pain or need-related. I understand you are not happy and hurting, and I'm here to help you as much as possible. I'll bring you some pain meds in an hour. In the meantime, we could attempt some ice, or I can activate some blood flow through gentle massage?"

"No thanks to that! Just leave me alone," I grumble.

"I will be back in to check on you with your medication in less than an hour now. Of course, let me know if you need me sooner."

She turns and walks back out of the room. I can feel my blood pressure rising. I close my eyes and count to ten. It's a technique my dad taught me when I would get frustrated, and I knew I couldn't lash out. Unfortunately for Chuck, I can't seem to keep that in check.

I open my eyes and my best friend is looking at me with a lifted eyebrow. "You should be ashamed of yourself for the way you treated Charlie," Sophie says. "She's only here to help you and PLEASE stop calling that sweet woman Chuck! What the hell is wrong with you? Every time your mother hears that she looks like she's going to cry. It's upsetting her watching you behave like this. So, stop! We understand you are angry, frustrated, and stuck in this damn bed but we didn't put you there! We're here to help you and get you back on your feet as soon as possible and you're fighting all of us each step of the way!"

I stare at her and don't say a word. When Sophie starts on a mad tirade, I know better than to interrupt her. "Are you done?"

"Honestly, Jax," she says shaking her head, "Please stop being a major asshole. This isn't you."

"I'm so sorry that I am making your life difficult," I say with as much sarcasm as possible.

Sophie sighs, "Listen, buddy, we love you, but your mom and I think it's best if we head home and not be the target of your anger. If you need us to stay, we absolutely will, but we don't think being here is helping you in any capacity. You have Charlie now, and she can handle your medical and mobility needs. She can ignore this new personality, but it's starting to wear thin on your mom and me."

"Fine, go home. It's not like I can do anything, and you don't need to be here to watch me lie here and be handicapped."

"We're going to look at flights home for tomorrow. That way, we can prep anything to make life easier for you."

"Great," I say with no enthusiasm.

Sophie leaves the room, and I exhale. Fuck my life. I hear Mom and Sophie talking to Chuck in the living room. I'm not sure if it's meant for me to hear or not.

"Charlie, I'm so sorry that my son is being so hateful towards you. I am so embarrassed by his behavior."

"Mrs. Turner, please don't worry about me. I've raised my own family and have worked with many patients who go through their own version of dealing with a major injury. Mr. Turner is not doing anything that is out of the norm for someone in his position. Unfortunately, being who he is and the public also being aware of his current state seems to be fueling his handling of the situation. I agree that both of you seem to be his punching bag, and I promise you that I can handle the next couple of weeks getting him back on his feet. He needs to focus on staying off that leg and not trying to lift himself with his broken wrists in casts. He is only making his recovery harder."

"I know he's angry, and I would be too, but I raised him better than this, and I apologize on his behalf. Sophie and I are going to fly home tomorrow. We can be here within a day if things change, but this can't continue. He needs to focus on getting better. My son is an active and vibrant young man and these injuries snapped all of that away."

"I promise I have this handled. He's dealing with the beginning stages of having a bad injury. His life isn't what it was a week ago. Honestly, I have a lot of experience in this type of situation, and it could get a little worse for him before it gets better. He has about three more weeks before he can move around independently. Once we get him there, physical therapy is going to start. He will be expecting to be where he was, but that will be another turning point for him. Let's focus on the immediate needs and move forward from there. You both have my cell phone and can check in at any time. I do think…"

Shit! They must have walked further away and now I can't hear what they are saying about me.

***

Sophie comes into my room with a big smile and her hands full of small tubes. "Since you've been such an ass, I haven't done this yet, but I'm leaving tomorrow, and I promised Stella that I would do whatever I could to make you better. She was really worried about your mental state, and now I'm beginning to understand. I think we can both agree it's taking a beating."

"Whatever Soph."

"Anyway…you're going to be a good patient and just listen. I do not need you to chit-chat with me unless you have something of value to say or I ask you a question. Got it?"

"YEP!"

"Stella gave me some oils for you. These little rollers are meant to help relieve some stress. She sent a few of them along in different scents. She said it's important to smell them and see if they shift your moods. For me, citrus

54

wakes me up in the morning or gives me a sense of happiness. Woody smells make me relax. So now is our Q and A session. Smell this.”

She puts a small bottle under my nose. It smells like lavender. It smells like my grandmother, and I smile. I used to love going there and spending time with my grandparents over the summer. “Not bad. Reminds me of my grandparent's house.”

“So, it brings you happiness or good feelings?”

“Yeah.”

“Okay good! Now smell this.”

She shoves another bottle under my nose. This smells woodsy with something sweet. It makes me think of the campgrounds at home or hiking in the woods in the Midwest. Man, those were some great times growing up. “This reminds me of home and growing up around the campfires and hiking the woods.”

“Another one for the good vibes category then?”

“Yeah, two for two.”

“This is the last one I have for you to smell,” she says as she shoves it again under my nose.

Holy hell that one is strong. It makes my eyes water. This has a minty citrus smell almost medicinal. It makes me think of being sick and mom rubbing the ointment on my chest to help me sleep better. “This is like mom's sick ointment, but it relaxes me because she used it when I had to rest and go to sleep.”

“Hmm, it’s eucalyptus so that makes sense. I always put it in my vaporizer when I’m sick too. Must be a mom thing, and now we know what will calm you down a bit. I’ll let Charlie know how they make you feel in case you need them. These have rollers so you can roll them on your skin, and they won’t irritate you. It should provide either happy thoughts or calm. You, sir, could use a bit of both. Maybe we should dump one of them over your head now?”

“Funny, har-har, Sophie.” I look at my best friend, “I’m sorry I am such a fucking asshole. I don’t know how to handle all this. I’m going to miss you, but I can’t keep you from your life either. That makes me add guilt on top of all the other feelings I have."

"I love you and know this side of you is coming from hurt and frustration, but it is a lot, Jax. I feel like I'm not helping you, and that hurts my heart because I'm letting you down. Your mom needs a break too, because she wants to help and fix things. But it's not up to us. It's up to you. We can be here as your cheerleaders or to wipe your face, but we are not able to heal you. I wish I had that magic wand to smack you on the head *hard* and poof you would be all healed."

"No one can speed up this process for me, because if they could, I would have paid millions for it. You guys head home and if I need you, I'll call, deal?"

"Well, I should warn you, we've decided if you don't start behaving, we're sending the dads in our place."

"Please don't."

"Then you, sir, need to behave and stop acting like an asshole."

"I will try harder. What else do you have in that bag you're holding?" I ask.

"Charlie is going to come back in with your meds soon, and she's going to do a gentle massage with Stella's oils. I told her what they were, and she was all over it. She's familiar with therapeutic massage, which you have been so hateful about and refusing. If you don't want her to do it, I am happy to use the oils and work them into your leg."

"I'll try to be better. At this point, I will try anything because my leg and wrists are fucking throbbing."

"You need to stop trying to get out of bed by yourself because you're only aggravating your injuries."

Charlie walks in, "Mr. Turner, it's time for your next dose of pain pills. How are you feeling?"

"Charlie, I'm honestly feeling a little nicer but could use those meds. Sophie said you are going to try to do a gentle massage?"

She looks over at my bestie and turns back to me with raised brows, "Yes. I think if we get the blood circulating through your knee area it will speed up the process of healing. I didn't realize that you had a holistic practitioner in your life. I looked at the oils Stella sent for you, and they should benefit sore muscles and spasms. Let's get your meds in you and see if we can calm that leg down a little bit before we get you ready for bed. Does that sound good?"

"Sounds great. Thank you."

"You are very welcome. Our goal is to get you healing and independent as quickly as possible."

Sophie says, "Jax, take your meds. Stella also sent along a barley bag that I wanted to heat up. I'm going to put a few drops of the eucalyptus oil on it so that it will help soothe your growly soul."

Standing she winks at Charlie and sashays out of the room.

"She's a good friend to have in your corner. Are you ready to try this oil and see if it gives your muscles a rest so you have a peaceful night?"

"Go ahead, Charlie. Do whatever you want."

She stops, laughs, and stares at me, "Oh, so you do know my name."

"Sorry. I'll try not to take my moods out on you."

"Not to worry Mr. Turner, my brothers all call me Chuck because I was the only girl in the family."

Chapter Nine

Stella

My evening class finished up and everyone cleaned up their area and left to go home, except for Sophie and Griffin who are both lying on their sides and having a quiet conversation. I'm worried about her because I know her heart and worries are still in LA with Jax. He told her and his mom to head home because there was nothing they could do, but I know she feels guilty for leaving him there without a friend or family to help since his injuries keep him from being independent. I walk over to my two friends and sit down next to them. "Hey, you two."

"Yoga was great tonight, Stella. I hope it calmed me down enough to sleep tonight," Sophie says to me.

"Sophie, what can I do for you? I know you're worried about Jax, but you know the nurse puts his health and wellness as her priority. You even told me that she sends text messages to you and his mom, so you won't worry. I thought he was finally not fighting her?"

"He's finally cooperating with Charlie and lets her work on his leg with gentle massage and your oils, but his mental state is still what I'm worried about. It's been a few weeks since the accident, but his moods are all over the place. One minute, he's so angry and yelling about life, and the next, he's quiet and second-guessing everything. The paps have been horrible to him. Once they found out about the accident, they started blabbing about whether he was drunk or he had caused the accident. He is immediately the bad guy because that story sells. He was so excited about this movie he was supposed to be working on. I just don't know how to help."

"Hmm…first, I'm going to lock up, then, if you have time, why don't you come up for a bit? I have something that I want to run past you and Griffin. I can make you a hot calming tea so you can sleep better tonight, and we can talk."

Sophie nods, "Okay, that sounds good. Go lock up, and I'm going to text Rob that I'm going upstairs for a little bit."

"Go head upstairs with Griffin. I'll be there in a few."

***

After I brew some tea for us and put out the lemon squares Mom snuck over to me today, I curl up on the couch with my friends. "I have something that I want to run by you, and I need your honest feedback if you think it's worth trying or not."

Griffin leans back against the couch, "Stella, I'm always game for whatever you want to do but please share."

"My wonderful mentor, Tillie from Sedona, who taught me everything I know about holistic practice is coming through town and is stopping here to see me Sunday. Since the studio's closed, I was thinking about asking her to do a sound bath session and make it invite-only. Do you think anyone would be interested in that, or will people think that is too outside their comfort zone?"

Sophie smiles, "Oh my god Stella I would LOVE that! Yes, please! Do it."

Griffin says, "I agree with Soph. I would be open to trying something like that. What exactly is it, other than being something cool I haven't tried yet?"

"There are all kinds of sound bath sessions, but Tillie uses a more holistic approach with Tibetan singing bowls. Everyone would come here for a session that lasts about an hour. You lie down or sit against the wall, so your body is relaxed. The sound from the singing bowl creates a full-body therapy experience. The vibrations move through you to restore your body, mind, and spirit to create a sense of balance and harmony. It's another way to open and clear your chakra and release stuck energy. Sometimes, it lets your emotions out. I've cried through sessions but in a

60

healing way. It should help release anything you have bottled up causing you stress."

"Can we ship her to LA? That sounds like something amazing for Jax," Sophie says with a wink. "Let's do it, Stella. What do you need from Griff and me?"

"Who should I invite? I don't want people to feel weird, but it is an amazing experience. I mean, even if no one shows up but us, it would be worth it to me to have shared it with the both of you," I say.

Griffin rubs his chin, "Why don't you send it out to everyone in a group text? Give them a shortened version of what it is and tell them it's free to attend and something you want to try. Then whoever shows up gets to try it."

Sophie nods enthusiastically, "I agree with Griffin. I think that is a great idea!"

"Thank you. I think you will love Tillie. She is amazing. Now, Sophie, I know you and Jax are like siblings and closer than just friends, but some of his healing he must do on his own. You can be there to offer support and provide him with tools to achieve it on his own, but he needs to be the one to do the hard work. I'm always here for you if you want support or need to talk about things. I'm also happy to reach out or send him anything I think may help if he's open to those things."

Sophie hugs me, "I appreciate having you in my life so much! Thank you, Stella. You are the best girlfriend I've ever had."

"Aw, aren't you two cute? I want in on this hug," Griffin says, before pushing his way into our hug. "I love you girls, too!"

***

After I get into bed, I grab my phone and send a group text to my family and friends in town. I spoke with Tillie, and she was excited to provide a sound session with the people in my life.

Me: Hey everyone! My mentor from Sedona is coming through town on Sunday and will be offering a Sound Bath session here at my studio. What is a Sound Bath experience? It's a session to release any blocked energy in your body. Tillie uses Tibetan Singing Bowls that produce vibrations. Come to the studio in comfy clothes, find a spot on the floor, get comfortable, and allow the vibrations to move through your body. Feel free to bring any other friends. I have yoga mats but feel free to bring a pillow or blanket. Sometimes during sessions, you relax and get chilled. If you have questions, reach out to me directly. If you want to attend, I look forward to seeing you on Sunday @ 11 a.m. in my studio at Mint & Sage. The session will last about an hour. xoxo Stella

Chapter Ten

Jax

Hollywood's Fallen Star: From Leading Man to Limping Liability! In a shocking turn of events, Tinseltown's once-mighty leading man, Jax Turner, has found himself teetering on the precipice of irrelevance after a catastrophic accident sent his career into a tailspin. The golden boy of Hollywood is now just a shadow of his former self.

The glamorous life of red carpets, flashing cameras, and adoring fans have been replaced with hospital beds, grueling rehab, and whispers of uncertainty. The question on everyone's lips: Can he bounce back from this career-crushing blow?

In the unforgiving world of Hollywood, where yesterday's sensations are today's forgotten relics, the road to redemption is steep and treacherous. Stay tuned as we continue to track the ups and downs of Hollywood's fallen leading man and discover if he can defy the odds and stage the comeback of a lifetime!

Charlie walks into the room and quickly turns off the television.

"Mr. Turner, why do you torture yourself with all that crap? You know those television shows are just live broadcasts of the tabloids. They only make you mad and frustrated. You have enough experience with this life that you know better than to focus on anything they have to say."

"I know it's all trash, Charlie, but I thought maybe it was better to know what's being said so my PR team can be on top of it." I give a shrug, and Charlie stops what she's doing and just stares at me. "What?"

"If you think I believe that for a second, you're crazy. Your PR team doesn't need you to tell them how to do their job. What did your manager say to you yesterday?"

"That I should ignore the tabloids and talk shows, and that my team is releasing facts and updates as needed to keep my image and reputation in check," I mumble.

"Exactly," Charlie says. "When did they say you have that interview with Good Morning LA? I think once that airs, it will take some steam out of the paparazzi sails, don't you?"

"It should," I agree. "My team is setting up the interview for tomorrow afternoon. Do you think you can help me look decent? I know it will be over a video call from here, but I'd like to be sitting somewhere other than in my bed and look like I have showered. Do I need a haircut?"

Charlie smiles at me and sits down across from me. "Can I be honest with you?"

"Please, I appreciate honesty. You know that, Charlie."

"You have some significant injuries. I think it's okay for the reporters to see that. We'll get you showered and cleaned up. You don't need a haircut. Shave—hmm, don't shave. I think if you feel good that will carry over to looking your best. You have injuries. They don't need to see your hands or your hurt leg. We can sit you up in a chair with your leg propped up and use the hospital table to put the computer on in front of you. They will assume you're sitting at a desk or whatever. Just be yourself and share what you're comfortable saying to them. You know how to handle yourself. This isn't anything new. Give them the raw facts and that you're healing as fast as possible and appreciate your fan's support."

"You are damn smart, Charlie. Thanks."

"You can handle this, and I'll make sure you look your best. I heard your manager say they could send someone here to spiff you up. Why'd you say no to that if you are so worried?"

"Because I knew you would make sure I didn't look bad, and I didn't want a stranger in my home. You've been good to me, I appreciate it, and I trust you."

"Just doing my job, Mr. Turner."

"Oh, so we're back to Mr. Turner. Why do I have to keep telling you that you can call me Jax? Mr. Turner makes me sound like an old man."

"Fine. Jax, can I get you anything else? Your groceries will be delivered any minute, and I will need to put them away. Are you still good with dinner being delivered from your friend Mattie?"

"He needs to stop sending us food. Between all the guys I feel like all we do is eat restaurant food. Next time he calls I'm going to say thank you but hold off on all the takeout. I just want some pot roast and salad. Not some five-star meal from a fancy LA restaurant."

Charlie says, "Please also tell him he doesn't have to always make sure I have dinner delivered too. It's very nice of him, but not at all expected or necessary."

"Charlie?"

"Yes, Mr.…Jax?"

"He said that is a big thank you from the guys since they can't be here and for taking care of my grouchy ass. Trust me, they appreciate you being here and helping me eat and bathe because Mattie said once was enough and he prefers not to need to do it again."

"I won't argue with that anymore then. How about I make you some pot roast this weekend? I could use some home-cooked food myself."

"That sounds amazing, and I would get up and hug you if I could right now but that is on the no-go list right now."

"Ok, I'll be back to check on you or yell if you need me sooner. Did the massage on your knee help again today?"

"Yes, and the next time you think something will help me and I refuse you, I want you to feel free to smack me. I wish I would have allowed you to do that sooner because it really is helping get rid of some of the muscle spasms."

"I'll remember you said that," Charlie says with a big smile and leaves the room.

Chapter Eleven

Stella

Tillie and I are enjoying a cup of tea and some scones that I got from Harmonious Bites earlier this morning. Tillie is here for the day before moving on to Chicago for a visit with another friend.

"I am so happy to see you Stella and the energy coming off you is so lovely. You seem to be very happy. Are you?" Tillie asks.

I look at Tillie, one of the best people in my life, and smile big, "I am happy. I feel like I finally accomplished something important in my life. You know I couldn't have done this without you."

"That is sweet to say, Stella, but you managed this on your own merit. I only provided the tools for you to get here, but I wasn't the one that did the work. You, sweet girl, did that all by yourself, and I am very proud of you."

I wipe a tear from the corner of my eye. "Tillie, sometimes I feel as though you are the only one who has truly ever seen me for what I could become or who I was. That means more to me than anything else in my entire life. I wouldn't be here if the energy of Sedona hadn't pulled me to your door."

"Maybe. Maybe not." Tillie muses. "On another day or another time, that energy may have pulled you somewhere else, but I do believe that you would have been guided to finding your way sooner or later. Sometimes that energy and timing only presents itself when you're ready for it."

"True. That's something that I try to continue to teach. I tell everyone in my classes that they need to listen to what is happening around them, or they may miss something important. I learned that from you."

"That's very good advice. What is our plan today? I know you asked me to do a session. How many are we expecting?"

I laugh, "I have no idea. I invited my family and friends, but honestly, Tillie, that could end up being a fairly big group of people. They should be here around eleven to start the session. I'd say let's plan on starting about fifteen minutes later to give time to those that are still trickling in?"

"That sounds perfect. I brought three of my singing bowls with me and my rain stick. Let's enjoy our tea a little bit longer and then you can help me set up wherever you want me."

"Perfect."

***

Tillie and I picked my biggest studio, and we're doing the finishing touches on the lighting and turning on the diffuser and salt lamps around the room. She prefers to have the lighting low so that those attending the session have an easier time relaxing. We hear voices and look towards the entrance of the room and see my family and friends start to arrive.

Tillie moves towards them and says, "Welcome, please come as you are and find a space where you can relax. Use a yoga mat or lean up against the wall. Whatever provides the space to let your guard down."

Logan, PJ, and Genie head in followed closely by all the girls, Sophie, Julia, her daughter Josie, Sam, Bree, Hillary, Ellen, Ruby, and Mrs. Turner. Then the significant others come up the rear, Edison, Jackson, Noah, Garrett, Paul, Scott, Griffin, and Rob. Wow! Everyone in my life is pretty much settling into a space on the floor. "Thank you all for coming. This means so much to me that you want to experience this with me," I say.

"I hope we aren't late!" A voice comes from the door as Gertie, our resident gossip, and her group of widowed friends walk in with her.

"No, we haven't started yet," I tell her. "I have yoga mats in the corner for anyone that wants some extra cushion under them."

68

I look for Tillie and see her talking with Logan, one of my friends, and a fireman from our town. He's in a deep conversation with her, and she is beaming. I wonder what's going on, so I walk over. "Hey Logan, thanks for coming."

"Stella! Is this something that you're going to do regularly?" he asks.

"Maybe? Is this all your stuff piled up?" I look down and see a thick blanket, bolster and pillow.

"Yeah, this is my meditation stuff," he says. "I use meditation tapes at home all the time, but I have never done a sound session. I was just talking to Tillie about how this works so that I can get the most out of it. She told me to be as close to her as possible and how to set up my stuff. I'm going to need a yoga mat from you."

"They're right over there." I point to the corner in the back of the room. "I'll save you a spot right here next to me in front. I wasn't going to join the session, but now that I see who's here, I think I will."

I grab a yoga mat and a couple of blankets, one for under my neck and the other to use over my legs so I don't get chilled during the session. Logan starts to create his space next to me. I ask Tillie to start explaining the session.

"Good morning, everyone, my name is Tillie, and I am a holistic practitioner from Sedona. Stella is one of my dearest friends and I am so happy to see that she has such a large group of people that support her holistic healing practices. Just out of curiosity, has anyone here done a sound bath before? Wow, only two of you and Stella, you don't count." Tillie smiles and winks at me. "The first thing is to find a space where you can relax. You can lie down on a yoga mat or sit against a wall. The session will last about an hour. You may fall asleep or just fall into a deep state of relaxation. So, don't be surprised or embarrassed if we hear some snoring in the room. Here is the breakdown of the way my session will flow. I'll ask you to set an intention and what you hope to achieve or experience during the session. Do you want to release stress or anxiety? Connect with your inner self or gain clarity? That type of intention. Our bodies are made up of energy and sound is made up of energy. When the energy in our body gets blocked, we can get sick. That is why this is a healing practice. You may feel the vibrations move through you, and sometimes, you may feel a tightness. Breathe through it. That could be because the energy from the vibration is getting stuck in a block of energy within you. It will shift and vibrate and break that blockage away. This could cause your emotions to shift, so just go with whatever your body tells you because you may feel a physical or emotional detox. There is no judgment here, and we all have our own blocks and worries. This exercise will help restore your balance because sound has the power to heal."

I look around the room at all the people who care about me and show up to support me and my heart warms. I look at Logan who has a huge smile on his face, and his eyes are huge and excited. "Logan, you ready for this?"

He glances at me, "I am ready to rock this sound session, Stell. This is so cool. Can we keep Tillie? Let's not let her leave."

"Well, as much as I would love that she does have other people to heal and help. If this goes well, I can find someone in the area to continue the sessions."

"That would be amazing! I would pencil this into my schedule every time. Thank you for bringing such amazing things to town."

I try not to let him see the wetness in my eyes. "Thank you, Logan. I hope you enjoy it."

I give Tillie the go-ahead to continue.

"I'll be using my three singing bowls today, which will create vibrations. You may hear some chanting thrown in. I honestly never have a plan and my energy will take over and tell me where to move and what to do. I'll end the session by bringing you back into a state of awareness using my rain stick. It will sound like soft rain outside. If you're ready, I'll ask you to get yourself in a relaxed position with your head facing me and your feet towards the back of the room. You want the vibrations to go through you from top to bottom. Set your intentions, and we will begin."

***

Tillie was amazing, and I feel in my soul the difference this session brings to me. I need to bring this back into my life in a normal routine. I slowly sit up, collect my thoughts, and look around the room. Everyone is slowly sitting up or lying on their side talking to the person in front of them. Tillie instructed them to take a minute to collect their thoughts. I see Rob gather Sophie into his arms. She has tears running down her face. I slowly stand up and move over to my friend.

"Sophie, are you okay?" I ask.

"Stella, that was amazing. I'm sorry I'm such a mess, but these are good tears. I just can't seem to stop them."

Tillie joins us, squats down by Sophie, and puts a hand on her shoulder, "Honey, let those tears flow. They need to come out and as they do, they will shed whatever is blocked in you. Just breathe through the process. Stella let's give your friends a moment to just sit and be still. You can walk around and help me answer any questions."

We move around the room gathering feedback and answering any of the questions being asked. Some of the group could feel areas in their bodies where the vibrations broke through what felt like a blocked area or injury and others noticed emotional releases like Sophie.

As I get to Hillary and Garrett, I see them talking animatedly. "Hey, you two, what did you think?"

Hillary hugs me, "Awesome, Stella. I feel like a million bucks. I was just telling your brother I am extremely horny now. Is that normal?"

"Honey, you are always horny," Garrett says.

I roll my eyes at my brother. "Actually, Hillary, yes, there is a study that sound waves can cause the growth of new blood vessels around the clitoral area and enhance nerve stimulation, which increases sensation. Tillie has some clients that she has routine sessions for that have some issues after having children."

71

"See! I told you it was more sensitive than normal, Garrett. Let's go home and take advantage of the gift we were given. Thanks, Stella, it was great! Keep doing the sessions and I will be the first one to sign up!"

The rest of the comments are positive, and Tillie is in a deep discussion with my mom when I see Logan walking towards me with gusto. Oh boy! He grabs me in his huge arms and picks me up with a spin.

"Ugh, Logan you are squeezing the life out of me."

"I adore you and Tillie. I feel A-mazing!" He puts me back down on my feet and gives me a big smooch on the cheek. I look at this big bear of a man with his tattooed sleeves and a big smile. No wonder the kids love having him at the school as Mr. Safety.

"So, you enjoyed it? More than your plain meditation?"

"You know, I've had a weird kink in my left shoulder, and I could literally feel the vibrations get stuck. Like they were building up and then finally they broke through like a bomb going off and the kink released. Once that happened, I was able to feel the vibrations move from my head to my toes. Ab..so…lute…ly ah..mazing!"

"I'm glad you enjoyed it. I always feel amazing afterward too. Even if you don't work through a block when you finish a session you usually feel better than before."

"Thanks again. It was super cool. I'm going to grab my stuff and head out but keep me posted on the schedule for more."

"Will do!"

I head towards Mom and Tillie and watch them hug. "This is nice. My two favorite women, I adore, hugging each other."

Tillie says, "I am so excited that I finally got to meet your mother and father in person. Your mom invited me over for dinner, and I would love to, but I have a prior dinner on my schedule with the friends I'm here visiting in the city. Maybe on my way back out towards Sedona I can swing by here again and see the both of you."

I give Tillie a big hug. "Tillie, you know you always have an open door wherever I am, and if you can make it back through on your way home, I would love that!"

"Stella, I am so proud of you and reaching for your dreams. I was sharing that with your mom when you walked over. From the people in this room today, I'd say you have a lot of people in this town that love you very much."

"I do and I'm honestly overwhelmed at everyone that came today. Even the guys came, and I think they enjoyed the session."

"What's not to enjoy from one of my sessions? I can spin a nonbeliever right around. Even your doctors in the room commented to me about how they will suggest this practice to certain patients. I said everyone can benefit from a sound session."

Gertie walks over and hugs me. "Stella, the ladies and I love this amazing studio you've created. I don't know what those singing bowls did to me, but I feel like a younger version of myself. It's like the fountain of youth just poured through my body and gave me the most wonderful sense of energy."

"Gertie, I'm so glad that all of you enjoyed the session. I think it was a hit, and I will talk with Tillie and have her help me find someone good in the area who can offer these sound sessions more often. I wasn't sure what type of reaction I would get since it isn't a known practice."

"Honey, if I feel like this after each session, I'm going to shout it from the rooftops," Gertie says. "I need to head out, but if you think you're going to continue these sound sessions, I will for sure be attending. I think the others feel the same. Make sure you put a nice charge on them, too! Get some extra bucks in your wallet for providing this type of euphoria."

Tillie smiles and brings me to her side, "I am so happy you enjoyed the session. I'll make sure Stella finds someone to continue providing sound therapy since everyone has enjoyed it so much. I love helping share holistic healing practices with newbies. There is so much we can do to help heal our bodies."

***

Everyone has left, including my friend Tillie, and I am alone in my apartment just catching my breath when Mom sends me a text on the group chat.

Mom: Gertie posted a lovely message in Harmony Hears on FB. Wonderful experience today with you and Tillie. Thank you for bringing us all a wonderful morning. We are all so proud of you and happy to participate and support you!

Her message keeps getting emojis attached to it by everyone and a few direct text messages come my way reiterating the same type of thank you message. I pull up Facebook on my phone and see the post.

A SYMPHONY OF RELAXATION WITH SOUND THERAPY

Imagine being cocooned in a symphony of soothing vibrations as if you're floating on soft fluffy clouds made of harmony. Sound therapy is like giving your soul a spa day, where stress melts away and inner harmony emerges. Keep your eyes on Mint & Sage for more sessions to come!

Chapter Twelve

Jax

Three long weeks have almost gone by since the accident that ruined my life. I'm still stuck in casts on my knee and both wrists, and one hundred percent still relying on Charlie and others to do everything for me. This sucks. My life is on hold, and I can't do anything for myself or be alone.

Charlie comes into the room, "Oh good. I see you're up. We're going to move you into the family room today. I already have the couch ready and the ottoman for your leg. Sophie sent a list of your favorite movies to me, and I have you all set up for a day of movies to get you up and out of that bed."

"Fine."

"Do you want breakfast now or after your shower?"

"I don't need a shower. Food is fine," I reply.

"Food or shower first. You are having a shower today, Jax. I've let you push it off long enough. You'll feel better after one. Even if you just sit under the rain shower heads, it will make you feel better. I can put you in there and leave you alone, but one way or another we are getting you cleaned up. Don't force me to wheel you outside and shower you off with the hose. I'm not above doing that you know," Charlie says with her hands on her hips.

I can tell she's serious. "Yeah, how about breakfast in here, then shower in the shower?" I lift my brow at her and see her nod in agreement. "Then you can stick me in front of the television."

"Great. What do you want to eat? Eggs? Oatmeal?"

"Can you whip me up one of your southwestern omelets?"

"Yes, I'd be happy to do that for you. Do you want toast or bacon with it?"

"Toast and some hot sauce. I feel gross and not myself today. Maybe the hot sauce and some movies will get my head in the right space. Did you eat yet?" I ask.

Charlie stands there just staring at me, "No, I can join you again for breakfast. Jax…I'm here to talk if you need it. I know your mom and Sophie are starting to worry that you're slipping into a depression. Know that I'm here to talk to or to listen in addition to being your hands and legs for the time being. I have good listening skills. I can get a referral from my kids or husband if you need it."

"Charlie, you've been great. Awesome really. I'm just not a guy that likes to sit around. I'm usually on the go and working out. Just sitting around here is starting to get on my nerves. I'm restless, but there's not a damn thing I can do about it."

"It's all part of the healing process, and I know it can take a toll on someone like you especially having to be dependent for even the little things. Let's work together to try to get you in the right headspace. Food and shower and then, what if we drag you into a vehicle and just get you the hell out of the house today?"

I look at Charlie and try very hard to not look like a pussy while I wipe my eye like it itches. "Charlie, there is a big bonus in it for you if you get me the fuck out of here today. I don't care where we go if I see outside of this house and my property."

"Works for me. You think about what car we can get you into the easiest. If you don't have one, I have my SUV here. We can always try that if you don't want me to drive your car."

"Hmm, actually let's take yours if you don't mind. No one will expect me to be in your car. I'll make sure to fill up the tank for you."

***

Charlie manages to get me into her SUV, and we're heading towards the Mount Wilson Observatory. This drive was her suggestion and even though I don't want to admit it, she was right, and I am already feeling better.

"I never seem to take the time to drive out here and see how pretty the area is," she says to me. "If I am not working, I am usually at home with my husband or one of the kids is over, and we're having a family dinner."

"You've been taking care of me for almost three weeks, and I just realized I haven't even bothered to ask you anything about yourself. That's a dickhead thing of me to not do. I'm sorry Charlie. How many kids do you have?"

Charlie smiles, "I have three grown kids, and the two boys are married. The youngest, my daughter who is in her late twenties, is single and not in any hurry to change that. She's very career-focused and says a family or husband isn't in her plans right now."

"Good for her. I'm an only child but many of my friends back home stayed single until their thirties or even early forties. I think our generation wants to be financially independent before we slow down and move into having families. At least that's what I see from my friends and what I guess I want."

"That's smart. My boys both married in their late twenties but they both met wonderful women that were ready to have families. I am the proud grandparent of six grandkids ages eleven to three months old."

"Wow, that sounds like a lot of fun when they're all together. Are they all out here in the area?"

"Yes. I'm lucky enough that they are all within an hour from home. I see them all quite often."

"Sorry if this job taking care of me is keeping you from them."

Charlie waves me off. "Nonsense. I don't mind taking care of you. It's a nice feeling to be needed again. On another note, we need to take you to the doctor tomorrow for X-rays. How are you feeling about that? This will tell us if the bones are healing or if you need more surgery on your wrists."

"I'm hoping that everything is healing as it should be and that some of these casts come off sooner rather than later."

"I hope so too, Jax, I hope so too."

"Thank you for getting me the hell out of my house. I enjoy your company and I'm trying to be more aware of my attitude."

"You are doing just fine, Jax," Charlie says as she pats my casted hand.

Chapter Thirteen

Stella

Wow, the response I got back from the sound bath session is incredible, and there is a high demand for me to continue offering more. Tillie was able to give me some names of her contacts to help me find someone close to Lake Harmony to provide classes. I will keep them scheduled on Sundays or late in the evenings if Sundays begin filling up too quickly. I've reached out to a few of her contacts to see if they would be interested. Maybe if I can have a rotation of a few of them, I won't feel so worried about having it as a recurring special class offering.

This weekend, I'm heading into the city to buy more supplies for the products I sell in the studio. Since the studio opened, and I have a regular flow of clients coming through, my products are selling out like crazy. Thank goodness when Griff is home in the evenings, he doesn't mind labeling all the bottles for the oils and bath salts. He will do anything if I pay him with my shredded chicken tacos and margaritas. Easy enough trade for the free help.

The studio is between classes, and I am putting things on the shelf when Logan comes into the studio. "How is my favorite yoga master doing today?"

"Hey, Logan, I'm good. How are you doing?"

"I thought I'd stop by and see how my favorite little lady is doing and see if you have any more sound sessions scheduled yet for me."

"I love how enthusiastic you are about those. I don't have anything scheduled yet, but I plan to have at least one session per month if not two in the beginning. See what kind of demand continues for it. I'm thinking most likely on Sundays since the studio is typically closed and so is Genie's shop until noon. I don't want the noise to disrupt her shop next door. I'm waiting to hear back from some of Tillie's contacts. My goal is to have one scheduled for two weeks from now. I promise to keep you in the loop. I'll be updating my website with Griffin, and we're going to add a class schedule and some information on the upcoming sound sessions. I'll text you as soon as one is confirmed."

"Awesome! I hope they are as good as Tillie."

"Each person has their style but I'm sure they will all be similar. Some sound therapy practitioners even use a gong. Those are my favorites, but Tillie doesn't travel with her gong. It's too big and she prefers the singing bowls for travel."

"Gong? Did you say gong like a big disc with a hammer? Gong?"

"Yep. That's the one. It does a similar thing with vibrations, but I feel like it can dig deep into your body and release more. The sound is incredible."

"Oh man, please tell me we can try that. I am getting all excited already."

"You will love it. And as much as you enjoyed Tillie's session, remember to always make sure you're positioned as close to the sound as possible. You would not want to be in the back of the room for a gong session."

"Got it. Thanks, cutie. I'm off to the station now. I start my 48-hour shift today." He hugs me and heads to the door.

"Stay safe, Logan."

He turns and says over his shoulder, "Always. I'm Mr. Safety. Safety is my middle name." Then he continues out the door of the studio.

***

Griffin and I finished eating tacos and we're on our second Margarita working on updating the website and adding class schedules. It's easier to keep the same rotating schedule for now since I'm running the classes. Eventually, I can pull in someone else but for now, paying one person to manage the front side of the studio while I am in classes is enough.

"I heard back from two of Tillie's contacts today," I tell Griffin. "Sara can start right away and is excited to help me branch out. She uses singing bowls and a gong, so Logan will be excited. The other person, Evander, is only available for one session a month. His schedule is busier than Sara's, but I want to have options. They are charging me the same for each session, and I can fit that into the budget. I'll make sure to put a tip sign out for each of them. They said they use a QR code and it will go directly to their account."

"Oh, what do we know about them? Do they have websites so we can check them out?" Griffin asks.

"Yes, I already did that but here…check them out yourself."

Griffin grabs my phone and starts typing away, "Oh lordy, Stella bug. This Evander is cute. Look at his eyes. I hope he's gay."

"Griffin! Oh my god, you are ridiculous. Don't harass my sound practitioners."

"He is so good-looking. I can't wait to meet him. They don't live too far away from here. Maybe if they have regular clients that follow their sessions you will get new people through the studio. Sounds like a win-win for you, either way. I love how everyone took to the sound session. *Sounds* like you've brought a product to town that all the old townies needed."

"Very funny you goof. I'm getting very nice feedback for the yoga classes and the sound session. Josie asked me to do a private yoga session with her dance troupe and their parents. It makes me happy that I can provide something fun for them. Instead of them paying me, I donated the cost of the class to her dance troupe for new costumes."

"Aren't you the sweetest Auntie ever? That was very nice of you to do for her and her friends."

"You know I'd do anything for my sweet niece. She is the kindest girl for her age. What other pre-teen do you know who isn't a bit of a hormone mess with multiple personalities? Josie is always so level-headed. My nephew Daniel was too. I guess it comes from awesome parenting by Julia and Jackson."

"Could be. They are level-headed themselves, and I agree. Josie is the sweetest girl. I love her. She's Julia's mini-me."

"I had Gertie and the Widow Crew in my gentle yoga session today. I told Gertie she doesn't have to wear a leotard like in the 70s, but she says she does it so her boobs don't drop out of her bra. I almost peed myself when she said that in front of my class. One of my regular moms talked to her about trying a sports bra. Gertie just kept saying, *I had no idea that's what those are for.*"

Chapter Fourteen

Jax

Charlie's driving me home after my latest doctor's appointment and getting x-rays to determine how my wrists and knees are healing. Thankfully something is finally going my way, and everything seems to be mending. I'm now sporting two splints instead of plaster casts on my wrists. I can take the splints off so I can wash myself, and as of tomorrow, I am allowed partial weight-bearing on my leg. That means I can use crutches but since I can't put weight on my wrists, the doctor said to put the weight on my armpits, which isn't how you should use crutches but for the next two weeks, it means I can finally gain back some of my independence.

"Jesus, this shit is ridiculous," I blurt out.

Charlie shakes her head. "Are you looking at those tabloids again? You know it is only going to upset you. You shouldn't waste your time reading that garbage."

"I know but listen to the latest, Charlie. The headline is *Jax Turner's Fall From Grace: Is He Fading into Oblivion? In a startling twist of fate, Hollywood heartthrob Jax Turner is reportedly in seclusion, nursing his wounds and nursing a bruised ego after losing his coveted leading role to rising star Max Thorne. The once-dazzling Turner, known for his magnetic screen presence, now faces an uphill battle to regain his status as Tinseltown's leading man.*

The blockbuster film that was supposed to be Turner's next crowning achievement turned into a crushing blow as Max Thorne swooped in and stole the limelight. Industry insiders are abuzz with whispers that Thorne's captivating performance has cast a long shadow over Turner's once-illustrious career.

Turner, who once held the keys to the kingdom, now finds himself on the fringes of Hollywood, watching as Thorne basks in the glory that was once rightfully his.

The question on everyone's lips is whether Jax Turner can ever reclaim his throne. Can he rise from the ashes of this career-shattering setback and again become the shining star he once was? Only time will tell if his injuries heal, and if so, whether he'll have the fortitude to claw his way back to relevance.

With Max Thorne's star on the rise, Turner faces fierce competition for the A-list roles that once fell into his lap. Directors, eager for fresh faces and dynamic talent, are casting a wary eye on the wounded star, unsure if he can still deliver the box office magic that made him a household name.

As the days turn into weeks and the weeks into months, the world watches and waits to see if Jax Turner can summon the strength to reclaim his former place at the top of the Hollywood hierarchy. Will Turner emerge from hiding and reclaim his throne, or is the sun setting on his once-blazing career? Only time will tell.

I sit back and laugh, shaking my head, "I almost want to reach out and ask if that was supposed to pump me up or tear me down. I suppose they don't have too much to write about with my interview on a newsworthy show two weeks ago. I have nothing to hide, and they did a good job of stating the facts and talking about my injuries. I was honest and said I was bummed out that I was dropped from the movie, but I know how things go around here. Every minute during filming costs money and they couldn't put everything and everyone on hold with pay waiting for me to recover. I know I have at least another month of recovery in front of me." I look over at Charlie, "Do you think in another month I will be walking and able to live my life like I did before the accident?"

"From what your doctor shared today I'd say yes unless you do something stupid." She looks at me with a raised brow, "You should be healed up and fine. I think moving into physical therapy in a week is a good start at getting your strength and stamina back, but you've been sitting idle for a month. I don't think you realize how quickly your body loses strength. It won't be easy to get you back to where you were but you can do it with some hard work. You also have restrictions for a bit longer, so be mindful of those, or you'll be facing more setbacks."

"I'm going to decide in the next day or so if I am going to do my therapy here in LA or go back to Lake Harmony," I tell Charlie. "Do you have an opinion? If so, I'd like to hear it."

Charlie says, "Since you don't need me around anymore, I'd feel better if you went somewhere that you have support. Just in case you overdo it."

"Charlie, are you tired of me?" I ask with heavy sarcasm and a pout on my face.

"Nope. You've kind of turned into one of my kids at this point. You allow me to say what I think, and I think you should go home and have your parents and friends to help you through this next month. I see you're lonely, and I think it would get you back in the right frame of mind while you try to build up your strength and mobility. I don't think you have a real picture of what physical therapy entails, and there may be times when you are too exhausted to do much yourself. Go home, Jax. Let your parents spoil you a little bit. Your mom has been worried about you. Give Sophie time to make sure you're doing whatever you need to be one hundred percent again. That friend of yours had to be convinced not to fly here at least three times a week since she left. Go spend some time with everyone. You said to the doctor you can line up your physical therapy at home, so do that."

"So, you ARE tired of me huh?"

Frustrated she says to me, "You are as bad as my kids. That is not at all what I said!"

I start laughing and look at her again, "I heard you, and I'm going to take your advice. You haven't pushed me in the wrong direction yet, and you wouldn't start now. And you're right. I could use some quiet but knowing a friend or parent is there if I need them is comforting. I'll call my security guy and see if he can quietly get me out on a flight home. Can you stay another day to make sure I get out of LA?"

"For you? I can do that. I'm going to clean out your fridge too, so you don't come back to molded food."

"Take whatever you want since you've been the one doing the shopping. I can restock when I come back later."

She pats me on the forearm like mom would do, "Jax, you are going to be okay, and you will get your life back. You just have a little more work to do to get you at that point."

"Thank you, Charlie. That means a lot to me."

"You are very welcome."

***

The first call I make is to my parents. Mom answers on the second ring, sounding out of breath, "Jax! Oh my, I've been waiting for you to call me. I've tried not to pester you today knowing you were going to the doctor. What's the update?"

"Hey, Mom, it's good news. The nasty plaster casts are off my hands, and I am now in splints, which I am allowed to remove to take a shower. My knee is healing, and I will be able to put some weight on it soon, but I can't put weight on my wrists so it's a bit tricky still but better anyway. The doctor said I can do my physical therapy anywhere I choose, and he will send the orders over to them. Do you think you can put me up for a couple of weeks while I figure out things back in Lake Harmony?"

"You're thinking of coming home for therapy? Of course, I can put you up. This is your home for heaven's sake. Dad will be home in the evenings, and I'm around now that I've retired and can take care of you. When will you be arriving?"

"I'd like to try to get a flight out by tomorrow night, but if you need longer, I can push it off. I should be able to get around on crutches well enough to not need the wheelchair. Don't make a big fuss over me. We'll figure it all out once I get there. I'll text you the information for my arrival as soon as I know so someone can pick me up. I'm going to fly into the private airstrip, so the paps don't clue into my whereabouts."

"Oh, alright honey. Just keep me posted. Should I call Sophie, or did you tell her already?"

"I've got it, she's my next call, Mom, but thanks. Talk soon. Love you."

"Love you too, honey."

I hang up and call my best friend. She quickly picks up, "Hey. How'd the doctor's appointment go? Please tell me it was good news."

"They are going to amputate my leg and the left wrist isn't looking too good."

"Fuck Jax! What the hell happened?"

"Sophie," laughing I say, "Oh my god, relax. Why the hell would they want to cut off my leg? Jesus."

"You are such an asshole. I don't know why you would even joke about that. I hate you sometimes. This is not the moment for that kind of bullshit from you. Don't ever do that to me again."

"Fine. I'm sorry. The doctor took those horrible casts off my wrists and put me in two splints. Thankfully, I can finally shower by myself, and I'll be able to put some weight on my leg but not my wrists, so that means my armpits will be sore but at this point, I just want out of the damn wheelchair and to gain some of my independence back."

"That does sound like good news. Did you get the all-clear to start therapy soon, too?" Sophie asks.

"Yeah, the doctor just needs to know where I plan on doing that and that's my next call. I've decided to come back to Lake Harmony for my physical therapy. That way if I need help, I have you and Mom and whoever can spare the time to help me. It sucks being here in LA without you or the guys around, especially being out of commission for at least another month. I'm going stir-crazy just sitting in my house. Poor Charlie was forced to do movie and pizza nights with me."

"She did go over and above for you, but that's because you are easy to love and worry about. I hope you realize how lucky you were to get her. I love that you're coming home for your therapy. I'm happy to help you get back and forth; although, it depends on where. With the two of us together that could cause a frenzy around here. When are you heading in? Should I fly out and try to help you get here?"

"I'm going to attempt to get home by tomorrow night. I'm going to call Sully and see if I can get him or Reese or someone from his security team to fly in with me on a charter like we did when we snuck you into Lake Harmony. I don't want to go through the big airports and have the opportunity for someone to get a picture to sell to the tabloids. I just need some quiet and another month to keep healing. I already talked to Mom, and I'll crash with her."

"You know you're always welcome to crash with Rob and me. It's not like we don't have room in one of our four spare bedrooms for you."

"Sophie, I love you, but you guys are still in that honeymoon stage, and as much as I love you and like him, I don't want to be in the middle of the two of you."

Sophie laughs on the other end of the line, "What are you trying to say, Jax?"

"You two are always touching and all over each other. God only knows what I'd have to listen to if I stayed there. I love you, but that makes me a little uncomfortable."

"Whatever. You're just jealous that I have fun naked times with my man. I wish you had fun naked times with someone too."

"Too much, Soph. Anyway, I'll text you with any updates on my arrival. I miss you and can't wait to see you."

"Miss you too, buddy. Love you. I'm happy you got some good news."

"Thanks, I've got another call to make, so I'll talk to you soon." I hang up the phone and make one more call.

I dial and wait for him to answer, "Dr. Roarke."

"Hey, Noah, it's Jax. I'm hoping you can help me out."

"I will always try, Jax. How are things healing on your end? Bree has kept me in the loop on your injuries and everything. What do you need?"

"I've been cleared for physical therapy and instead of being stuck here in LA and avoiding the tabloids, I decided to come back to Lake Harmony and do it there. Can you find out for me what orthopedics group my doctor from here can transfer me to so that I can line up the therapy?"

"You got it. I'll reach out to my buddy tonight, and I'll text you the information for your LA doc. When will you be here?"

"I'm hoping to arrive by tomorrow night and have therapy lined up to start by next week."

"Let us know when you get here and if there is anything you need. You know we're both here to help get you on your feet and you need to come see little Jameson. You won't believe how big he is already at two months. He is so damn cute and starting to get kind of chubby. I wish he would sleep through the night a little better, but my son is always hungry."

"I can't wait to see him. The pictures Bree sends are adorable. I appreciate the help Noah, and I'll watch for the contact information for the ortho group."

"See you soon, Jax!"

I look over at Charlie and she has a happy smile looking at me. "What?" I ask her.

"Do you know that talking to your friends right now puts a sparkle back into your eyes and the biggest smile across your face that I haven't seen in person since I met you?"

"Don't embarrass me…and what are you talking about?"

"I think going back home to finish your recovery from the accident is a great decision based on how happy you were talking to all the people back at home." She grabs my hand and squeezes, "You are going to be just fine Jax, just fine. You have people at home that love you a lot, and now I can relax and not have to worry about you after I end my care.”

I look over at her, “Charlie, I don’t think you can get rid of me that easily.” She quickly looks at me with concern. “You’ve helped me through one of the shittiest experiences of my life. I don’t think I’d be here without you. You aren’t just my caretaker; you’ve become my friend.” I watch as her eyes grow watery.

“You’ve become more than a patient to me, too.”

Chapter Fifteen

Stella

Sophie and I are over at Mrs. Turner's house turning the downstairs den into a guest room. Rob brought the guest bed down for us, and we're throwing the sheets and comforter back on.

"Girls, thank you so much for coming over to help," says Mrs. Turner. "I didn't even think to bring the bed down so he could avoid the stairs. This will make things a little easier on him. I just wish we had a full bath down here, too. He'll need to go up to shower."

"Noah thought he may want to shower at the clinic after his therapy. He may work up quite a sweat trying to get through whatever they throw his way. Noah asked, and he can use the facility there before he comes home," Sophie says.

"Oh, that's good. I didn't know they had that set up over there. Good to know," Mrs. Turner says.

"As long as he has a bed and can manage to get to the bathroom here in the hall he should be fine," I chime in. "Some movement is good for him, I'm sure. And I think having the wheelchair here for him in case it becomes too much with the crutches is a good idea."

Sophie bites her lip, "I'm not sure he'll think of it that way, but he isn't one hundred percent weight-bearing on his wrists or knee, so after therapy, Rob and I thought he may appreciate the wheelchair to get around. Maybe not, though. Depends on how his moods go, ya know."

"Better to be prepared than to need something and not have it. I have a shower chair for him too if he needs to take a shower here, but he'd have to get up the stairs to do so," his mom says.

"What time is he expected to arrive?" I ask.

"He texted me when he got on the plane," Sophie says. "They should be here around eight o'clock tonight. Rob and I are going to go pick him up from the airstrip and get him back here to his parent's house."

"If you need me, just text me okay? I'll be around and ready for whatever you or Jax need."

"Thanks, Stella." Sophie gives me a quick hug. "I appreciate it so much, and thank you for bringing more of those oils here. He said he's been using them on his knee a lot and that the roll-ons have helped him relax when he gets anxious."

"I'm happy to help however I can."

We finish setting up Jax's room, and his mom pulls us into the kitchen for a treat. We're all sitting around the table lost in our own thoughts. "Jax may still go through some different emotions he isn't expecting," I tell them. "Therapy is a new chapter in this journey of healing. I want you both to be ready for an emotional setback if it happens."

"Stella, do you think that will happen? Charlie told me he's been upbeat about his situation and was looking forward to coming home," Sophie says.

"Soph, he has been sedimentary at home. The only movement he's had to do is go from bed to couch. Now, he's going to be expected to move from house to car to therapy. Throw in whatever they'll be doing in therapy, and he's going to be exhausted. I'm just worried that with how he reacted initially his mood may shift back to that when things don't go as quickly as he expects. He's been idle for a bit now, and his body lost a lot of stamina." I look at both Sophie and his mom, "Just be prepared. It may not be as easy for him as he's expecting and he's already lashed out at those closest to him."

"Girls, my Jax is not a patient person, and I think you're right, Stella. He's going to expect to come here and be able to move around swiftly and get in and out of therapy and feel like it's another workout. If healing were that easy, we wouldn't be so careful to avoid getting hurt. We should be prepared for his moods to shift. Thank goodness there are enough of us to spread the moods around. Can you girls prepare all his friends that we need some support over the next couple of weeks? I'm just not sure I can keep his father from strangling him if he lashes out at Mitch, or if he hears Jax lash out at me like before."

"Mrs. Turner, between family, friends, and their significant others, we'll be able to help out. Please just let us know if and when you need a break. We're all here for you. That's what family does," I say.

Chapter Sixteen

Jax

I got in late last night with the help of Rob and Sophie, and traveling was exhausting. Using crutches but trying not to put weight on my knee or wrists isn't as easy as I had hoped. I'm frustrated that Mom changed up her entire first floor so that I could move around freely including putting a bed in the downstairs den. It's not like I can't move around a little better than I did. Sophie made sure to add everyone's numbers to my phone in case I needed help. Mom and Dad are going to take me to my therapy sessions, but first, we're on our way to meet the orthopedic doctor to talk about next steps moving forward.

"Dad, you didn't have to make time today to go with Mom and me to the doctor."

"Son, I want to make sure you get the best treatment, and I also need to hear what the doctor wants you to do. I know you, and you're going to push harder than you're meant to. I just need to hear the doctor's directions myself."

"It's not like Mom couldn't tell you," I say.

"She could, but I want to hear it myself, and here we are already at the clinic. Dr. Roarke said this is the best group to use?" Dad asks.

"Yeah," I tell him. "Noah made sure I got set up with their best physical therapist and doctor. My team already got all the NDAs done so my treatment plan is secure. I told them to relax because of medical HIPPA, but they wanted a second layer of confidentiality."

"Better safe than sorry I suppose, son. Let's make sure to get a handicapped parking pass for the car too, Katy. That will make Jax going to and from a bit simpler for the driver."

"Oh, good idea, honey. I'll talk to the staff while we're waiting for Jax."

"I'll pull up to the door and let the two of you out. Jax, better put your hat and glasses on just in case. Katy, I'll come find you after I park."

Dad pulls up to the door, and Mom jumps out and comes around to the passenger side with my crutches. "Do you want me to go inside and see if there's a wheelchair, so you don't tire yourself out getting to the doctor?" she asks.

"Nope, just hand over my crutches, and I'll use them today," I say with more gusto than I have in me.

"Okay, just take your time."

I grab the crutches and use my good leg to push up out of the car seat. I sway a bit until I get the crutches under my arms.

Mom grabs my shoulders and helps settle me, "Good lord, don't scare me like that. You got it? Remember, nice and easy. No rush to get there, Jax."

"I'm good, Mom. Let's get inside. Dad will probably catch up to us before we can even check in at the rate I'm moving."

"Take your time, Jax, I'll be there as soon as I find a parking spot. Katy, be ready to grab him if he starts leaning over wrong."

***

Mom looks around the doctor's office while we wait for him to come in. "This is a nice office. The girls up front were very professional when they saw you walk in the door. I admire that they didn't pester you for an autograph."

I say, "I usually don't get harassed too much when I'm in Lake Harmony. That's one of the biggest reasons I decided to come home to do my PT. I can be myself here and not have to keep my LA brand on all the time."

"You have enough to deal with right now," Mom nods in agreement.

The door slowly opens and the doctor comes in. "Mr. Turner, it's good to meet you," he says as he shakes my hand. "I'm Doc Madden, the head ortho for Lake Harmony, and I've spoken a bit to Dr. Roarke about your situation.

Seems like you got some pretty good injuries from a recent car accident. How are you feeling?"

"I'm ready to start feeling more like myself, but I'm better today than I was a few weeks ago," I say.

"I understand. When we get injuries that interrupt our normal day-to-day routine, it can put a new perspective on life." Doc Madden looks around the room and his eyes settle on my crutches. "I also see that you're quite determined and are already using crutches, even though life would be easier and less exhausting if you were still in a wheelchair."

"I'm done with the chair, doc. I need to get back on my feet as soon as possible."

The doctor shakes both of my parents' hands, and they have a silent conversation while I watch. Doc Madden then goes to his desk and takes a seat opening my file. "Your doctors in LA did a great job, and looking at the accident and injuries it caused I'd say you got jerked around a good bit. You had injuries to both wrists and your right knee. You currently have a fifty percent weight bearing on all those injuries. How's that going, considering you walked in here on crutches." He crosses his arms and leans forward on my file and stares at me.

I hear mom gasp, "Jax!"

I turn and stare at her then look at the doctor and answer him, "I am on crutches, but the doctor in LA told me to use them with my armpits taking the weight, not my wrists. I try to balance on my good leg while I move the crutches with each step. I'm only doing the amount of weight I'm allowed to do. I won't lie, though. It's exhausting, and I just want to do whatever it takes to get to the point where I can walk again without extreme caution."

"That's got to be killing your armpits, but as long as you're not putting the pressure on your wrists or knee and causing issues with the fractures not healing correctly, I will trust that you are being careful." The doctor stares at me a second longer than what is comfortable making a strong point. "However, if you do overdo the weight-bearing limitations you currently have, let's talk about what that could look like." He glances at my parents and then back towards me, "If you apply more weight than that to fractured wrists, at this point you'd most likely end up in surgery having pins put in to support the fracture that hasn't healed properly. The knee being reinjured could also mean surgery and six to eight more weeks in a wheelchair with no weight bearing. We don't want that."

He stares at me again for a long second, and it's very clear to me what his expectations are. "Right," I say. "Follow the plan and don't put more than fifty percent weight on my injuries."

"Great! Glad we have an understanding. Let's talk about your PT. I have you set up with Keller. He's my best therapist here and will also be strong enough to push you along. He is great at healing fractures and has worked well with other patients who have lost strength and stamina. You'll get some homework to do at home but again," he looks directly at me, "no more than fifty percent and follow directions."

"Sounds good. When do we start?"

"Tomorrow. I've already made your schedule since you said to go ahead and get you set up. You're going to work on mobility first. Nothing crazy, but I think you will see that a little PT pushes you a lot in the beginning. I'm going to give you a prescription for anti-inflammatory meds to help ease any discomfort. During PT, you'll be working on mobility stretches along with massage and electrical stimulation. If there is any scar tissue in your surgical areas, Keller will help work through those areas. How is your current pain level?"

"I'm at about a four or five most days and can get by with some ibuprofen."

"Good, I don't like giving pain meds out if you don't need them. You will be sore, so I advise you to take an ibuprofen either right before the session or directly after. Don't let it go too long before you take something if it's needed. Stay ahead of the pain. Keller will also make sure to send you home with some ice packs you can wrap around your wrists and knee. You'll learn more from him about what to do at home. I'll be in contact with him during your therapy, and any signs you're not following directions, I'll be told, and then we will be forced to find a better solution to the situation. Any questions?"

Mom leans forward and asks, "Dr. Madden, should Jax be using the wheelchair instead of the crutches still? I don't want him to cause more harm to his injuries."

"Jax seems to be doing alright with the crutches, but he hasn't had to use them to go too far. He will need to listen to his body and let you know if he is too fatigued for the crutches. If you have a chair on standby that's a good plan, and if not, let's make sure you have one at home for his use just in case."

"Mom, I'm fine with the crutches."

Dad looks at me with a stern scowl, "I'm glad you can get around on those, but you may be too exhausted after PT with Keller to move. Let's just be prepared for it in case. It's no big deal for us to keep a chair in the garage. Your energy needs to go into PT and healing, not trying to crutch your way around. Right, Doc Madden? Can we also get a handicap card for the car for parking?"

"Yes, when you check out the front staff will have that ready for you. Jax, focus on healing and PT. The chair is there for you to move about and not use your energy. Remember to focus on what the important factor here is...healing and getting back on your feet one hundred percent."

"Thank you, Doc Madden, I appreciate you taking the time to work me into your schedule and get me set up with therapy. I'm home to get whipped into shape as quickly as possible."

"I am happy to help, Jax. But remember...healing takes time. The more you push, the slower it will be. Listen to Keller and listen to your body. You know what you can handle. We just want you to get back up to the level of health that you had before the accident. Reach out with any questions or situations that arise."

Chapter Seventeen

Stella

Griff and I are hanging out at Cooper's Corner and some of the gang came in to have dinner and join Trivia Tuesday. "Hey everyone, nice to see you," I wave.

Julia comes over and gives me a big hug, "Jackson and I have a night to ourselves and thought we'd come out to see you and have some wings and cold beer. How are you doing, Stella?"

"I'm good. Guess what? I got two people to agree to do sound sessions at the studio moving forward, so I should be able to have at least two sessions a month for now. Logan has been stopping in or texting me since the session with Tillie, so I didn't want to waste any time. He is so excited about the sound sessions. It cracks me up!"

"That sounds great! I love how much he enjoyed that with Tillie. Sometimes looking at him you forget he is a big loveable teddy bear," Julia says.

"Who's a loveable teddy bear?" Jackson asks as he comes up behind Julia and hugs her around the middle.

"Logan." We both say at the same time.

"Ah, yes, that fits. How are you today, Stella?" Jackson asks.

"Good. I was just telling Jules that I have two sound therapists lined up for sessions."

"You better let Hillary know. She's been harassing both Jules and Garrett about when her *Vajayjay therapy* will continue," Jackson says with a chuckle and shaking his head.

"Oh my god, seriously?" I look at my sister and she's nodding and laughing. "Hillary is insane! God bless our brother. He has his hands full with her."

"I think Garrett can handle it. He needed someone to keep him on his toes and well…Hill…fits that mold," Julia says. "They are good together. Keep it feisty."

"And with that comment, I'll go check to see if Griff needs anything else. Hey Coop, we should be good to go in a few."

Cooper nods at me and takes a pitcher of beer and glasses to the table where Julia, Jackson, Ellen, and Scott are sitting. "Hey, who's all coming tonight? Need another table?" he asks them.

I walk towards the front of the room where Griff is setting up trivia night.

"I'm about ready, Stella bug," Griff says. "Want to walk around and hand out the trivia sheets for me?"

"You got it. Oh boy, here come Garrett and Hillary. Save me tonight. She's all about her *Vajayjay therapy.*"

"Um, her what?"

"You heard me. I guess she's been talking about when the next sound therapy is scheduled but has been calling it her *Vajayjay therapy.* You haven't heard her talk about it at work?" I ask him.

"No!" Griffin insists. "Although…we haven't been at the same event or in the shop together much for the last week. I know the last time I saw her she was talking about the crazy sexy times she and your brother had after Tillie's session and I told her to stop it because it was making me jelly. *Vajayjay therapy*…that is fan-fucking-tastic. That girl! Oh look, Sophie and Rob just came in. Gotta kiss my sweetie, be back in a second honey."

Griff runs off towards Sophie and Rob and gives Rob kisses on both cheeks. Sophie grins up at him and says, "What? Am I nothing to you?"

"Oh sweets, I'm happy to give you kisses too," Griffin says, kissing her on the cheeks.

"Hey, nice to see you two," I say to Sophie and Rob. "How's Jax doing Sophie?"

"Maybe we shouldn't discuss him tonight," Rob says with big eyes at me warning me to avoid the topic.

"The jackass? Is that who you are talking about?" Soph asks.

"Nope?" I answer.

"He's back to being a jerkwad. Yelling at his poor mom and being very short with me."

"What, why? He was fine when he got home a few nights ago. How has he moved from fine to jerkwad in just a day or so?"

"Because he has been pushing too hard to get better and now he had a setback," Sophie tells me. "His mom took the crutches away after picking him up from PT where he was madder than a nest of bees."

"So… he's been lashing out?"

"Oh yeah. He is unbelievable. Rob took my phone away before we came here because I was yelling at my text messages."

"Come here, friend," I pull her into me and wrap her in a big hug. "You can't fix him. I had a feeling he was going to react this way. Be there for him but as a friend, not as a punching bag." I hear her sniffle.

"I know, but it's so hard to watch my best friend hurting. Physically and mentally. I can't help him or fix it. I don't know what to do anymore."

I look up at my big brother and wink, "It's not your fault. He needs to figure it out. Let him know you're there for him when he needs help but not there to be abused. Focus on you and your happiness right now. When he needs you, he'll reach out. He did last time. Maybe if you and his mom aren't his punching bags, he'll stop lashing out again like last time."

"His poor parents are stuck with him."

"Actually…" I pull back and look at my brother Rob. "Do you have anyone in the rental Sophie used?"

"The love shack, no, not right now and not any time soon since the summer renters have all left. Why, what are you thinking?" Rob asks.

"Stella, what are you thinking?!" Sophie says.

"Let's take a seat and brainstorm with everyone, but I have an idea that may help his situation and take the pressure off everyone else."

Chapter Eighteen

Jax

I've had three days of PT with a lot of stretching and sweating, and now I'm not allowed to use crutches unless going to the bathroom because I'm overdoing it. What the hell is this bullshit? I'm working my ass off to get better, and they treat me like I'm some handicapped invalid. I'm sick of this shit. I'm in my room ignoring my parents and any texts or calls that have come in since last night when I told my best friend I'm sick of her and tired of her harassing me and then yelling at my mom at dinner when she tried to serve me in my room. I don't need to be here and take this shit. I'm Jax fucking Turner the Hottest man in Hollywood.

"Knock, Knock," I hear at the door and watch as Aunt Gertie walks into the room.

"Hey."

She walks over and kisses me on the cheek and then smacks the back of my head.

"Ow, what was that for?" I rub my head.

"Do you honestly need to ask? Your mother is a nervous wreck in her own home, and Uncle Pete and I had to get your father out of the house this morning before he barged in here to kick your ass."

I jerk my head up and look at her. "Huh?"

"Jax," she says while shaking her head at me and sits down on the bed next to me. "You're angry and frustrated. I understand that. You have injuries that keep you from being who you are meant to be but that does not give you the right to become an asshole and treat people who love you like shit."

I'm staring at my Aunt Gertie and my jaw is most likely on the floor.

"What?" she asks.

"You don't swear, Aunt Gertie."

"Well, thanks to you and your idiotic behavior, you've forced me to swear, and that makes me even more pissed off."

"Uh-huh."

"Anyway, while your Uncle Pete has your dad out trying to calm down this morning, I'm here to pack your shit because kiddo you are moving out!"

"WHAT! Where the hell am I going?" I ask.

"Anywhere but here with your parents. I cannot watch you behave this way and treat your wonderful parents with such disrespect. You have managed to piss them and your best friend off. Sophie called your mom last night and said they're moving you out of everyone's target range. If you want to act like an asshole, you can do it while being alone."

"What if I need help?"

"Then you are going to have to ask for it. But, in the meantime, you won't have anyone around to be your punching bag."

"Why do I continue to be the one that keeps getting the shitty treatment? I'm the one who's injured!" I yell at her.

"Yes, you are," Aunt Gertie agrees. "But your words to the people you love are hurting them, too." She grabs my jaw in her hand and turns my face to look at her. "No matter how old you get, Jax Turner, you will always be my little Jaxie, and I am not going to allow you to hurt the people you love because you're hurting and frustrated. We're going to put you somewhere safe where you have time to heal, and where you can't harass other people. You need to stop and reflect on your actions, buddy. You are mobile enough to handle moving about with a wheelchair or your crutches, and we'll make sure you get fed and transportation to and from your therapy. What we won't do is allow you to continue to attack people around you who just want to love and help you. Understand?"

"Fine. Where am I going?" I ask.

"To the love shack."

"The what?"

"Rob's rental house where Sophie stayed when she was here hiding. It's all on one floor and has a walk-in shower. You should be good to go. It has a security system so if anyone should bother you outside of friends and family, you can handle that too. Any questions.”

“No,” I shake my head, knowing when I’ve been bested. “I guess I’ll get myself dressed and ready to go.”

“Good idea, kiddo. I’ll give you some space unless you need help dressing?”

“Nah, I got it. Aunt Gertie?”

“Yeah, Jaxie?”

“I’m just frustrated. Life is throwing me curve balls, and I don’t have a mitt to catch them.”

“Jaxie, you just gotta take a deep breath and forget the mitt, and use the goddamn bat!”

I smile at my crazy aunt and watch as she marches out the door. Before she walks out, Aunt Gertie turns and says, “Don’t make me swear again, Jax! Ladies don’t swear. Yell if you need me. We leave in an hour after you eat some breakfast.”

Once she’s gone, I grab my phone.

Jax: I’m sorry
Sophie: I know
Jax: I love you
Sophie: Love you too. I’ll be by to check on you later @LS
Jax: LS?
Sophie: Love Shack, I’ll bring lunch and we can have a LONG talk
Jax: thank you for not turning your back on me
Sophie: Never! Although I REALLY want to kick your ass right now
Jax: Understood

I carefully get my sore ass up off the bed and change. Looks like I’m being kicked out of my parents’ house for misbehaving. What’s next?

***

I’ve been transferred over to the Love Shack rental by Aunt Gertie. She got me inside and unpacked my suitcases. I’m on the couch with my leg up, rubbing the tender area, when I hear the alarm beep and look over to see Sophie and Rob walk in.

"Hey."

Rob looks over, "Hey." Then turns to Sophie, "I can stay if you want me to."

"Nope. My best friend," she turns to me with a pointed look, and then back to him, "and I are going to have a long heart-to-heart, and he's going to learn to understand how things are looking moving forward."

Rob kisses her and looks my way, "Good luck, buddy. She's been pretty pissed at you."

"Understood."

Sophie walks him out and then comes back to me. She looks down at me rubbing my leg, "You, okay? Hurting today?"

"Yeah, my knee is throbbing today, so I just started massaging it like Charlie used to. Can you go to my room and grab the oil from Stella? It's probably in the bathroom where Aunt Gertie unpacked my bathroom things. It's the yellow labeled one."

"Yep, give me a second." She pops up and comes back after a few minutes. "Looks like it's almost gone. I'm happy to see that you've been using it."

"It helps the spasms more than I thought it would, and right now, I need something to help get my leg to stop throbbing."

"I'm happy to help you. Why don't you lean back and relax and talk to me while I try to help? What's going on in that head of yours Jax?"

Sophie gets the oil out and starts rubbing it around my knee and, between her warm hands and the oil, the throbbing starts to settle down a bit. "I'm sorry, Sophie."

"Mm-hmm."

"I was feeling pretty good back in LA. I was given the go-ahead to use crutches if I didn't put a lot of weight on my injuries. Once I got here, I started going from Mom's over to therapy…" She looked up at me with concern and then went back to massaging my knee, "…and then with the back and forth and Keller pushing me to my limits, I broke. My knee and wrists started hurting more than before because he was stretching the scar tissue and working on mobility. I refused to use a wheelchair because I'm an idiot and so my pain and frustration spiraled."

She stops and looks at me, "What changes are you going to make now with this situation you are in?" She waits, and after I don't immediately answer, she goes back to focusing on my knee.

"I don't know."

She looks up and her hands stop moving, "You don't know."

I bite my lip, "Other than not being a jerk to everyone around me…that's probably a good place to start. I need to focus on taking better care of myself, so I don't have a bigger setback."

She doesn't look up but says, "Keep going…"

My bestie is full of piss and vinegar because of me. I continue, "I'm going to listen to the people around me and focus on healing. I am going to follow the doctor's orders. I will ask for help when I need it. I will patiently wait for you to not be angry with me."

She exhales and her worries seem to lift along with some of mine, "That's a very good start. Are you going to listen and accept the help we want to give and not be a stubborn jerkwad and think you can do it all alone?"

"Yes. I promise I will accept whatever help is given without being a major ass."

"Great. Tomorrow, Rob is coming to get you for dinner and poker night with the guys. Wheelchair or crutches--it's up to you--but he's ready to help with either, and you WILL accept his help. We are all worried about you. I thought your being here was going to be better for your healing because you have so many of us who want to help you, but instead, you pushed us all away and thought you could handle it alone. YOU CAN'T. You have to learn to accept that right now you still need to lean on anyone that offers help. Take it.

Don't be embarrassed by needing help. Okay? Can you do that for me? Because I don't like being angry with you."

"I can do that for you. I can't promise I won't lash out a little, but I'll try harder not to be a jerkwad. Do you forgive me?"

"I forgive you."

"Are you still pissed at me?"

"A little bit. I was REALLY mad Jax. You were horrible!"

"I'm sorry, I'll be more mindful of taking my frustrations out on everybody moving forward."

"Good. How's your leg feeling? Did that help a bit?"

"Yeah, buddy, it helped a lot. Wanna come over here, snuggle, and watch a movie with me?"

"Yep, let me go grab the sandwiches and chips I brought for lunch. You pick the movie…nothing gross since I have to eat while watching it."

Chapter Nineteen

Stella

It's my last yoga session of the day, and I'm walking the room while the class relaxes in the restorative pose, Shavasana. During this time, I like to put a touch of essential oil on my participant's foreheads with a light touch on their shoulders to deepen their relaxation and help promote stress reduction.

Sophie came in for this class and once everyone else left, she cleaned up her space and headed my way to fill me in on her talk with Jax earlier.

"Sounds like you got through to him. How did he feel about moving out of his parents' house?" I ask.

"He didn't fight too hard. Stella, I think this will be a good thing for him as long as he doesn't keep pushing his injuries too much. He needs to be more aware of how much he can do—his limitations."

"That's true. With any injury or loss of independence, we don't always realize how bad things are until we need to do things for ourselves. I know you and his parents are making sure he'll have warm meals and not need anything, so I do think this could help him. How was his mental state?"

"At the time, a bit….reserved? I think he was shocked that Gertie moved him out of his parents' place and over to the rental."

"Was he in any pain or working through it?"

"When I got there, he was rubbing his knee. Said it was hurting bad. He even asked me to get the oils you had sent to him in LA. The yellow one was almost gone, so he must be using that a lot."

"Oh good. Yeah, that was the one to help with muscle spasms. I'm glad he's using that stuff. It should help."

"I'm going to head out, but will I see you at book club tonight?" Sophie asks me, then continues, "The boys are having poker night and Rob is taking Jax with him. I feel like I deserve a night with the girls after being so worried."

I nod, "I plan on coming over. A night with the girls is usually a good time, and you need a night not to worry. Rob taking Jax to poker night is perfect. I'm going to clean the studio and lock up for the day. If you need anything, let me know."

Sophie walks with me to the front door, "Thanks, Stella. See you later." She waves goodbye from the sidewalk and heads to her car.

I go around the studio locking up and stopping in the front at my product display. If Jax is almost out of the oil, I should make sure he has enough. I grab another bottle, and as I walk to the register, I also grab one of the journals I sell and a small salt lamp. Why not?

***

I pull into the drive of the rental, or the "love shack," as everyone calls it, and pause. I hope I'm not overstepping. I don't know Jax well. Of course, we went to school together, but we weren't close. We also both graduated and left Lake Harmony shortly after. In the last decade, he found his way to Hollywood, and I traveled the country finding my happiness. Now we're adults with nothing in common.

Stella, you have the knowledge to share, and he needs all the support he can get right now while he heals his body and spirit. Share what you've been taught. Don't be a chicken. It's just Jax. You don't give a crap if he's a Hollywood star or not. To you, he's the dork that was in school plays and tried to join the choir. Here we go!

With a determined mindset, I grab the items I brought from the studio and walk to the code box in the garage. Rob gave the code to me earlier, so I entered it to let myself in and knock, and as I open the door, I announce myself. I don't want Jax to freak out that someone is invading his space, and I don't want to surprise him in an uncomfortable situation. "Jax, you decent?"

I hear his laugh coming from the other room, "Yeah, come on in. I'm on the couch."

"It's Stella," I say. "I'm just dropping some things off for you." I turn the corner and see him in the family room on the couch. He's in basketball shorts, a tight t-shirt, and barefoot. "Hey."

"Hi, Stella. How have you been? I haven't seen you since Sophie's birthday."

"I'm good. The better question is how are you?" I look at his knee, and the scar is bright red. "That looks like it hurts."

"Yeah, I've realized that even though I'm only in splints on my wrists, I still can't manage to massage my leg as easily as I want. I was sitting here trying not to aggravate my wrists while trying to soothe my knee. Therapy was rough today."

"Well, then, today must be your lucky day. I've got time to spare and…" holding up both my hands to him, "two good wrists."

"It's okay. I'll manage. I know you've got better things to do tonight than sit here with me."

He looks like he needs help but doesn't want to ask for it, "Cut the shit, Jax. I'm here and I can help you. From what Sophie shared, you're going to be humble and accept all help coming your way, right? I think that's the latest." I smile at him and do a gimme gesture for the oil. "Hand it over."

"Don't tell Sophie I tried to deny help, please. But, yeah, if you could help me right now, I think it would help the spasms. Your oil has been awesome. My home nurse in LA, Charlie, used it every day on me."

"I'm glad I could help. Let me work on this knee for a bit, then I'll show you what else I brought you."

"You didn't have to bring me anything."

I stop opening the oil and look at him with a raised brow.

"Thank you for your help, Stella."

While I'm working on his knee, we fall into an awkward silence. We don't know each other well, and we haven't been alone in years. I try for small talk, and he answers, and then we resume the silence.

"Stella?"

"Huh," I answer while not looking up.

"This shouldn't be so awkward being alone together, right? We've known each other our entire lives, and we aren't exactly strangers."

I laugh, "Oh, my god! Why is this so awkward between us right now? I've known you forever and this was just kinda weird."

"It shouldn't be. Okay, I'll start....Sophie seems to be close to you and Griffin. Thank you for welcoming my best friend to town and treating her like a normal person."

I stop what I'm doing and say, "Sophie is normal. Why would I treat her any differently? She is one of the sweetest and most sincere people I have ever met, and she loves Griffin, which is very important to me. She has become one of my best friends too."

"I know Sophie is normal, but a lot of people just see the Hollywood version of her. Not the real person."

"Jax, I see Sophie for who she is and how she treats others. I don't view her by her job. I don't give a crap about your Hollywood status either. I see you as the dork from high school who loved being in the plays and should never, and I say never, have tried to broaden your ability and add singing."

"Oh my god. That was horrible. Every once in a while, the gossip rags will pull that footage of me, and it's released into the world reminding me to never sing outside the shower. The guys make fun of me all the time, and when we're all together they try to get me to sing with them as a joke."

"The guys? OH…you mean the band guys. Which band is it again? Rock band, right?"

"Are you seriously asking this right now?"

"Um…yep. Why?"

"What rock band? Brick Row is finishing up a world tour and it's what band…oh those rock guys. You kill me."

"Rock Band, Hollywood Star, blah blah blah. That is the job that you do--not the person you are."

He stares at me for a few minutes while I continue to manipulate the muscles around his knee.

Jax says, "That feels amazing. How did you get it to loosen up so fast?"

"Magic. Now while we're talking, I brought you a refill on this oil so you never run out. If it's working, then keep at it. Do you get massaged at therapy?"

"Yeah, Keller usually ends my therapy session with a massage or electric stim after he works my injuries to death. Why?"

"Take your oil with you to therapy and have him use it when he does massages. No reason that you can't use it more often."

"Oh, good idea, yeah, I can do that tomorrow."

"Also, I brought you a salt lamp. I'm going to put it in…" I look around the room, "…in here, I think. Is this where you spend most of your time when you aren't at therapy or out?"

"Yeah, the couch with my leg up is the most comfortable spot if I'm not in bed."

"Okay, so yeah, I'll plug it in here. It will also be a good nightlight, so you don't fall if you get up at night. Salt lamps help detoxify the air you breathe and will calm you." I hesitate and bite my lip feeling worried.

"What's wrong?" Jax asks.

"You know what I do and what I believe in right? A holistic approach to wellness?"

"Yeah. Sophie shares all the stuff she's been learning from you, why?"

"How do YOU feel about holistic healing and that stuff?"

"I'm open to anything that works to make me better."

I smile, thankful that he's open to this, and put my hand back on his knee. Jax is staring at me hard, gazing into my eyes and his eyes move around my body like he's memorizing me. I watch him scan my face, my hair, and my chest, while I continue talking, "I'm always nervous with new people when I don't know how they feel about my holistic beliefs. I just want to help and sometimes taking a holistic approach gives that little extra bump toward making someone better, you know?" He's still checking me out with his roaming eyes. "JAX!"

"Shit. Sorry, did I flake out?"

"Yes! You were just staring at me and didn't hear a thing I was saying. Where'd your mind take you?"

He blushes, "I was just thinking…about all the stuff Sophie's done with you and at your studio."

I feel like he's not telling me everything, but continue, "OH, anyway…I was saying I would like to try to help you with your healing if you're open to it."

"I'm open to it. What are you thinking?"

"I brought you a journal and I want you to start using it every day. Write down whatever comes to mind. Feelings, pain, frustrations, good things, bad things, stray thoughts, whatever."

"You want me to write in a diary?"

"No, I want you to journal. It's a proven fact that writing your thoughts and feelings down on paper about anything challenging or upsetting can help you move forward because putting those thoughts and feelings down on paper symbolizes you releasing or letting go of them. I think it could help with the frustrations you're dealing with."

"I'm frustrated that it's taking so long to heal and be back to normal."

"What if normal never comes?" I stare at him waiting for a reaction.

"Why wouldn't it?"

"All I'm saying is your normal before the accident may not be your normal now, and it could trigger your frustration and that throws off your ability to heal. You have other frustrations too. Sophie said you were upset you lost this last film. You had worked hard to prepare for it. Frustration. You see the crap the tabloids are saying. Frustration. You aren't independent, yet. Frustration. Your body doesn't work like it used to. Frustration. Your car is wrecked. Frustration. You just got kicked out of your parent's house. Frustration. Should I continue or are you getting the point?"

"Are YOU trying to cause me FRUSTRATION Stella, because you are doing a damn good job?"

"No, but I'm bringing them forward because if you try writing in the journal like I suggested maybe some of that FRUSTRATION will ease and give you some breathing room. How are you sleeping at night?"

"I only sleep a couple hours and then I move and either put stress on my knee or my wrists and wake up."

"We need to work on that, too. Your body needs rest to heal, and if you aren't getting solid hours of sleep that isn't good enough. Did you try using any of the oils for relaxation at night before bed?"

"I think I tried the roll-on one once or twice."

"Have you ever tried meditation or sound therapy?"

"No. I can't meditate. I feel dumb and my mind starts listing all the things on my to-do list."

I pause and take a cleansing breath, "If I want to try something to help you sleep, would you be open to it?"

"I promised Sophie I would accept all the help offered. It's not something weird, is it?"

"Nope. Just some meditation with oils but I think it could help you. Tomorrow I'm going to come over, and we are going to do a meditation session, massage your knee, and get you set up for a restful night." Jax hesitates as if to say something, then just nods at me. "This is great Jax! I think this could help you so much!"

Chapter Twenty

Jax

This poker night is some serious shit. Garrett has a food spread that covers all the counters in the kitchen. Rob picked me up as directed, and we are both staring into Garrett's kitchen.

"Holy shit, Garrett. What's with the food?" Rob asks as he helps me over to the dining table.

"Hillary had a big event, and this was the food they never served. That's why I texted everyone to please show up hungry."

"Jax, you good? Should we prop your leg on another chair?" Rob asks.

"I don't want to be a bother."

Rob crosses his arms, "OH no buddy, that ain't gonna fly here. Sophie made it very clear that you're not to stress your injuries and have a good time. We're propping that fucking leg up and you're gonna love it. Then I'm going to make you a big plate of food and shove a beer in your hand. That good, man?"

"Sure, sounds great. I appreciate all your help during my time of need." I smile big and play along. I do appreciate their help.

He smirks back at me catching my sarcasm, "Great. I hope you brought cash because I plan on cleaning out your wallet tonight."

The rest of the guys slowly walk in as I'm enjoying my first beer and eating some of the food off the plate piled high in front of me. I don't know these guys too well because the Stone brothers were a lot older than me. Same with the spouses of their sisters. Cooper, I know from going to Cooper's Corner for food and drinks when I'm home. Everyone treats me normally except for the occasional sarcastic jab at my most handsome man status. This is why I came back to Lake Harmony. My soul needed some recharging.

Noah asks, "How's therapy going? Are you still in the 'it gets worse before better' phase?"

"Yeah, it's been brutal. Keller works my knee like it should be able to bend to the point he expects, and while he's torturing me, I'm crying inside like a little girl. Then he moves on to deep tissue massage on my wrists, and I hurt so bad by the time I get home, I can barely move. Thank God Stella came over yesterday after I got to the couch and rubbed me down." All eyes quickly move to stare at me.

Rob leans forward, "What was that about Stella?"

"Ah…she stopped by to bring me more of the oils she sent to me in LA for the muscle spasms and caught me trying to massage my knee and helped me instead."

"Don't hurt my little sister," Garrett says with a straight and very serious look.

I'm looking around the table, and all the guys that five minutes ago were shooting the shit with me, now seem to have their hackles up. Taking a deep breath and exhaling, "I like Stella. I've known her my whole life, even though we don't know each other well now as adults. We were just talking and reconnecting, and she felt sorry for me and helped put oil on my knee and loosen up the muscle. She wants to try some meditation exercises tomorrow to help me sleep better. She was very bossy about it. I didn't feel like I could say no to her."

Rob stares at me, leans forward, and rests his arms on the table, "Stella has a huge heart. Don't abuse it. She will stand her ground, trust me, but she tends to see only the good in people. Don't disappoint me by taking advantage of that, and don't get Sophie mad because that is her best friend here alongside Griffin."

"Stella and I are friends or becoming newly re-acquainted friends. Seriously, I have no bad intentions."

"Keep it that way," Cooper says under his breath looking like he could snap me in half.

Noah claps his hands together, "Anyway….Jax, have you been cleared for any light exercise yet? I've been swimming in the lake this summer and when you get the all-clear I'd be happy to take you with me. It would be a good soft movement for both your leg and wrists."

"Not yet, but that sounds great, Noah, thanks. I'll let you know."

"Can we get back to poker and me taking all of your money now," Jackson says to bring the mood back to relaxed.

Chapter Twenty-One

Jax

Sophie dropped me off at therapy, parked the car, and then snuck in after me in her rocker chick disguise. Keller laughs when she walks back to the therapy station where he is stretching out my leg.

"Sophie, do you still need to wear a disguise around town?" he asks her.

She flops down on the chair next to the table I'm on, "Probably not, but I'm trying not to freak the town out by spotting both of us out together. The last thing we need is for people to think Jax is here and that we are hooking up as a couple. The townies have been great about allowing me to become one of them, and I try to be out and about and stop to talk to anyone local when I bump into a fan. I figure the more they see me, the less of a shiny new toy I am. I would love to be at the point where Jax is and not have to worry about it at all."

"Soph, I grew up here, so most of the townies don't give two shits about me," I tell her. "The only ones who do a double take are the summer tourists or new people who move into town and don't realize I grew up here. I think going out around town and to yoga will get them adjusted to you now living here."

"He's probably right, and it doesn't hurt that you are connected to the Stone Family. They're highly respected in Lake Harmony, plus you have direct ties to the sheriff," Keller says. "Although it is kinda cool that you're both here, I get that people who don't know you and just see you in films may see you as a couple due to proximity."

Sophie nods, "Yeah, and right now, my best friend here needs to focus on his healing and getting back to normal. Plus, Rob enjoys the disguises."

I look at my best friend, "Please don't elaborate on that further."

She sits back and laughs, "Gotcha. So…Keller….how is my best friend doing? Will he be ready to join Dancing with the Stars next season?"

Keller stops my stretching and looks at me, "Are you doing that show, man?"

Sophie is trying to hold it together when I answer, "Don't listen to Soph. She's pulling your leg."

"Actually…Jax, Keller is pulling yours," she says and starts cracking up as we both give her a look. "Come ON! You left yourself wide open for that one!"

"Have you been talking to your brother Ollie?" I ask. "Because that was totally one of his bad one-liners."

"He was just here for a couple of weeks shadowing Rob and the guy building that green home. I guess I didn't tell you because that was right after your accident, and I wanted you to focus on getting better."

"I need to reach out to your family, Sophie," I say. "They've been checking on me, but I haven't responded with more than a text. That's kind of shitty, and I'm sorry, but I wasn't in the headspace to discuss my injuries."

"Hey," Sophie leans forward and puts her hand on my shoulder, "Mom and Dad and the twins love you. They only wanted you to know they cared and were worried about you. Don't feel bad. They understand you're dealing with a lot of different emotions. I've kept them in the loop, and when you feel up to it, I know they'd love to hear from you. But no pressure and no guilt. Got it, buddy?"

"Okay, I'll make sure to reach out to them soon."

Keller walks over to get the towels before he massages my leg, and I sit up and grab my bag. "Hey, Keller, Stella told me I should see if you can use this oil from her when you work on my knee. She sent it to me after my accident and it seems to help the spasms." I hand it over to him and watch, as he reads the label.

"There's some good stuff in here. Does she sell this at her studio?"

Sophie smiles at me, "I'm glad you're using that a lot." She turns her attention to Keller in answer to his question,

"Stella gave him that and a few others when I went to LA right after the accident. She makes the oils and sells them in her shop. She has a bunch of different ones."

I add, "Yeah, my home nurse would use it daily, and I could tell the difference. Stella seems to know her stuff. She also brought me a salt lamp, and she's coming over tonight to work on meditation."

Sophie's eyes snap to mine, "She is?"

"Uh-huh. I told her that I have trouble sleeping, and she wants to try some meditation."

"And…you agreed to that?"

"Sophie, I promised I would accept all the help. I'm trying hard to do that, and she even has me journaling."

"Oh my god! You are journaling too?"

Keller is massaging my knee with the oil while Sophie and I exchange this semi-funny banter. "Yes, Stella thought that if I write down my thoughts it may help me move through some of the things that trigger high frustration levels for me."

"Cool, I've journaled during tough times Jax. It works if you are open to putting your true thoughts into it," Keller says.

"You've journaled too? I feel a bit stupid so far, but I've started writing in it. Most of it seems like random thoughts, but maybe the more I write, the less stupid I'll feel. Is that part of the process?" I ask him.

He looks up, "Yep. Think of it as stretching your brain. The more you write, the more you stretch the muscle and the less it will hurt to do."

"Mmm….this is so interesting. I never wrote in a diary but maybe I should try this too," Sophie says to us.

"It's not a diary!" Keller and I both say at the same time.

Chapter Twenty-Two

Stella

I'm upstairs gathering supplies for the meditation session with Jax, but probably overthinking it. I don't know what will work for him because everyone prefers different types of meditation. I can explain the different techniques, and we could try a different one each time until he finds one that he can continue doing himself.

"Stella bug…what are you so focused on and humming about," Griffin asks.

"Hi Griff, I didn't even hear you come in."

"I know because you've been standing here humming and looking through your box of supplies. What's up?"

"I'm heading over to work with Jax on meditation. He hasn't been sleeping well since the accident, and if he doesn't sleep, his body won't heal. I'm just sorting through these things to see what I should take with me tonight."

"Has he done meditation before, or is he a total newbie to it?"

"He said he tried it, but his thoughts went out of control."

"So, he's a meditation virgin then. I'd aim small. Go with the basics. Focus on trying to get him to relax first. Go from there."

"You're probably right. I'm thinking too big. Thanks, Griff."

"Always here for ya. I'm gonna relax at home tonight and order a pizza. Want me to get enough for you?"

"Thanks, but no. I was going to grab dinner for Jax and me since I'm not sure if he can cook. I'll catch you later. I better go before he's starving to death."

"Have fun, toots."

***

I turn off the alarm and let myself in, "Hello. I'm here." I probably should ask if I should stop letting myself in…but he doesn't need to get up off the couch if I do. So, whatever.

"I'll be right out. Give me a second," Jax yells from the back.

I hear him struggling and cursing under his breath. "Are you okay? Do you need help?"

"Stella?"

"Yeah?"

"I'm in the shower, but I slipped on the wet floor and the crutch went out from under me. I can't get off the floor."

"Oh my god. Don't move!" I jump up and run to the back, "Don't hurt yourself. I'm coming!" I turn the corner and see he's on the floor somehow between the shower and the toilet, his bad leg stretched out in front of him, the crutches thrown out the other direction. "Did you hurt yourself?"

"Just my pride."

"Okay, let's just take a minute to figure out how to get you up. You still can't put weight on your wrists or knee. If I can somehow get you up onto your elbows…" I'm looking at the room visualizing the movement he needs to make.

"Stell…you can call my dad or Rob if you need to. I don't want to put weight on my injuries, but I don't think you can lift me."

"Shh…I'm thinking. I'm a lot stronger than I look, Jax. So, we just need to get your good leg back under you first. I'm going to stand in the shower and try to lift you by the armpits. If we can get your good leg under you that will work, and you roll onto the toilet with the weight on your chest or elbows. Let's try that. You ready?"

I move behind him and put my body against his in a squat. My arms are wrapped around his body under his armpits, and I slowly start to rise from a squat position.

"Holy fuck, you ARE strong…"

Holding him a little off the ground, "I'm okay still, can you move your good leg under you yet?"

"I've got my elbows on the toilet so take a breath."

I release the tight hold on him but don't move away. "Why do men refuse to dry off before leaving the bathroom?"

He chuckles, "Because we are lazy and dumb?"

"Is your good leg under you?"

"Yeah, I'm on my knee…but I'm afraid when I stand up the towel is gonna drop," he says over his shoulder.

Of course, this is when I realize I'm pushed up against and laying a bit on top of an almost naked Jax, and without that towel, this situation could get a lot more naked.

"I've seen a naked man before, Jax, and with the parts of you exposed in your movies, there isn't much left to see. Let's just get you safely off the floor. I'll close my eyes if it makes you more comfortable."

"It's fine, Stell…I just don't want to offend you if I'm standing here bare ass naked in a second."

"Let's do this, mister. We're going to slowly stand up, but I'm not going to let you go until you tell me you're steady. Then, I'll grab the crutches and make sure you get to your room safely to change. Ready?"

"Ready."

We move slowly and we manage to get him standing and yes, the towel drops. "Whoops," he says.

I watch my hands slide down his chest in the mirror in front of us before they go back to my sides and when I look up he is watching me through the reflection of the mirror. "Are you steady? If so, I'll grab the crutches and hand you the towel."

"You just want to check out my ass."

"What? I do not."

Chuckling he says, "Just trying to break the serious mood. I'm steady."

We watch each other through the reflection of the mirror. My eyes slowly take him in and follow his chest down. His abs are ripped, and he has those sexy indents at his hips that point down to…

"Eyes up here, Stell."

I jerk my eyes back up to his in the mirror and smirk. "I just wanted to see what all the fuss is about. Figured you must have something special to have earned the hottest man title. Not too shabby, Jax. Thank God getting older was good for you." Then, I bend down, hand him the towel, and walk over to grab the crutches for him. Before I turn around, I ask, "Are you decent?"

He answers, "For now."

I turn around to see him chuckling and shaking his head as I hand him the crutches. "Do you think you can make it safely to your room and get dressed alone? I have dinner waiting in the kitchen for us and then we'll make sure you didn't hurt yourself in that fall and get our meditation on."

***

"What did you do all day today?" I ask.

"Sophie took me to therapy, and when I came home, I made the mistake of looking at the tabloids. They are so fucking idiotic."

"Why would you do that? Those things are all full of garbage. I remember when Sophie was in the spotlight with her stalker, and it was so frustrating to read all the lies they printed just to make a buck."

"My team has one or two journalists that we use that will give me some extra privacy if we give them some occasional dirt. I wanted to see what's being spread before I call them tomorrow to discuss if we need to provide something legit. I came across mostly bullshit."

"Like what?"

"If you grab my phone off the coffee table, I'll show you."

I hand him his phone. "Just make sure it isn't messing with your head, Jax. You can't let that garbage influence your healing."

"Here, this is the most comical one I saw today." He hands me his phone back, and I read the article.

130

In a shocking turn of events, Hollywood heartthrob Jax Turner, once the shining star of Tinseltown, is now hiding away in an undisclosed location, attempting to mend not only his battered body but also his wounded pride after a disastrous Fourth of July accident that left him scarred both physically and emotionally.

Close friends of the star spilled the beans on the emotional toll the accident took on Jax's self-esteem. "He's been spending hours in front of the mirror, contemplating the reflection of a man who once stood at the pinnacle of fame and success. It's not just about physical recovery; it's about rebuilding the confidence that was shattered on that fateful night," confided an anonymous source.

Rumors suggest that Jax Turner is not only focusing on physical recovery but is also undergoing a secret self-improvement journey. Sources claim he's immersed himself in meditation and yoga and even taken up painting to find solace and rediscover his true self.

As we eagerly await Jax Turner's grand comeback, one can't help but wonder: Is this fallen star truly on a quest for redemption, or is he merely hiding from the prying eyes of the paparazzi, healing his wounded pride in private? Stay tuned for more exclusive updates on the elusive star's journey of redemption, only here at CelebSecrets!

Shaking my head, "Jesus, they are ridiculous. At least they got the meditation right. How do you feel about yoga?"

"Let's wait on that until all my injuries are healed," Jax says.

"Good idea. Anyway, I want to talk to you about some different types of meditation. We'll start with something very basic, then we can try some of the other techniques."

"How many are there?"

"A lot. The nine most popular are mindfulness, spiritual, focused, movement, mantra, progressive, visualization…"

"Stella."

“Huh?”

“So, a lot. Maybe give me a quick overview?”

“I think we should start with a basic technique, but honestly with meditation, it comes to what feels comfortable. You learn how to meditate by practicing. To begin, I need to get you comfortable and quiet. Once you relax, I’ll walk you through a guided meditation tonight.”

“I’m looking forward to it.”

“I think it will help you rest at night. If you like the guided meditation, I can set you up with some apps on your phone that will help you continue to practice.”

“Thank you, Stella. I appreciate your help even when I’m naked.”

“Jax?”

“Yeah?”

“Shut up.”

Chapter Twenty-Three

Jax

After a restful night's sleep, I wake up and realize someone's warm body is wrapped around me. Without moving, I open my eyes and see Stella with half her body lying on top of mine. Her arm is across my chest, and her head is snug under my chin on my shoulder. We are on top of the covers and fully clothed. We must have both passed out with the meditation app. I move slowly so I can turn my head enough to look at her. Her soft breath warms me with each exhale. She is beautiful, and her kindness and warmth make her even more tempting. I move her long dark locks from her face and watch her beautiful blue eyes start to flutter open.

"Morning," I say.

"Morning. I think we can say that meditation helped you rest last night," she replies.

"Yep, it worked so well looks like it knocked us both out."

"Sorry, I'm hogging the bed and on top of you."

She doesn't move away though. "Nothing to be sorry about. I slept great last night. Thank you." I turn a little more and kiss her forehead. "Thank you for…being you, Stell. You've been a huge help to me, and I want you to know that."

"Jax, you don't have to thank me for helping you heal. That's who I am and what I like to do. I'm so glad that you're receptive to my help and that it's working for you. I don't like to see people I care about hurting in any capacity."

"I'm someone that you care about, huh?"

"Yeah. Somehow, the goofy boy I grew up with seems to have become a decent man, and believe it or not, someone I care about. You're interconnected to my friends and family, so I suppose I'm stuck with you."

"Oh gee, thanks. I'm happy to know that you care about me because I care about you, too. I'm happy we're stuck with each other."

"Jax?"

"Hmm," I say but keep holding her and I'm twirling one of her locks of hair around my finger.

"I'm going to head out because I have an early class this morning, so you are going to need to let me up."

"Eh…I don't want to."

Stella looks at me and bites her lip, "Even though I've seen you naked, and I suppose you have reason to be proud of your hottest man title, I do need to go home so I'm ready for my class. Can I do anything for you before I head out? Do you need breakfast? Please don't fall again when you shower, or I'm going to tell Sophie to get you an alarm button."

"I promise to be more careful when getting in and out of the shower. I'll have Mom bring a non-slip rug over later to put down in there to avoid that problem. I'm good. I've got some breakfast casserole from Bree I can heat up. Then I'm going fishing with Rob and his buddies."

Stella sits up and looks at me, "Fishing with Rob? Oh god, don't get drunk with those idiots. At least I know Logan can carry you home if needed."

"It'll be fun. I'm looking forward to it."

"With that, I'm heading out. Don't overdo it. And use that app again tonight. At least we know you got some good rest last night."

She stands up, stretches her arms straight up, and bends forward in a gentle sweep to touch her toes. Damn, she is beautiful, and she needs to NOT bend over in front of me like that in the morning. She looks at me over her shoulder as I'm staring at her ass and smirks. "You're welcome," she says with a wink and sashays out of my room.

I yell after her, "You are trouble with a big T, Stell. You totally did that on purpose!"

"You know you loved it," she hollers back at me.

***

Rob and I pull up to the marina where his dad's pontoon boat is stored. "I thought you had a ski boat?"

"I do, but when we fish, we take out Dad's pontoon, so we have more room to move around. And I figured it's a hell of a lot easier to deal with crutches on the pontoon for you."

"Ah, you're probably right."

I see PJ and Logan heading our way, and Rob and I get out of his truck and head towards the docks with them. When we get to the boat, Logan puts his hand out to stop me.

"What's up, Logan?"

"Okay, little man. I'm going to help you with the boat because we don't want any injuries to your injuries. Sophie would beat my ass if I let you hurt yourself, so I'm going to just pick you up and get you on the boat."

With that PJ grabs my crutches, and Logan throws me over his shoulder in a fireman hold. I'm caught a bit off guard since I wasn't expecting to be handled like a sack of potatoes.

"I don't think this is necessary you guys," I say as I hang over Logan's shoulder.

Logan gets us onto the pontoon and puts me back down on my good leg. "I wasn't taking any chances, Jax. You and I know that being on the angry side of little Sophie is not a place a man wants to be."

"What did you do to make her mad?"

"I haven't done a thing, but I sure have enjoyed watching my buddy Robert here be afraid of her."

I give Rob a look, "What'd you do?"

Rob pushes his hand through his hair, "Which time? I'm either too worried about her safety or being annoying and doing too much for her. She sure likes her independence, so it's been a learning curve for us as we navigated the beginning of our relationship."

"It started with her having a stalker trying to kidnap her, so I understand you wanting to be protective of her."

"THANK YOU! Why can't she understand that?"

"Aw, boys," Logan says. "Sophie is the best. I just love that little lady. Now how about telling me why I saw Stella's car in your driveway all night?"

Rob, PJ, and I all look at Logan. Then Rob and PJ turn to look at me.

Rob stands with his arms crossed in front of me, "I hope we don't have a problem, Jax."

"No problem," I answer. "Please, relax. Stella and I are friends. We grew up together and have known each other for thirty years. I'm not going to hurt your little sister or my best friend's-best friend."

"Then why was her car at your house all night? Did she break down? Tell me she broke down and left it there until she could get it looked at. Logan, did she call you to look at the car? Or you PJ? She didn't call me," Rob says.

"Let me sit okay." I hobble over to the seat on the boat before they throw me overboard. The guys move in around me all on guard. "She came over last night to do some meditation with me but when she got there I had fallen getting out of the shower. She found me struggling to get up and helped me. Once I got up off the floor and went to get dressed, we had dinner together. Then, we did a guided meditation. Since the first one helped me relax, she thought we should get me ready for bed by lying in bed and doing another one. Her goal was to get me relaxed, so I could sleep through the night."

I'm watching the guys as I try to explain myself, and their eyes keep moving between each of them. It's like they're having a silent conversation.

"Still doesn't explain her being there all night," Logan says.

"We fell asleep," I shrug.

"Let me see if I understand this correctly. My little sister came over to help you relax. Finds you naked on the floor in the bathroom, helps you, has dinner with you, then does meditation with you to help you relax, then you both go in your BED and fall asleep during more meditation?"

"Yeah, that about sums it up."

Logan smirks at me, "She found you naked on the floor, huh?"

"I had a towel around me. Well, until it fell off, and she looked me over in the mirror." Rob's jaw gets tight. I can see that he's holding back. I try to reassure him, "Really, nothing happened. We did a meditation app that's super cool and fell asleep. I woke up this morning with her wrapped around me. I slept fantastic for the first time since this accident."

"Oh, buddy. You were doing okay until you added how you woke up," PJ says, chuckling. "Come on, Rob, we've known this guy since he was a little twerp. It's all good."

Rob takes a breath and says, "I'm going to say this once more and give you a heads up, because I love your best friend, and I don't want any bad vibes between us. My little sister loves hard. She will do anything for anyone that needs her. Do not take advantage of that. I don't know what life is like in LA and you being you, but this is Lake Harmony, and I do not have a problem showing you how we handle guys who take advantage of sweet girls. Got me? Plus, these two would die for Stella, so you don't want to piss them off either."

"I got you, but Rob, seriously—we are just friends. Is she beautiful? Absolutely. But I don't live here, and I wouldn't hurt her like that."

"But you do live here. Sometimes" Rob points out. "Isn't that why you're building that house next to ours? So that you and Sophie never have to give each other up. All I'm saying is watch yourself. I don't want any problems, and I don't want my sister hurt when you head home to LA and your life there."

"I promise to treat my friend Stella, your little sister, with respect. Are we good now?" I ask.

Logan rubs his hands together, "Let's catch some fish. My belly is hungry, and it wants to eat fish fry tonight!"

Chapter Twenty-Four

Stella

I'm feeling restless because I scheduled my part-timer to do my afternoon class sessions for me. But Sophie called this morning and told me to grab Jax and head to her house. She has a surprise for us. So, here I am, pulling up into his driveway when he walks out the front door. I wave, and he gives me a sexy smile and wink. I go around and help get him settled in the passenger seat and throw his crutches in the back of my VW Bug 'Sunny,' which is bright yellow. I love her.

"Jesus, this is a tiny car. I should have remembered that you drove a bug before agreeing to this field trip with you over to Soph's."

"Stop your bitchin' you fit just fine."

"In your mini death trap. Sure."

I spin to look at him, "Shit. I forgot to ask you if you have any kind of PTSD from being in a car. Do you?"

"Not too much. It's more if a car seems to be coming at me faster than expected. That's what happened you know. I was coming around a curve in the road and they were heading straight at me. They lost control and the back of their car hit mine and spun me over the side and into the tree line. God, that sucked ass. I still hear the metal tearing and glass shattering around me sometimes."

I shake my head, "You're lucky to only have the injuries that you do. If you would have been hit going faster or head-on, you may not be here at all."

"That's what the police and EMTs said when they cut me out of my Audi."

"Anyway, let's not focus on that memory. Do you have any idea what Sophie's surprise is?"

"Not a clue. I would think if they got engaged, we'd have heard about it right?" Jax asks.

"Agree. I don't think that's it. Rob is going to propose, but I think he wants to make sure Sophie is ready. Although, my brother isn't getting any younger, and they have a bit of an age gap."

"Age doesn't matter. He doesn't act like he's in his forties. He threatened me just like a high school bully when we were fishing."

"What? Why? What had him all pissed with you?"

"Logan was so helpful and mentioned that your car was at my place overnight. He wanted to make sure that I understood that if I hurt you, he was going to hurt me and Logan and PJ would assist."

"Rob is an idiot. Just ignore him. I am surrounded by big idiot men in my life."

"Thanks."

"I wasn't including you in that list, but I can later, so watch it. Rob needs to mind his own business. If I want to have dirty, sweaty, naked sex all night long with you, then Rob won't be stopping me." I look at Jax after pulling out of the driveway, and his mouth is hanging open. "Stop it. You cannot tell me that you haven't heard women telling you about having sex with you or that they want to wrap themselves around your naked body and do dirty things to you? You are one of Hollywood's Hottest Men are you not? I expect that you have a lot of dirty suggestions and offers coming at you all the time."

"Stella, I think we need to change the subject because you talking dirty to me right now is not a good idea."

I look down at his lap, because of course I look down, and see he is turned on. "That...turned you on?"

"I'm a man, and you are talking about having sex with me. You turn me on. So, yes. Please change the topic of discussion so I don't continue to embarrass myself in front of you and Sophie. God forbid Rob is home and I walk up to the house with a semi."

I laugh and start singing to the radio, which happens to be playing a Rolling Stone song and when I sing, *I can't* *get no, satisfaction…*I look over at Jax and sing it to him and he rolls his eyes at me.

"You are going to be the death of me today," he says.

***

We walk up to the front door at Sophie's and ring the doorbell. "COME IN YOU GUYS," Sophie yells.

"You'd think living with my brother she'd know better than to leave the door unlocked and invite people in without checking," I say to Jax.

"This is Lake Harmony, what's gonna happen?"

"Being kidnapped by a stalker?"

"Done and over with…now back to boring Midwest and worrying about football playoffs."

I hold the door while Jax moves into the room. Sophie yells, "Hurry and shut the door before she escapes." Then, the cutest little puppy comes barreling around the corner, its feet bigger than its body.

I sit down on the floor, grab the puppy, and give it kisses while it licks my face clean. Sophie walks in with a big grin on her face and sits down next to me.

"Isn't she the cutest puppy in the whole world," Sophie says while she watches the puppy in my arms acting like a squiggle monkey.

"She's adorable! Is this the surprise?" Jax asks.

"Yeah. When I was getting to know Rob, I mentioned that I always wanted a dog, but that I didn't think it was fair to a puppy since I travel so much with my films. He convinced me that if I got a puppy, and we trained it, she could either come with me on set so I wouldn't be lonely, or she could stay home with him. So, we heard there were these cute lab mix puppies at the shelter and went over early this morning to bring one home. This pretty girl is my baby, Betty."

"She's adorable, Soph," Jax says. "Can we move somewhere I can sit easier and play with her too since you ladies are hogging the baby. I want to share puppy kisses, too."

141

Sophie says, "Shoot. Sorry, Jax. Let's go to the family room where she has her toy basket, and we can all play with her. She is so sweet, and so far, she's doing pretty good with going potty outside." A timer goes off on Sophie's Apple watch, "Oh it's pee-pee time! Go on in the family room and get comfy while I take Betty out. *Come with momma baby girl, it's time to go pee-pee and poo-poo.*"

***

"Stell," Sophie whispers, "Let's go have a drink in the kitchen while those two nap together on the couch." Jax and Betty are lying on the couch sound asleep. The puppy is all curled up on his chest, so I doubt he slept well last night. I stop and stare at him for a minute, Soph pulls me by the arm into the kitchen with a smirk.

"You are so good for him," she says.

I quickly turn to look at Sophie, "Huh?"

"You and Jax. You're rubbing off on him, and I like what I'm seeing. The changes in him. He seems more…grounded, or maybe more at ease than he's been since the accident."

"I'm not doing anything that I wouldn't do for any of you."

"Stella, it's a good thing. Now, want to tell me your side of the story on how you ended up having a sleepover with him last week?"

"Seriously? My brother is still bent out of shape about that?"

"No, I've got your back, girlfriend, and set him straight, but I do want the deets. Is there a romance brewing between my two besties?"

"Simmer your jets, lady. We are friends, but I can't say looking at him is too hard on the eyes. But…he isn't in a place for anything romantic, and he isn't staying here in Lake Harmony. His life is in LA. I've done my days of traveling around the country. I'm here now, where I want to stay. He'll be moving on as soon as he doesn't need help."

"Alright, I won't bug you about it. But it would be so awesome if something were to happen between you both. He does seem better, though. Less angry. So, whatever you're doing seems to be helping."

"I think he's been journaling, but he hasn't shared anything about that with me. I hoped the meditation was going to help him sleep, but seeing as he is currently snuggled up with your puppy and sound asleep, I'm worried he had a bad night. Did he say anything to you?"

"When I took him to therapy, he was talking about journaling with Keller. Keller told him he had done it to work through his situation and that it helped him, so Jax shared he had been doodling a bit with thoughts. Then, I mentioned the word DIARY, and they both shut down and moved to a new topic."

"Good, I'm glad he's been journaling. At least it's one way to work through what he's feeling. I know therapy takes a lot out of him, but he seems strong. His body sure hasn't lost any of its form." And…I just said the wrong thing. Sophie has stars in her eyes. "What?"

"So, it's true? You did see him naked, and you liked what you saw?" she asks me wiggling her eyebrows up and down.

"Dear lord! I'm not blind or stupid. He's a beautiful specimen of a sexy man. Of course, I liked what I saw. I had to almost wipe the drool off my face!"

Sophie grabs my hand and squeezes.

"Soph, do not let your mind wander down the road of white picket fences and matching lives. I'm not you. He is not Rob. We are not in the same time and situation that you are in. I love you, but I'm not moving in that direction."

"Fine," she says and pouts.

"I have enjoyed getting to know him again, at least as an adult. As kids, we didn't move in the same circle of people. I have always been a bit of a dreamer and the kids thought I was a flake. He was in the popular group of kids and involved in sports and theater. He's always been a bit of a sporty nerd. Those two personalities don't jive as kids, but now as adults…yeah, we have more in common. At least I think we both enjoy the other's company."

Sophie's watch goes off again meaning it's time for a potty break. We both get up and look into the room at the nappers. "Should I wake her up and take her out? I don't want to wake him up if he's finally resting."

"Let's let them both sleep a little bit longer. How often are you taking her out?"

"I set it for every thirty minutes."

"Did she potty the last time?"

"Yep, my big girl went pee-pee like a star!"

"Then I think you can skip it, let's just let them be and see how things look in another thirty."

We head back into the kitchen, and I ask her, "So…are you done with the movie thing or what's your plan?"

"Still on my break, but I have some scripts I've been reading. I think I may do one over the winter. They are shooting it on a tropical set, and Rob and I thought we'd both go, if possible. He may have to move between work and there, but he's trying to set it up to work. I like the script. It's a cute single-mom story. I kind of like the idea of practicing that role."

"I'm so glad you found each other, and that he will try to make the time to be with you while filming if possible. The happiness radiates off you."

"I'm so in love with him, and I am so happy. I never really thought I'd have this love and family in my life. LA was so cold and lonely. The only one I had there for me was Jax. Now, I have all of you, a community I love, and my parents are only a couple of driving hours away. I love my life. Now I wish I could get Jax to move home. I thought that was a given as he is building that fancy house right next to ours, but he keeps saying he isn't ready to make that his full-time home yet. He wants to keep LA as his home base. Maybe that'll change, but maybe not. At least, he'll eventually move back here. I miss him so much when we're so far apart."

"This accident took a toll on him, so LA may not be the happy normal it used to be. Only he can decide. But thankfully, he's healing and moving in the right direction. Although, he may steal your dog."

"Right! I wish he was more mobile. I'd love for him to go and pick out one of her siblings."

"Puppies and crutches are not a good combo."

Chapter Twenty-Five

Jax

I finally got clearance to put weight on my leg as long as I wear the Velcro brace, so Keller is working on getting me up and walking. My gate is off because I'm not used to using both legs equally. He keeps laughing at what he calls my drunk sailor strut. Feels weird to be walking on both legs again.

"I'm trying not to laugh, but every time I have a patient that gets to use both legs after being on no weight-bearing status for at least a month, it's as if everyone forgets how to balance," Keller says.

"I may look like an ass but I'm damn happy that I can ditch the crutches. My armpits have taken a beating since I couldn't put the weight on my wrists."

"You're looking pretty good, but now we need to start putting some strength training into the mix to get you back in shape. That leg is a little leaner since you've been off it. You think you're up for some light leg work?"

"Let's do it. I need to be back to normal, so I'm up for whatever you've got lined up."

"What else is new with you? What did the doc say about the wrists?"

"He wants me to wear the splints on my wrists for at least another week or so. The bones are more fragile, and he figures he'll let me deal with getting back on both feet before totally letting me loose."

"He increased what you can do while splints are off but don't go nuts at home. Listen to him. You're so close right now to being off any limitations so don't push it okay?"

"I won't. I'm meeting with my team after therapy. They were waiting for the doctor to give me the clearance to walk without support. I'm praying they have something in the works for me. I've been asking for scripts, but they kept pushing me off saying I wasn't healed enough, yet. What they don't understand is I'd like to have time to prepare, so if doc thinks I'll be closer to healed in a few weeks, there's no reason not to start reviewing scripts."

"I'm sure you're ready to focus on more than just therapy at home."

"I am, but I'm not."

Keller looks at me and tilts his head, "What's the pause? Something keeping you from moving forward?"

"I just want to make sure I'm better and don't screw myself by jumping back into things too quickly."

Keller scratches his jaw, "Uh huh."

I stop doing the leg machine, "What?"

"You sure it's not *someone* keeping you here longer? Seems to me, you've been spending a lot of time with Stella Stone."

"We're good friends, and it's nice to have Sophie around again. I'm just making sure I'm strong enough before I take off."

"Okay, for what it's worth, Stella is a cool chic."

I give him a look that's clear I don't want him sniffing around her, and he puts his hands up in a surrender pose.

"Good friends--got it. I won't go there. We're good. She sure is pretty though. Ten more."

"You're an ass, Keller."

"So I've been told."

***

Once I'm back at home, I take the scheduled Zoom call with my PR and management teams in LA.

"You are looking good Jax. How are you feeling," my manager asks me.

"I'm cleared to walk without crutches finally, so that's a relief. I'm still wearing the brace on my leg, same as both wrists, but I'm not feeling as handicapped as before. Today, we started working on some strength training on my bad leg, and I'm going to start swimming in the lake here when I can. A buddy of mine trains in the lake and said he'd go with me."

"Glad you've got some good friends and support there. It was a good choice to go home for your therapy. How are you feeling otherwise?"

I look at my team and clearly say, "I need to find some work to focus on. I'm healing. Doctor thinks I should be good to go in a month, and I want a project so please tell me what you've got for me."

"Happy to hear that. We have a couple of things we'll send you today. There's a rom-com and a new drama that would be the first of a trilogy. Look at them, and let us know if either grabs your interest. They're casting in a few weeks, and both want to start filming in about two months. You think you'll be ready by then?"

"I'll be ready."

We discuss who's producing and directing each, and of course, my interest is already leaning towards the drama. I've done the rom-com thing, and I want to push myself into something else. I don't want to be one of those actors who gets stuck always playing the romantic character. Give me a drama or action hero. Shoot, give me a bad guy, but enough with the love scenes and gooey storylines.

"How are you dealing with the tabloids and gossip rags, Jax?" my PR rep asks.

"I'm trying to ignore all of them. Why? Has something new popped that I'm not aware of, yet?"

"Nothing major. Just the continuation of you hiding and licking your wounds. I can't believe they haven't figured out that you're back in your hometown. Those people there sure do protect you and Sophie. I'm glad that you can have that privacy."

"Yeah, that's why I love being able to come home."

The PR rep continues, "We decided to share that you're busy reading new scripts and will be back to work soon. That should spin some of that garbage onto a new victim."

"Sounds good. It's the truth. We're looking forward to my next role, and I am healing. I'm ready to get back to work, so please send me whatever you've got. I'll keep working on getting my strength back, and we should be back in business soon."

We end the meeting, and I lean back and relax. I do need to work on my strength. I grab my phone and text Bree.

Jax: Hey Bree, Noah mentioned training in the lake. Can you ask him about that when he comes home later?
Bree: Hi friend. Sure thing. How are you doing?
Jax: Doc gave me the clear to walk with both feet so I'm doing a little jig of happiness
Bree: You probably shouldn't be dancing yet
Jax: Figure of speech Bree LOL
Bree: Whew...do you have plans tomorrow night?
Jax: Glorious plans of watching TV here at home
Bree: Terrible, I'll be by to pick you up at 5:30 tomorrow and you can come see Baby Jameson and have dinner with us and plan the lake time with Noah directly
Jax: Would love that. What can I bring?
Bree: Yourself. Earplugs. Jameson is teething ugh!
Jax: LOL See you tomorrow.

I barely put my phone down when it buzzed again.

Rob: You home?
Jax: Yes
Rob: You busy?
Jax: No, what's up
Rob: Going to grab you and bring you to the showroom. We need to look at cabinets, colors, hardware, faucets, etc.
Jax: Cool. See you soon

Chapter Twenty-Six

Stella

Griffin and I are home watching one of our favorite Housewives' shows and eating Thai food. I haven't talked to Jax in a few days. I know he's been busy with therapy and trying to get a handle on things, but I'm starting to miss him.

"And then, I went into the lake and the shark ate me. Thank god the elephant pulled me out of his mouth safely and took me to get donuts," Griffin says.

I give my friend a *what the fuck* look, "What about a shark, elephant, and donuts?"

Griffin gives his head a tilt and frowns, "Oh…THAT you heard. Jesus, Stella bug. I've been asking you a question over and over like five times, and you finally heard that? What's rolling around in that pretty head of yours? You better spill before you hurt yourself."

"Ha, ha. I was just…thinking."

"About a sexy, dark-haired man who happens to be spending a lot of time with you?"

"Not lately," I say a bit rejected.

"Oh… I see. Are you *maybe* missing him a little bit?"

I spin to face Griffin, and he does the same and takes my hands in his.

"Talk to me, Stellie. What's troubling you? Tell Griffin all your woes."

"Can you be serious for just a moment? I do have something on my mind, and I am not sure what to do about it."

"Go ahead. I promise to listen and only comment if you ask."

"Jax and I have spent a lot of time together. I know we both find each other attractive and there is A LOT of chemistry, but we haven't gone there. Neither of us has made a move that pushed us into more than being aware of the chemistry. He won't be here much longer, Griff. I don't want to get my heart and head wrapped around someone that won't be here. What do I do? Stop spending time with him now, so that when he leaves, I haven't put more energy into us?"

"Can you do that? Can you go back to just seeing him in passing or when you both might happen to be at the same place? He texts you all the time!!! I bet he sent you a text in the last couple of hours. Can you end that and go back to being just an acquaintance who runs into him a few times a year when he comes home? Better yet…how will you feel when you see someone else on his arm?"

"I don't like the sound of that, Griff," I say and shake my head.

"Or…you can remember that you are Stella Stone, my best friend, and kick-ass woman who takes what she wants out of life? If you want him Stella bug, which I can't see how that isn't the answer because, *YUM*, go get your man. So what if he leaves in a month or two? Make him miss what he walks away from. Sophie is here and would love for him to make Lake Harmony his home base like she has. What's saying he won't if he has a reason? Be the reason, sweetheart. Next time you find yourself with him, instead of putting on the brake, girl, press down harder on the gas, and take that sexy beast of a man for a ride! I know you want to. You just admitted so yourself. I mean, he is so beautiful."

My cell buzzes, and I look at Griff.

"Five bucks I know who it is," he says with his smirk and flutters his lashes at me.

Jax: Hey! I can walk on two feet!!! *dancing emoji*
Stella: Excellent – don't be a hero and overdo it
Jax: Don't ruin my joy, Stell
Stella: I'm happy for you. Should we celebrate?
Jax: Yes, I'm taking you to dinner tomorrow. When will you be free?

Griff is sitting so close, that he's reading the texts at the same time. "Oh my god, Stellie…Jax just asked you out on a date."

"It appears so."

"Please, if you love me do this. Go on that date, then get down and nasty with him. I need you to do this. You know he's my first choice, but since he likes lady parts, I'm giving him to you. Go love on that man for the both of us."

"You are ridiculous, but I think I'm going to do exactly that."

"You are," Griff says with a huge smile and clapping, "And I'll want all the juicy details."

Stella: My last class ends at 6 pm. Is that too late?
Jax: How long do you need to get ready?
Stella: I can pick you up at 7 pm.
Jax: Nah, I got the all-clear to drive…I'll pick YOU up at 7. Be hungry because we are going to Bella Roma's for dinner. I miss you. You haven't come by to check on me. What if I had fallen and couldn't get up again from the shower?
Stella: Then you're an idiot because once was enough. You didn't though, did you?
Jax: No but thank you for being worried about me. I'm doing better. Walking without crutches!! Writing in my journal. Using the meditation app. Starting to feel like myself again and you know why….BECAUSE OF YOU.

Griff makes some excited noises, "Holy crap. Seriously, if you don't get naked with this man, I'll be ashamed to call you my best friend. He is so dreamy, and I believe he's smitten with you."

"He is something, that's for sure."

Stella: I only gave you the tools to get better, but it makes me happy that you're using them. I want you to feel like yourself again. Your head is too big for a weak body to carry around by itself.

"Woman, what are you doing?" Griffin says with alarm.

"It's fine, it's our banter."

Jax: It's not the only big thing I have to carry around. Yes, I went there, and you know you know because you took a long look when I was standing naked in the bathroom

Stella: Yes, I did.

Jax: You liked what you saw.

Stella: Yes, I did

Jax: See you Friday, sweetheart. I'm looking forward to it. I'm sure we'll talk tomorrow *winking emoji*

Stella: Use your journal and app to get some rest. I know you're doing more than you should and healing takes time. Don't jump the gun now that you have a little more freedom.

Jax: I promise I won't. I think I'll need my strength. *winking emoji* Nite.

Stella: Nite

I put the phone down and look at Griffin, who is fanning himself. "I am so jealous of you right now. He is hot. H.O.T. and a dirty talker. I am so jelly of you, Stella bug."

"Looks like I have a date with Jax Friday." Griffin gets up and drags me into my room. "What are you doing?" I ask.

"Honey, we need to find the right outfit for you. I'm not here tomorrow because I'm running a dinner event for Hillary, so we need to find your date outfit right now. You go figure out the sexy bra and panties, and I'll start going through your closet for a dress. Oh, what about that flowy bohemian dress that falls off the shoulder and is a bit sheer? I love that dress on you with your skimpy shimmer heels. Maybe that, or maybe that dark blue wrap dress that matches your eyes. Come on, we're just going to have to try them all on. Should we call Sophie over? Nah, let's just get her on Facetime."

"Griff, she isn't going to want to sexy me up for a date with her best friend."

"Stellie, are you crazy? Of course, she is. She would love nothing more than to see Jax living here next door to her and Rob full time. I know this. You know this. Rob knows this. Let's help her make it happen. Now, put this on!"

Chapter Twenty-Seven

Jax

I've got a bouquet for Bree and a six-pack of beer for Noah. After I ring the bell, Noah opens the door. "Hey, man," he says. "I'm so glad to see you. Come on in. I would have been happy to come and get you tonight."

"It's good. I got clearance to walk and drive from the doctor. I just have to keep wearing the brace to support my leg for at least another week, but I'm almost back to where I was before the accident."

"That's good to hear. How's your strength and stamina? That also coming back?"

"Slowly, but I think so."

Bree comes in carrying their little boy. "Noah, don't harass Jax about his medical status. Turn the doctor off, babe. Can you take your son, please, so I can hug Jax?"

"How about Uncle Jax takes that little booger and hugs you at the same time?"

"I didn't want to assume you could manage, but he's all yours. I love my son, but I'm also happy to share him. He's been teething and a bit on the crabby side, so it's nice to have a breather. Come on in, and let's have a seat. Noah was just about to heat the grill. We're having steak and some veggies. Hope that sounds good."

"Sounds great."

Noah lifts the beer I brought, "Want one of these or a cold one from the fridge?"

"I'll take a cold one, and you can restock yours with what I brought."

The baby is cooing and looking at me with his big blue eyes. He has started getting a little fuller now and is turning into a chubby little fellow. "Hello, Jameson. Are you being good for Mommy and Daddy or causing a lot of fuss getting those horrible teeth in?"

"Good god, my ovaries are crying right now," Bree says.

I look up, "Huh?"

"Seeing you with a baby in your arms is a pretty picture. Do you want to have a family one day, Jax?"

"I do. I want it all. The wife, the family, the dog…all of it. The problem is it's nearly impossible to find, especially in LA. I don't date because it's usually someone who is using me to get herself seen, or my agent sets me up with someone else through their agent to help them get seen. It's all so fake in LA, so dating isn't a priority for me there."

"That does sound horrible. How did Mattie meet his wife? I'm sure being in a famous rock band takes the same type of toll on them."

I keep smiling at the baby but answer Bree, "Believe it or not, Mattie and his wife were high school sweethearts. They're the real deal, and she puts up with a lot with the band groupies, but they're solid. Jeff too. He's the only other one that's married. He met his wife in the beginning. She worked in the studio where they were recording. Neither of them wants kids right now, so when they tour, she goes with them. Devin and Josh just date or find what they need, when they need it…but LA isn't the place for me to find my forever."

"It's a good thing then, that you'll have your house here. How much longer do you have before it's done?"

"I was at the shop with Rob this week picking out finishing touches like cabinets, colors, faucets, all that stuff. He thinks they will have it done in about a month or so."

Noah comes back in with a beer, puts it in front of me on the table, sits next to Bree, and pulls her into his side. Noah asks, "Wow, so you and Rob will be neighbors. Are you planning on making this home then?"

"Nah. I'll furnish it and have it so when I'm home, I have my place. Or if anyone in the band needs to get away from LA, they have another option. But I think I'll keep LA as home for now."

"Now that you're back on two feet, Bree mentioned that you wanted to train with me at the lake," Noah asks.

"I was hoping that the timing would work out. I'm working with Keller on strengthening my hurt leg, but I want to also try swimming. The swelling still gets bad with the scar tissue and strengthening it may be easier in the water and help my wrists. I've always loved to swim, but I'm a little nervous about being out in the lake myself."

"I'm happy to take you with me. We can stick close to the shoreline just in case you cramp up or need to rest. Let's get it on the books starting Saturday morning."

"Thanks, Noah, I'd love that. Just tell me where to meet you."

The baby starts to fuss, and Bree gets up and takes him. "It's not you, it's him. He's getting hungry. He's always hungry."

Noah smiles at his wife, "He's a growing boy, babe." When Bree leaves the room, Noah leans forward, "How are you mentally dealing with all this?"

"I'm doing okay. Stella gave me some tips on how to deal with my feelings and frustrations about this mess. That's been working well so far. I like working with Keller. He doesn't take my shit and pushes me when he knows I can do more. Between the two of them, I'm healing faster than I honestly thought I would."

"Injuries can cause so many different issues, especially to your psyche. I'm happy to hear that you have a good handle on that. Stella is quite good at what she does. Have you done a sound treatment with her yet? That was the most amazing thing that I've ever experienced."

"No, I think she has one coming up, though, so I'll have to ask her about it tomorrow."

"Tomorrow? You two have become close, huh?"

I sit back, take a sip of my beer, and smile at my friend, "We are going on a date tomorrow."

"No shit?" Noah sits back too with a chuckle. "Rob know?"

"Don't know. Don't care. I like Stella, and we have been tiptoeing around with each other for weeks. There's a lot of chemistry between us, and I decided to go for it."

"Go for what?" Bree asks as she comes back into the room with the baby and a bottle.

"Jax and Stella are going on a date tomorrow."

"Oh, this I love," she says. "How is that going to work when you head back to LA?"

"I'm not sure, but I can't ignore it anymore. We've been getting close and there's a lot of chemistry between us, and if I don't see if it's something, I think I will regret it. No, I know I would."

Chapter Twenty-Eight

Stella

I decided on my favorite off-the-shoulder bohemian style dress, and I looked in the mirror as I applied sheer lip ointment. I love this dress and the way the fitted princess bodice frames my body. *Eat your heart out, Jax Turner.*

I've got about ten minutes until he arrives. I told him I'd meet him downstairs, but he insisted on coming up to the door. I'm not sure the steps are a good idea, but he said he could manage and wanted to be a gentleman and ring the bell. Bella Roma's is just on the other side of the town square, so we can walk over from here. That way, he can park behind the store where I keep Sunny my Beetle. I straighten up and go into the kitchen to leave Griff a note.

Heading out with Jax for dinner. Hope you had a good event. Talk tomorrow over coffee. Kisses! Stella

I hear a knock at the door and look over to see Jax smiling in from the outside. I walk over and open the door, "Hello there. You made it up the stairs okay?" He's smiling, and his eyes are scanning slowly from my feet up my body causing tingles. When he looks into my eyes, I see desire.

"You are beautiful. The stairs were not going to be a problem and could never keep me from being with you."

I feel my face warm and know I'm blushing, which doesn't happen often. "Thank you. You look handsome tonight." He's wearing dark slacks and a blue dress shirt with the sleeves rolled up. I love his forearms and the strength in them. "Come in for a moment, and I'll grab my purse. You okay with walking over to the restaurant?"

"As long as you hold my hand."

"I can work with that." He smiles, it's the smile that reflects in his eyes, the smile that is only given when he is being sincere. I grab my purse and head to the door. I feel his hand on the small of my back. "The door is locked so just close it after you, please." I walk slowly down the steps, giving him time to make it safely down behind me. I watch as he takes his last step. "Are you wearing your brace, Jax? Not even your wrist splints!"

"Ah…no." The guilty look he gives me pushes me forward.

"I didn't think so. Why are you not wearing your brace?"

"I got the all-clear to walk, and it wouldn't fit under my slacks, and I didn't want to wear it over them."

Letting out a frustrated sigh, I put my hands on my hips. "This is exactly what you aren't supposed to do. What if you accidentally hurt your knee? That will set you back again. Now I'm a little hesitant to walk to the restaurant."

"Stella, it's literally across the street. I'll be fine. Plus, you're going to hold my hand and keep me from catastrophe."

I can't with this guy. Men and their machoism. "If at any time your leg starts bothering you, do you promise to tell me?"

He stares at me for a moment until I finally see his resolve. He takes my hand and runs his thumb across the top of my hand, "I promise. Sorry if I caused you to worry. I want tonight to be perfect."

"Come on, let's go enjoy dinner and celebrate that you're off crutches and hopefully stay that way."

We make our way through the town square, past the fountain in the park, and toward Bella Roma's. This is the town's favorite Italian restaurant. They make four or five main dishes based on fresh ingredients, and it is always packed table-to-table, and it is delicious. Jax opens the restaurant door for me, and we walk in just as Maria, the owner, heads over to us.

"Good evening, you two. Don't you both look lovely! Jax, I have your favorite table ready for you. Let me show you back."

We follow Maria, and Jax again has his hand on my lower back as we make our way through the restaurant. Of course, we see familiar faces, and we smile and say hello.

I've never been here without at least seeing a family member or someone I know from the community. Maria takes us to a quiet table in the back corner, and Jax pulls my chair out for me.

"Thank you."

"You're welcome, sweetheart."

Interesting. Jax sits down next to me instead of across from me at the table and thanks Maria for the perfect table.

"Before I walk away, let me share the menu tonight. Antoni has been busy today, so we have Lasagne alla Bolognese, Melanzane alla Parmigiana, Pollo alla Cacciatora, and Spaghetti alla Carbonara. He also has his tiramisu for dessert. Do either of you care for a glass of wine?"

"Stella, would you like to share a bottle of wine?"

"That sounds wonderful. How about a Cab or Merlot?"

"Maria, could you bring us a bottle that would go well with dinner? You pick. I know you usually have something good you're hiding in back."

"Of course, I will be right back with your wine and will ask your server to bring you some sparkling water and warm bread."

"Thank you, Maria. So, what sounds good to you, Stella? I could eat any of those choices."

"Their food is always delicious, but I may just go with the lasagna. What are you thinking you want to eat?"

"I'm leaning on the parmigiana or chicken dish."

"I haven't tried their parmigiana yet, but I don't think you can go wrong here. Or get both, we sample everything, and you take leftovers home for tomorrow?"

"Now you're talking, but only if you promise to help me eat dessert later?"

"I never say no to dessert, Jax. Never."

***

163

We sit back in our chairs, the bottle of wine long gone, and our dinners enjoyed. Maria makes her way over to our table, "You both look satisfied. Did you enjoy dinner?"

"Absolutely. It was delicious, and I have leftovers to enjoy later," Jax says.

"Can I interest you in dessert? Antoni saved a piece of tiramisu for you."

Jax looks over and raises his eyebrow, "Do you have room for dessert still?"

Smiling at him, I turn back to Maria, "Could we take it to go, Maria? That way we can let our dinners settle a little before we dive into his delicious dessert."

"Of course, Stella. Let me go box the piece up for you."

"I told you, Jax, I never say no to dessert, but I have no room for it right now. I guess that means you'll just have to come upstairs with me and wait for our dinner to digest a little bit."

"Ah, I see. You're inviting me up for a nightcap?"

Jax looks at me with his typical smirk, and I smirk right back, "You'll just have to come over and see what happens."

Jax pays the bill, and he escorts me out of the restaurant and back through the town square holding my hand. "Thank you for a delicious dinner tonight. I had a great time with you tonight."

"It's been the best date I've had in as long as I can remember," he says.

I catch my breath. It was a date. Of course, it was a date, Stella. Why would you think it was just two friends going out? He's held your hand or been touching you since he arrived.

Jax squeezes my hand, "Stella…where did your thoughts just take you?"

We're at the bottom of the stairs that lead up to my apartment, and I turn to him. "It's silly, really. I got caught up that you said this was a date."

"Did you not think this was a date? More than just two friends going out? If not, I better up my game and make my intentions clear."

"No, no…I thought it was a date but when you said it out loud, it just started me thinking about being on a date with Jax Turner, and I kind of spiraled for a moment after that because yes, you are Jax Turner, but to me you are just Jax."

"Hmm…I think I understand where you went just now, but let me see if I'm right. Yes, I am Jax Turner, the actor from Hollywood. Yes, I am Jax Turner, the idiot childhood friend who never bothered to get to know you better. Yes, I am Jax Turner, the guy who came home after a horrible accident battered and bruised, and who is so thankful to have gotten to know the girl from my past better because now he has significant feelings for her."

"Significant feelings for me, huh?"

He runs his thumb down my jaw, "Yes, some significant feelings, so what should I do?"

"Kiss me."

Jax puts his hand behind my neck and pulls me closer to him letting his lips gently brush against mine. I gasp as the energy between us feels magnetic and feel him smile against my lips. He leans back in and runs his tongue along the seam of my mouth and without hesitation, our kiss becomes more heated and filled with passion. After a moment I feel him start to shift his weight from leg to leg, so I pull away.

"Come on, Romeo. Let's get you upstairs and off that leg. I can sense that you're starting to hurt."

"Yeah. Probably should've worn the damn brace, but I wouldn't want to give you the pleasure of being right again."

"Come on…take your time up the stairs."

I get to the top and turn. Jax is a few steps behind me. "I'm glad that you're going slow."

"I am, but I was also enjoying the sway of your ass in front of me."

"Ah, always the charmer. Come on up and take your pants off. I need to take a look."

"I'm not even upstairs and you are already getting me naked?"

"You bet."

I unlock the door and leave it open for Mr. Stubborn, then walk to the bathroom to grab my oil. I meet Jax back in the living room. "Off with the pants and take a seat, please."

"What are your intentions once the pants come off," he asks with his smirk.

"I'm going to rub you down with my oil, then most likely put some ice on your knee while we enjoy our dessert."

He moves so quickly to shed the pants, that I have to laugh, "You are ridiculous."

"All I heard was rub me down with oil. Done."

Chapter Twenty-Nine
Jax

My date with Stella has been perfect so far. Now, I'm upstairs in her apartment and taking my pants off. Didn't think the night was going to spin this way, but I had hoped. My pants are off and I take a seat on the couch in my boxers. "All set. Please have your way with me."

Stella looks at my knee, which is tight and hurting.

"You over did it didn't you? Be honest with me," she says with a frown.

"Yeah, I did. I should have worn the brace for sure. Especially with the stairs."

"Oh, Jax. I told you that I would meet you downstairs."

"No, this is on me not you. I wanted tonight to be perfect. You deserve to be treated with my best, and if I wasn't dealing with this injury, I'd have come to the door to pick you up like a gentleman. I'm not allowing this injury to hold me back any longer."

She gently moves my leg up onto the table. "Does this hurt?"

"No, it feels good to be straightened out a bit. Thank you."

She sits in front of me on the coffee table and pulls the bottom of her dress nearly up to her waist.

"Jax grab that small pillow next to you, please."

I grab the small pillow and hand it to her.

"I'm going to slide under your leg and put this pillow under your knee. That will help support it while I work the oil into your knee. If it becomes too much, please let me know. Okay?"

"Okay."

"Bend your knee just a little bit until we get settled." She lifts my lower leg, puts her other hand under my knee, and slides herself in front of me. She gently lifts and slides the pillow under my bent knee and puts my foot in her lap to rest.

"How does this feel? Is the extension of your knee, okay?"

I take a deep breath, looking over my knee at her exposed thighs. "All good." Is she trying to kill me right now showing off her beautiful, sculpted legs?

Stella puts some of the oil in her hands, "I'm going to warm the oil up, then we're going to do a deep tissue massage. Knowing you're hurting, I want to avoid any bad spasms later. I should smack you for not wearing your brace."

She begins to gently work the muscles around my knee, focusing on the incision marks and area where the scar tissue is tight. I watch her strong hands as they start to take the pain and tightness away. I finally feel some relief and relax back on the couch.

"How is the pressure? Is it too much?"

"No, I can handle more--it's starting to relax."

"Good, just tell me if I need to back off. It's still pretty tight, so let's get your knee feeling better, then we can put some ice on it while we eat dessert. Sound good?"

She's leaning forward while working the muscles around my knee, which gives me a direct view of her breasts, and I can see she isn't wearing a bra. Good god, she is going to kill me. I groan and put my head back and stare at the ceiling. Her hands stop and I look back at her.

"Did I hurt you?"

"No, feels great. Thank you, Stell."

Her hands continue to move around my knee and then start to work up my thigh. Is she fucking serious right now? I start thinking of anything to avoid making a fool of myself. *Granny panties. Aunt Gertie in granny panties. Fish guts. Ten times forty. Ten times eighty. Dead kittens. Garbage dumpster. Oh my god, that feels so good and her hand just skimmed my cock.* Yep…all control is lost. I'm getting a full boner. I look at Stella as my boxers start to tent. She of course notices and bites her lip as her eyes come up to meet mine. Her hands continue to skim my cock, now possibly on purpose, and her smile gets bigger.

"You are trying to kill me tonight, aren't you?"

"At least your knee doesn't seem to be hurting too badly anymore."

"Stell?"

"Hmm?"

I beckon her closer with my finger, "Come here, please."

She slides out from under my leg gently putting it down on the floor, stands up, pulls her dress off over her head, and stands in front of me in just her lacy throng and gently straddles my lap putting her hands on my shoulders. "I'm here. What did you need?"

"You took off your dress."

"I didn't want to get oil on it, and I figured it was coming off anyway. Was I wrong?"

I put my hand behind her and pull her into me. Her warmth sitting directly on top of my hard cock. "Not wrong," I say before my mouth finds hers. There is no gentle kissing between us this time. It's a pure hot need. She is grinding against me, and I'm so turned on from wanting her for the last couple of weeks, I have to slow things down before I cum in my boxers like a young kid. I pause and rest my forehead against hers. She continues to move against my cock.

"Stell, give me a second, baby. I'm trying hard not to embarrass myself here."

"Jax, why don't we move this to my room before Griff finds me naked and riding you and wants to watch."

That pulls a genuine laugh from me. "Okay, beautiful. You take the lead, and I'll follow. Are you sure? I can leave, and we can finish this another time."

She traces her finger across my lips as she continues to rub herself up and down my cock. "Jax," she looks into my eyes. "You aren't going anywhere tonight." She stands, puts her hand out to me, and we walk to her room.

I stand in front of Stella's bed, and she slowly starts unbuttoning my shirt. She moves it off my shoulders and it drops to the floor. She then puts her thumbs into each side of her lacy thong and shimmies them down her legs and steps out of them. I am transfixed looking at her. She is in front of me completely naked and almost shaved bare. She smiles.

"You are beautiful, Stella." I look her up and down and when I get back to her beautiful blue eyes, I ask, "How the fuck did I get to be the lucky bastard to be here with you?"

She gives me a gentle kiss on my mouth and slowly starts moving down my chest with her mouth. She slowly takes my boxers off, and I feel a gentle kiss on my cock before she rises and stands before me.

"You're going to lay on your back and enjoy this tonight. Since you can't be on your knee, can you let me be in charge tonight?"

"There are a lot of things I can do while laying on my back tonight, babe."

With a wink, she says, "Oh, Jax, I'm counting on it."

"Fuck!"

"What? What's the matter?"

"I didn't bring protection. I honestly didn't think things were going here. I mean I hoped eventually, but those weren't my expectations."

She leans in to kiss me. "No problem, I live with Griff, and he has a large supply. Let me go grab a handful."

"A handful?"

"Don't worry. I promise we won't hurt your injuries, but we may as well be prepared. Are you sure you feel up to this? I want to be with you, I haven't been with anyone for a long time, but we can wait until your leg is better."

"It's been a long time for me too, Stell, but if I don't get inside of you tonight it may kill me."

She kisses me again, "I think I've been waiting for you too, Jax. I don't sleep with someone unless I feel a strong connection to them. There's amazing energy between us, and I hope you're open to exploring that with me."

"I feel it too. I can't wait to be inside you. Go grab the handful of condoms beautiful and get back to this bed."

I watch her walk gracefully out of the room, then move to the bed, and lie down. My heart is racing knowing this is the first woman I will be intimate with that I have real feelings for. There is pressure on me to make it perfect, to make it a night both of us will remember. She comes back into the bedroom, shuts the door, and stops to look at me.

"That's quite a sight, having you in my bed. I want to remember this moment."

"You know, I was just having that same conversation with myself about you."

"Were you now?

She walks toward the bed and crawls up from the bottom of the bed all while running her hands up my thighs. She bends down and licks my cock from the base to the head and runs her tongue around me. Her hands then continue to run up my abs towards my chest and she hovers above my thighs.

"May I," she asks with a condom in her hand.

I just nod while I watch her open the condom and roll it down my cock. Once I'm suited up, she grabs me and slowly lowers herself down while watching my eyes. Once she's seated fully, her head falls back, and she begins to move. My hands go to her breasts and their fullness rests heavily in my hold. I pinch her nipple, and she groans. She is so wet that the sounds coming from her movements turn me on even more. Her body is sculpted and strong, and she knows how to chase her pleasure. Her mouth finds mine, and we get lost in a passionate kiss as we both seek out our pleasure. I help her move her hips up and down as her breathing gets quicker. I know she's close. Her hand reaches behind her and she massages my balls putting just enough pressure on them to increase the sensation that I'm feeling. My cock grows even bigger inside her heat.

She begins to rock faster, and I watch as she explodes, her warm pussy grabbing my cock with such force I follow her over. She continues to rock against me and enjoys her orgasm through all the pulsing until she gives me the most beautiful smile I have ever seen. "That was amazing. Did I hurt you? Are you okay?"

I pull her mouth down to mine, "I'm fantastic, and you are simply amazing, baby." I run my other hand up and down her spine while I lose myself in her again.

Chapter Thirty

Stella

I wake up with a warm hot chest against my back, and what I can only assume is Jax's hardness up against my backside. He is slowly running his hand over my hip. I turn my head over my shoulder to look at him. "Good morning. Did you sleep okay?"

"Morning, beautiful. I slept well in the few hours since we closed our eyes."

I face him, "How is your knee doing this morning? I know we were careful and kept it out of harm's way, but are you feeling okay for real?"

"Now that you ask, there is something that you could do to help me feel better," he says as his hand moves and he rubs my lower lip with his finger and searches my eyes.

"Oh yeah, what would that be?"

He rolls us so that he is on his back and I'm on top of him. I start to grind on his cock that is somehow hard again. "Does this seem to help?"

"It's good, but I think we could make it even better." He reaches over to the night table and grabs a condom.

Thankfully, I grabbed a handful from Griff's stash last night because we used all but one, along with giving each other pleasure with our mouths. This is the last of the handful. I lift myself off him and watch and he moves his hand once up and down his cock and then rolls the condom on. Then I slowly start to lower myself down on him, slower than he wants apparently as he lifts at the same time as I'm pressing my hips down. We both groan as we allow this moment for my body to relax around his size. Then, all bets are off, and this becomes a passion-filled race to see who gets their pleasure the fastest. I am riding him hard, and I lean myself backward while he rubs my clit in fast circles. My orgasm is just out of reach, but the tingles start, and my body knows that the pleasure we are seeking will be delivered. With his other hand he pinches my nipple and the combined pressure on my clit and nipple helps me fall into a state of bliss, and I moan so loud I'm sure the neighbors hear me. Jax follows shortly after with a groan of release.

We lay in each other's arms catching our breath, when we hear clapping outside the door.

"Is that clapping I hear," Jax whispers.

The clapping is then followed by my best friend's voice, "That was magnificent you two. I am so proud of you both. Once you're decent, you can join me for coffee and cinnamon rolls in the kitchen. Oh and, Jax, your pants are neatly folded across the back of the couch where I found them. Same for your dress, Stella Bug. Congratulations on finally having sexy times. Beautiful. Bravo!"

"Be out soon, Griff," I yell. I watch Jax's reaction as I lean down and give him another kiss, "I guess Griffin is home. Has he scared you off yet?"

"Nah, your best friend is important to you, and he's a great guy. I hope he's willing to share you, though."

"Oh, you don't have to worry about that. Griff is one hundred percent looking forward to sharing you with me. Come on, let's grab a coffee and enjoy our walk of pleasure."

"I like the sound of that! *Walk of pleasure*--It most certainly was. I don't know how I am going to ever go hours without being inside of you Stell." He kisses me and holds me tight.

"Since I am off today, we are going to spend the day together because I have big plans for you, so you won't have time to miss me."

"Sounds perfect to me then. Let's have breakfast with Griff, then let's go to my place where I can remove all your clothing and continue where we left off."

***

After a hilarious breakfast with Griff, who gave us grief about keeping him up and horny all night, we went to Jax's house, so he could shower and change. He knows we have plans. I just haven't clued him in on them yet. Jax walks toward me from the bedroom. His hair is damp and combed off his face, and he's wearing camo shorts and a tight black t-shirt, which clings to his upper body. He also has his knee brace on, which tells me he did overdo it last night.

"My shower would have been way more fun if you would have joined me," he pouts.

"Next time. If I had joined you, we would have ended up having sex for a few hours, and there's something we need to go do. I see you're wearing your knee brace. Nothing on your wrists, though? Are you sure that's a good idea?"

"My wrist splints are in here by the couch, and yes, I'll put them on. I'm following the doctor's orders."

"Thank you. Are you ready for a little adventure?"

"Yep. Where are we headed?"

I take the keys off the kitchen table, "First I need to drive us there, and second...you'll have to wait and see."

He walks over and puts his braces on each wrist. "Okay, babe, lead the way, and I'll follow," he says leaning into me and kissing me.

We head to Jax's car, and after he gets in and buckles up, I start driving towards our destination. He keeps asking questions, trying to figure out where we're going. He has no clue because our destination is new since he moved away to LA. I'm not even sure most of our community knows that they are up and running already. I pull the car into a warehouse-looking structure and park. "We're here."

"Hmm...I'm not even sure what's in these old warehouses anymore. Did you bring me here to kill me, babe?"

"Nope. Come on...we have someone to meet." He gets out of the car a bit hesitant. "Trust me. This is going to be great. I promise." I hold his hand as we walk around the corner of the building to where there's an entrance, and we go inside.

"What are you up to, sweetheart?"

We step up to the counter, and Trish comes out from the back room. "Hey, Stella. I'm so glad you came in. I was about to call you and tell you to hurry in."

"Oh no, are we too late?"

"Not yet, we have a couple still, but not nearly as many as before."

"Well, I'm happy to hear that. That's good news for you and them, and hopefully, we'll create better news before we head out." Jax stares back and forth between Trish and me with a confused expression. "Jax, this is my friend, Trish, and she runs this place. Trish, Jax here requires some support, and I'm hoping you have the answer."

"Nice to meet you, Trish. I'm sorry, but Stella has kept me in the dark here. I don't even know what this place is."

Trish smiles at me, then looks back at Jax, "Nice to meet you too, Jax. Why don't you bring him on back, Stella, and we'll see what we can find to clear up the confusion."

"Jax, let's go see the surprise I have in store for you." I take his hand and pull him with me around the corner and down the hall to where Trish is waiting.

"I put everyone in this room here for you. If you find one you like, just come grab me. Take your time and have fun. I hope you brought your energy with you."

Trish walks away, and Jax still has no idea where we are or what we're doing. "Promise to trust me," I ask him and kiss his lips softly.

"Always."

"Then let's go play."

"Huh?"

I open the door and pull him inside the room. We are barely inside when Jax gasps happily, and we hear the little yips of four little roly-poly puppies in a caged-off play area.

Jax grabs me and hugs me so tight, I barely catch my breath. "You are amazing. I love this and don't be mad at me, but I'm going in to play so you'd better hurry up and follow."

I watch this big guy get inside the caged play area with four little fat puppies and start baby-talking. He is being attacked and kissed by them all and loving every second of it. I pull my phone out and take a quick picture to send to Sophie.

Stella: Guess who is in puppy heaven? *Picture of Jax on the floor with four fat puppies climbing on him*
Sophie: O.M.G. I am crying at all the love in this picture. Was he surprised?
Stella: Totally...and now he's baby talking to all of the puppies. My ovaries are exploding.
Sophie: I hope he picks one. Keep me posted, please.
Stella: Will do.

I watch him laughing and playing with the four puppies, when he looks over at me, "Are you coming in to join us?"

"I was just giving you a moment to enjoy all this love yourself. They sure are cute, aren't they?" I climb inside the play area, and one of the puppies comes over to see me, I start playing with him while keeping my eye on Jax. He's talking to them and having a conversation about how cute they are, and how they are going to grow up to be big and strong. Trish told me there were two girls and two boys left. I'm hoping that he will fall in love with one of the puppies, so we can take it home with us today. These are from the same litter as Sophie's puppy, Betty. She and I talked about Jax needing a puppy, especially now that he can walk again without those crutches. A puppy may give him a little more comfort once he flies back to LA.

Jax is lying on the floor so that the puppies can crawl all over him. He's the silliest thing ever, and I'm having just as much fun watching him enjoy this moment. If only Hollywood saw him now. He catches my eye and smiles. "I'm in puppy heaven right now."

"It looks that way."

"They are so cute. Is this the shelter? I didn't even know we had a shelter in Lake Harmony."

"Trish just opened about three months ago. She moved here from Missouri with her husband. She inherited the land and buildings from her uncle when he passed away. Her husband is going to open his vet practice in the building next door, and since we didn't have a shelter, she's been filling that need in our area. These puppies are from the same litter that Sophie's puppy came from."

"They are adorable. It's so cool that they decided to use the buildings for this." He picks up a big black puppy with a white nose, "You are just so cute. Yes, you are," he says as the squirmy puppy gives him a face full of kisses.

"Would you like to adopt one of these little puppies, Jax?"

He stops talking to the puppy and looks at me without saying a word. I can tell he is thinking about it. He looks at the puppy he's holding and smiles at him before kissing it on the nose. "Do you want me to be your daddy? You may have to learn to move around a lot, but I think you are meant to be my baby."

The puppy is still squirming and loving Jax. The other two have already walked away and are playing with some toys, but the puppy in his hands hasn't left him since he sat down.

"Looks to me, like you have your answer."

A huge smile is plastered across his face. "Looks like I have a puppy to take home and spoil. Thank you, Stella. How'd you know that this is what I needed?"

"Sophie and I watched you with Betty, and we were waiting for you to be done with the crutches. Trish has been keeping me in the loop about how many were left. I was hoping that you'd want to take one home. Sophie was worried about you being lonely when you go back to LA."

"Yeah, that won't suck nearly as much now if I have a puppy to give me kisses. Thank you for bringing me here."

He stands up and walks over to me to help me stand up. He pulls me in for a kiss with the wiggling puppy between us. "Thank you, sweetheart. This is an amazing surprise."

"I want you to be happy Jax. Let's go adopt your baby and make sure we have all the food, toys, and necessities that you will need. What are you going to name him?"

He looks down at the squirmy little puppy, "This little fellow's name is going to be Blue."

"Blue? Is that because of his eyes?"

His eyes move from the puppy to me, "Nope. It's because you found him for me and when I look at you, I always feel like I can get lost in your beautiful blue eyes."

"Wow, thank you. That's very sweet."

He puts his arm around me as we head back to the front of the shelter with blue in his arms. Jax is back to talking to the puppy about all the amazing adventures they are going to have together. My heart is full but also breaking a little as he talks about them moving back to LA soon.

Trish is up at the front when we get there. "Looks like someone has stolen your heart," she says to Jax.

He looks at me and answers, "Yeah, you could say that."

He adopts Blue and is also very generous and provides a substantial donation to the shelter to assist with whatever start-up costs they may still have. He also asks Trish to let him know if any of the other puppies have trouble finding a home. Then taking his phone out of his pocket, he hands it over to Trish and says, "Trish, do you mind taking a quick picture of the three of us? I can post it on my social media and ask for more donations and help in getting the others into happy homes."

He pulls me into the picture with him and Blue while Trish takes the picture. "Thank you. We appreciate any donations that come in. All donations go into the care and shelter of our rescues that need a new home."

"I'm happy to support a good cause, and since Blue here is heading home with me, I want to help his siblings find the same happiness."

Trish looks between Jax and me, "Thank you both again. You two enjoy the rest of your day and thank you for the generous donation."

"Absolutely, Trish. Stella, I think Blue here needs to go to the store and pick out some toys, a new leash, some cool dog bowls, and a big boy bed. Ready for some shopping?"

"Come on, boys, let's get your things and get you settled at home."

I hear Jax talking to Blue as we head back outside, *"Betty, your little sister, lives with my best friend. You will get to see her again soon. I know you may be afraid right now, but I promise it's going to be awesome little buddy, and I'm going to give you the best life you could have ever imagined."*

Chapter Thirty-One

Stella

I'm at the studio and about to open the doors for the day when I see Mrs. Turner walking briskly down the sidewalk from Ellen's coffee shop. She stops in front of my door and yells, "Good morning, Stella. Can you help me inside? My hands are full."

"Good morning," I say as I hold the door open for her. "It's nice to see you today."

She puts the drink tray and bag down on the front table. "I'm so glad I caught you before a class, sweetheart. I wanted to come in and see you myself, so I could give you a big hug and thank you."

She wraps her arms around me with a little squeeze and whispers, "*Thank you so much.*" Then, she pulls away and smiles at me while still holding my upper arms.

"You are an amazing young woman, and I don't know what we would have done without you these last couple of months. Jax called us last night and told us about the amazing weekend he had with you and the surprise of him adopting Blue! He's just....he's....oh Stella…you fixed my broken boy. He is happy again, and I know you had so much to do with his healing and change in attitude."

"Mrs. Turner, I only helped him with some tools to get his head moving in the right direction. He did the work himself."

"Yes, but you've also given him hope of a happy future, my sweet girl. He told us all about your date, and how you surprised him with the puppy. Everything about our conversation was Stella-related. I've been so worried about him out in LA and the women who just use my son for their personal gain. Sophie was a blessing to us, but I've been so worried about him since Sophie relocated to Lake Harmony. I had hoped that he would follow, and now with you, well…I hope he does."

Oh no, I hope her heart isn't dead set on him moving here right away. "Mrs. Turner, I do care about Jax, and we've gotten a lot closer since he came back, but I think he plans to stay in LA."

"But what about you? He isn't moving back? What does he think you're going to do? Follow him? That's nonsense when you just started your business. He has to move here! There isn't another option!"

I can feel her anxiety growing as she starts to spiral. "Mrs. Turner, Jax is the one that needs to make that decision. What did you bring this morning? Would you like to sit down and enjoy your coffee before it gets cold?"

"Oh goodness, I almost forgot. I stopped in at Harmony Bites and got us each a warm drink and muffin. Ellen said you prefer tea, so I got you a chai latte and blueberry muffin. Do you really have time to sit and talk to me for a few minutes?"

"I do. My first class isn't for thirty more minutes. Let's grab our treats and sit on the front bench."

We sit down, and Mrs. Turner says, "I'm going to go stop at the house later and see the puppy. Jax is at his physical therapy right now, so it gave me time to come here and see you. I try not to put added pressure on him, but I do hope he has a change of heart about his living situation soon. I know Sophie would love to see him make that big house he's building his primary home."

"I haven't seen it in person, but from what I hear from him and Sophie, it sounds beautiful."

"You should have him take you over there. He can use all the help he can get in getting it furnished, and that way, you'll like what he picks."

Oh boy. "I'll make sure to mention that to him. It would be another thing he can focus on while he continues healing and moving forward. He's definitely getting better. He told me he has a doctor's follow-up after his session with Keller today."

"Yes, and I think he's hoping to get rid of the splints on his wrists. He said Blue was trying to eat them off his hands. Silly little puppy," his mom says.

"I'm glad he's healing as quickly as he is. The strength training in his leg and hands will still take some time, but it should come together, and he will be just as strong as he was before the accident. I think Rob and his buddies had talked about doing strength training as soon as he got the clear on his wrists."

"I'm so glad that with Sophie and your relationship, he has grown closer to the younger people here. Since he's been gone so long, he hasn't kept as close to the people his age at home. Now, he's been able to reconnect. I thought that would sway him to move back home, but you're right, it's his decision to make."

"I know it's hard. Trust me, I'd love for him to stay, but I can't be responsible for that kind of decision Mrs. Turner."

"I understand. I do. He doesn't have a date to head back to LA yet. So, I suppose I have to be patient and see what he decides to do."

"I think that's all any of us can do, but at least when he leaves, he'll have Blue with him, and dogs are the best at giving unconditional love. Hopefully, he won't feel as lonely."

"Did you see your cute picture in Harmony Hears?"

"No. I must have missed it. Jax must not have seen it either, or he would have mentioned it. I know he was going to put something on social media."

"He sent the picture of both of you with the puppy to Gertie. He wanted to make sure she posted about the rescue and the new vet in town. Here, let me grab my phone and show you."

Mrs. Turner is shuffling through her big purse and then hands me her phone. "Look how cute you all are together."

I look at her phone and see the picture that Trish took and the Facebook post from Gertie.

I hand her phone back, "That is so cute. I know he wanted to post about the rescue on his social media but then decided against it until he was ready for the paparazzi to know exactly where he was. Instead, he posted a cute picture of Blue with his toys and just commented about playtime antics to cuddle sessions. Blue has already stolen his heart. There were some nice comments from fans about it helping him heal from his injuries, then of course, the typical trolls saying only a puppy wants him around. I don't know how he deals with that negative narrative. It would drive me crazy."

"That's part of the glamour, though. You take the positive with the cruel. He typically doesn't pay attention to it, but I agree, hearing those negative things would start to take a toll on me."

Mrs. Turner looks around the studio and pats my hand, "You've done a great job with your studio. I hear great things. How's the business doing?"

"Thank you, it's going great. I have a lot of regulars, especially moms in the community. During the summer months, I decided to run packages for tourists who come in for the week. Julia gave me that idea, and some of her guests take advantage of it. I'm also working on building my sound therapy sessions. I have my second one this weekend. Have you ever tried a sound therapy session?"

"I haven't done a sound session, but I've heard all about it from Gertie. She loves your studio and the sessions. I'm so happy it's taking off for you. Our town needed something like this to draw in the younger generation."

"Why don't you come to the session this Sunday? It will be at eleven o'clock for an hour. Wear comfortable clothes and bring a pillow or blanket. I have yoga mats for everyone. It's a neat experience, and so far, I've had great feedback. I'm even dragging Jax to the session this weekend. He just doesn't know it yet."

"Stella, I'd love to. Is it okay if I bring Mitch with me?"

"Absolutely. My parents will be here and the guys all come with their significant others. Logan said the guys from the firehouse are coming to this one, too."

"Wonderful!" Mrs. Turner stands, "I better get out of your hair, so you have time before your class starts. Thank you again, Stella." She hugs me again and heads out.

Jax you are going to break your mom's heart when you leave. Mine too.

Chapter Thirty-Two

Jax

I finally got some good news from the doctor. I no longer need to use the hand splints, unless I feel I need extra support, and I can take the brace off my leg at home during normal conditions, meaning nothing strenuous.

I just got off the phone with my agent and manager, and I should be getting a script delivered to me today about a new drama that will take place in Chicago. My agent thought it would be a great opportunity for me to spread my acting wings in a more serious role. I'm excited to see what the film is about. He didn't elaborate and wanted a genuine reaction once I read it through.

Before Mom gets here, I grab Blue and put his collar and leash on, "Come on Blue. Let's take a potty break and walk down to the water." Blue barrels toward the door like he was shot out of a rocket. "Whoa….slow down buddy before you smack into the door again." Using the hand gesture and command from YouTube, I tell him to sit. Yeah, that didn't work. I try again, "Blue, sit!" Huh, at least he stopped squirming to try to listen. "Blue, sit!" Closer. He's at least lying down. "Good try. Time to get you outside."

We walk slowly down to the lake since Blue is too busy stopping and smelling the lawn every two steps. He goes potty and continues to walk and wiggle his way down toward the lake. I love sitting down here by the water. Rob and Garrett own this rental. Sophie stayed here during her stalker situation and would sit out here often, so they decided to keep two of the chairs down here by the water's edge. I sit down, and Blue tries to jump up onto my lap and falls over. "Good try, Blue. You're a bit too small to make that jump, and when you are bigger, I'm not sure I want you in my lap. But since you are still just a baby, I'm going with Bree's advice that you cannot spoil a baby." I pick the puppy up, and after he gives me a couple of kisses, he rolls up into a ball on my lap and falls asleep.

While he's sleeping, I pull my phone out of my pocket and shoot a text off to Stella.

Jax: Home from Dr. I got the okay to remove hand splints and use them only as extra support if needed. Same with the knee brace. So if I'm careful I can be on top *winking emoji* although I love watching you ride my cock and seeing your breasts bounce. Nothing better than that. Mom is heading over soon to meet Blue who is sound asleep on my lap down by the water. Big walk for the little man *laughing emoji* Miss you. Need you. Text after your next class babe. I'll make dinner for us. Come over after you close the studio. I'll be here reading the new script *fingers crossed emoji*

I hear a car door and turn to see Mom's car in the drive. I stand with the puppy in my arms and wave at her. It's faster carrying him than letting him do the slow wiggle-walk back. "Come on buddy, let's go meet your grandma."

Mom walks around the back of the house, and I yell. "Hey Mom, we're heading back up."

She yells back, "I saw you down by the lake when I came up the street." She stands on the back deck and waits for us. When I get closer Blue is happy and squirming in my arms, "Hold on buddy, let's get you closer to Grandma before I put you down." He starts kissing my face and making his cute puppy noises. Once we're a few feet from Mom, I put him down, and he bounces over to her as she squats down.

"Aren't you just the cutest little thing, Blue."

Mom picks him up and gets a face full of kisses too. "Sorry, he's still a baby and thinks puppy kisses are his main goal in life."

"Oh, honey, he is the sweetest puppy and there is nothing better than puppy breath. Plus, Grandma already loves you to pieces."

"He just had a short nap, so we can take him in and wear him out with his toys. You got him okay?"

"I can handle a little wiggling puppy son, don't worry."

We get inside, and I'm pouring us a glass of lemonade when the doorbell rings. "Let me grab that. I'm expecting a script today." I head over to the front door where I find exactly what I was expecting. I walk back to Mom as I pull the script from the overnight delivery envelope and exhale a deep breath.

"New script already? Are you healed up enough?" Mom asks.

"Yeah, and my agent thought I would like this one. It's being filmed in Chicago."

I hear Mom inhale before I look up at her. "What?"

"That means that you'd be a little closer to home again if you get it. That would be nice for you."

"For me, huh?"

"Honey, yes. And for your dad and me. We love having you so close to home. I know you didn't end up here for good reasons this time, but I'm always hoping something, or someone, keeps you here."

"Mom, you know LA is my home base. I'll have the house here and eventually move back, but I'm not sure that time is now."

"I understand, it's your decision to make. How did your therapy and doctor's appointment go today?"

"Therapy is good. Keller is working on getting my knee stronger, and I've been able to swim in the lake a little with Noah. Now that I have the okay to use my hands, I can start to strengthen my arms and upper body. I feel a little bit out of shape not having been able to do much the last couple of months. I need my life back, and that means I have some work to still do on getting myself back to where I was."

"You're doing great, Jax. I know how hard this was on you, and even though you feel like it's taken forever, you've gotten stronger and healed faster than how things were looking when we finally found Charlie."

"Charlie was great. I miss having her around, but she called to check on me last week and told me she has another actor she's working with. They are a lot easier than I was at accepting help."

"You were absolutely horrible. Gosh, I don't even want to think about those days. I'm just so thankful Stella got you back to my sweet son. I went by and saw her this morning."

"What? You went to see Stella?"

"Yes, dear. I wanted to stop by her new studio and say hello. She invited your dad and me to join her sound session on Sunday. I can't wait to see what it's all about. Your Aunt Gertie loves the sound sessions."

"Huh, I didn't know she had one planned. She hasn't mentioned it."

"I know. That's what she said, but she is planning on you going with her, so I guess we will see you there."

"Cool. I'm open to trying anything that Stella thinks will help. She was spot on when it came to those oils and my journaling." I watch Mom and the smile that spreads across her face. "Dare I ask what is going through your mind right now?"

"I like you and Stella. She brings a certain balance to you, and even though you may not be aware of it, I am."

"I like me and Stella too."

"You seem very happy with her. What's that going to look like in the future? She won't leave here with her new business."

"I don't know. We haven't talked about it, but she knows that I plan on going back to LA. Maybe we can make it work long distance. I just haven't thought that far ahead to be honest. It's new, and right now, we're enjoying each other's company."

Mom stands, "Well then, I won't dig for any more answers. I'll head out because I know you're dying to get your eyes on that script. Call me if you need me. Otherwise, I will see you Sunday." Mom walks to where Blue is chewing on his bone and pats his head, "Bye, sweet thing. Grandma will bring Grandpa over soon to meet you."

"Come on, I'll walk you out."

***

I've spent the last few hours reading through the script, and I love it. The story is strong, and it's a drama focused on a detective and his partner in Chicago. This is the first of a trilogy. I'm writing down some notes I want to ask my agent when my phone buzzes with a text message.

Stella: Woot-woot on the ability to use your hands and knees. Although so far, I have no complaints about your ability to pleasure me. You've done quite nicely taking me from behind while I'm up on my knees or when I sit on your face. But... always open to new positions as long as your cock can push me to my orgasm. Miss you too. Your mom was so cute this morning and brought me tea and a muffin. We had a nice chat. I have one more class and then I will head your way after I shower.

Jax: Come straight here. I'll be happy to help you shower off *winking emoji* I have some chicken to throw on the grill and salad and potatoes.

Stella: mmm, shared shower...do you promise to make sure you wash all of me?

Jax: EVERY.SINGLE. SPOT. TWICE

Stella: Yummy...and dinner sounds delicious too *laughing emoji* How is Blue today? Being a good boy for you?

Jax: He is learning how to sit, and Sophie has me on the 30-minute potty breaks with (fingers crossed) no accidents today!

Stella: Yay! Good job, Blue!

Jax: Sound session?

Stella: Sunday * Smiling emoji* we can discuss later. I forgot to tell you, but you will love it. See you in an hour *winking emoji*

An hour for me to marinate the chicken and make the salad before Stella is here, and I distract her long enough to fill my need in the shower. I have one more text to send, then I can start dinner.

Jax: Dr gave the okay to carefully start weight training. Still cool to work out with you and Logan?
Rob: Awesome man! Yeah, I'd love to kick your ass in the gym and show you how it's done since you are a weak little bitch right now

Sophie: Sorry Rob was so rude to you and if he doesn't apologize to you he will be sleeping in the guest room and Betty will be with me in the master bed.

Rob: I would like to apologize for my comment. Sophie saw that and well…shit. Yes, Logan will be here at 7 am tomorrow so just come over
Jax: Cool. See you guys then.

Oh boy!

Jax: He apologized but it was just man-speak Soph…no hard feelings.
Sophie: Okay. It wasn't nice though so I'm glad he said sorry
Jax: It's all good. See you tomorrow. Can I bring Blue to visit with Betty while I work out?
Sophie: OMG…YES!!!!!
Jax: Cool, he is doing great but I can't wait to get them together. I want them to be BFFs like we are
Sophie: Of course! They are siblings who love each other and will be neighbors soon
Jax: We will be there in the morning *smiley emoji*

The alarm goes off on my phone, "Blue, let's go potty. Daddy is feeling a lot of pressure from some of the ladies in my life. We have some serious thinking to do in the next couple of weeks, boy."

Chapter Thirty-Three

Stella

I sit back and rub my stomach, "You made too much food. I feel like I'm going to roll out of this chair. Your chicken was amazing, and please feel free to make that anytime you want for me. I love that you learned how to cook with your mom. I don't think I've ever dated someone that cooked for me."

"I'm glad you enjoyed it, and I'm happy to cook for you any time you want. I can make pretty much anything on the grill or in the oven. The only thing I never really mastered was baking. Although, I can whip up some mean brownies from a box."

"It was all delicious. Hey, since it's not dark yet, how about if we go for a walk down at the park? We could take Blue, and he'd have some new areas to smell. Plus, it would help tire him out tonight."

Jax stands up and walks towards the counter. "Sounds good. Let me clean up the food, and we can take off."

"How about you put the food away, while I put the dishes in the dishwasher? That way it's done when we get home."

"Perfect."

***

Blue's on his leash, and he has sniffed every bush and tree we've seen so far at the park. Any time we see someone running, biking, or walking towards us on the trail, they stop or comment on how cute Blue is and that they saw our picture on Facebook.

"I think Blue is more famous than I am right now after Aunt Gertie posted our picture from the rescue," Jax says.

"He is quite the star now. You better be careful, or he may outshine yours."

"Aw, I'm happy to give him the spotlight right now. He's been a great puppy. Have I told you how happy I am that you took me to the shelter to find him?"

"Yes, but it makes my heart pitter-patter to hear you say it. I think he'll be a wonderful companion for you when you go back to LA. I know your mom and Sophie worry about you being lonely."

Jax stops walking and turns towards me. He puts his hands on my hips, "You won't worry about me?"

I look into his eyes and take a moment to find the words I want to say to him. "I do worry that LA won't be the same for you. I know you've done a lot of soul-searching and healing. Your friends from that rock band will be back from touring when you go back. If LA is home for you, then I accept that, and I'm happy for you."

"I know we haven't talked about later and what happens, but I do need to go back to LA. My life is there, Stella. I don't have any answers other than I have to go back there. I also need to call Mattie and the guys and let them know you still refer to them as *that rock band*. It would do them good after the world tour to be humbled a little bit."

I kiss his lips gently and touch his face, "You're ridiculous. I know you need to go back, and I won't keep you or make you feel guilty. My life is here in Lake Harmony, Jax, and I don't want to change that. I also admire that you know what you need to do. We haven't talked about what happens later, and right now, I don't think we need to. Can we just enjoy the time we have? You aren't leaving tomorrow, so we have time, and I don't want to waste it worrying about what's to come."

He kisses me again and leans his forehead on mine. "Did you ever think that you and I would be in an intimate relationship like this?"

I pull away and look at him, "With the Nerd-Jock? Absolutely not."

"Wow! Rough, but I get it. As kids, we didn't circle the same orbit, but as adults, I can't seem to gravitate away from you. It's like you are a magnet pulling me towards you, and I can't stop myself."

I kiss him again and pull him back into a slow walk with Blue, "I saw the script and your notes on the table when I came in today. Why don't you talk to me about the movie? What is it about?"

"The movie is a drama called, Windy City Shadows. The main character, Ace Donovan, is a Chicago detective who navigates the complex web of crime with his partner, Lucy Steele. As they investigate, they start to uncover the underbelly of Chicago and its darkest secrets. I like it so far, and I'm going to let my agent know I want it. I haven't done anything like this story so far. It's the first of a trilogy, plus it's on location in Chicago, which brings me closer to here."

"So how does that work? You get a script, read it, if you like it, you let your agent know, and then you get it?"

"Well…kind of. Usually, the script goes out to a couple of actors to see who will bite, and once they have the lead, they try to match the supporting characters with actors that have some on-screen chemistry. My agent did tell me that the producer of this one came directly to him and said that I'm their first choice for the lead. They even stalled for a bit knowing I was recovering from the accident. My agent reached out to them the minute I was off crutches and said I should be good to go in a few months, which is usually how long it takes before they start filming."

"Did your agent tell you anything else about what the producer is looking for?"

"No. He said they made it sound like they aren't even sure who they'll cast for the female lead until I let them know if I'm interested or not. He did say they're hoping to start filming before winter, and I'm usually on a film set for two to three months."

"Your house will be done by then, so will you live here in Lake Harmony while filming?"

"I hope so because I'd have Sophie to help with Blue during the day instead of him being stuck in my trailer."

"It sounds like you have a plan in place. That's exciting. Please keep me in the loop as you learn more details. I wonder who will be cast as your partner. There are so many choices with all these young starlets these days. It would be funny if Sophie was cast, but that's not her usual genre, either."

"I don't think Sophie has any immediate plans to go back to work, do you?"

"No, I think she's enjoying playing Susie homemaker right now with my brother. She mentioned something about a movie that was going to be somewhere on an island, but I haven't heard anything from her lately. She did say that she won't do more than one or two films a year, and when she does sign up for a film in the future, she and my brother would do their best to navigate him going with her at times."

"I'm so glad she has Rob. He's a good guy. I couldn't have picked a better person for her, and I like knowing that she has you and Griffin as her best friends here. I'm happy sharing that role with the both of you, especially when I can't be here for her."

"We love Sophie. She has been a great addition to our group. Even my sisters and their friends love Sophie. She has a lot of support here in Lake Harmony, just as you do, Jax."

"Being home this time was different. I came home to heal and hibernate from all the bullshit of Hollywood. Of course, I knew all of you from growing up, but it has been cool getting to know your brothers and their friends better. I finally feel like when I come home, I have a strong group of friends here again. After I left to go to LA and would come home to visit, my friends from childhood either left the area or got married and had young families. We don't have the same things in common, and although I know I could call them up, it just wouldn't be the same. Now, especially since Bree had her issues, I feel reconnected to the community and the people here. I'm not just former resident, Jax Turner, coming home to get away from Hollywood and the spotlight. When I come home, I have friends and family here that I can do normal things with. It's made it different being here now. I feel normal. I sound stupid, I know. I mean, everyone here always respected my privacy and didn't treat me like a star, but now…now I have friends that honestly do not give a shit about who I am, my connections in LA, or how much I have in my bank account. Rob called me a little bitch earlier."

Jax is laughing, but I stop and stare at him, "WHAT? Why did Rob call you a little bitch? What's his problem now?"

Jax pulls me into his arms, "Relax, babe. You sound as upset as Soph. He was just talking smack after I told him I was cleared to start weight training with him and Logan. It's fine."

"Fine. He can be an ass sometimes, and it's not like he knows we're sleeping together."

"Oh, I'm sure he's aware. The reality, though, is that it isn't any of their fucking business."

"Yeah, good luck, buddy. Logan is probably worse than Rob."

Chapter Thirty-Four

Jax

Stella and I are on our way to Sophie and Rob's for dinner and puppy chaos. Blue is on Stella's lap licking the passenger window, while his entire rear end wiggles with excitement.

"He's being so good in the car," Stella says. "Although, you will have to clean the window before you turn this rental in later. I can barely see out of it through all the slobber."

"Blue, are you excited to be in the car? You're going to see your sister tonight. Isn't that awesome? Betty is going to be so happy to see you. Remember, you have to go potty outside, but I bet Betty has some good spots picked out for you already."

"You are so ridiculous. But I love it when you talk to him like that. He's starting to recognize his name."

"Do you think so?"

"Yep. When you said it just now, he turned to look over at you, waiting to see what you were going to say next. It was cute."

"Aw, he loves his daddy." Blue is now licking and kissing Stella's face, and she is giggling. "I think he loves you too, Stell." She looks at me and smiles.

"He is pretty easy to love."

I pull into Rob's driveway and park the car. "Are my favorite girl and puppy ready to go inside?"

"Yep, let's go. We should probably let him pee before we go in the house. Then we can start him on the timer."

"Good thinking. Sophie probably has her timer going. He can buddy up with Betty. Blue and Betty. So cute."

Sophie comes out of the door before we even climb the first step, "Hey you three! OMG…he is so adorable. I love that you picked the puppy with the white nose. He is so cute." She squats down as the puppy bounces over to her.

"Hi Blue, I'm Sophie, and your sister Betty is so excited to see you! Come on in."

Sophie holds the door, and Blue runs in so fast, that Stella drops the leash, "And off he goes." We hear chaos coming from the family room and head to the back of the house where we see two little fat black puppies wrestling and playing with the biggest stuffed bear. Rob is on the couch next to them drinking a beer and laughing.

"Hey guys, come join the madness. Soph and I are hoping that Blue here is going to wear his sister out tonight. I've got all the toys on the floor so that they stay busy."

"Hey, buddy, thanks. Look how happy they are to be back together. A puppy reunion!" I say.

Sophie sighs, "It almost makes you want to go and get another one doesn't it?"

Before I can say anything, Stella and Rob both shake their heads and say, "No!"

I laugh, "You both answered that rather quickly."

Rob says, "Stella and I grew up with dogs. Especially labs. They tend to stay pretty feisty for a couple of years, unlike my sister's Great Pyrenees, Duke. He was a mellow lump of white fluff since he was a puppy. You'll see. I'm hoping since they are both mixed with something else that the mutt in them will make them more chill."

"I didn't have a dog growing up. I always wanted one, but we always had cats. Sophie, you didn't have a dog growing up, either. I guess we get to learn together."

"Looks that way. How is Blue doing with the potty training? Betty hasn't had an accident since the first day we brought her home. She's a genius."

"Blue is doing good too. I've been doing the timer schedule with him as you told me, and he's not had any accidents. Speaking of, do you have your timer set?"

Rob laughs, "Oh yeah, it goes off every thirty minutes while we're awake. He'll be fine. Let's get our pizza order in now since it'll take about an hour to be delivered. Sophie, why don't you and Stella order those up, and I'll make sure everyone has a drink?"

Rob walks over to Sophie and kisses her, "You know what I like. You want a glass of wine?"

"Yes, please," Sophie answers.

Rob looks at me and Stella, "Wine or beer?"

"Beer for me, and," I look at Stella and ask, "Wine, babe?"

"Yes, please."

Rob is standing there with his hands fisted at his side. "So this is happening then," he says, looking back and forth at the two of us.

Sophie moves closer and puts her arms around his waist while smiling hugely at us.

Stella comes closer to me and wraps her arm around my waist. "This is happening, Rob. Can you believe that I'm old enough to have a thriving sex life with this sexy and delicious man standing here with me? It's almost like I've grown up or something. Shocking, I know."

I lean down and whisper in her ear, "You may be pushing this a bit."

Stella turns to me, "Both of my brothers would like for me to stay a little girl. Little do they know that she grew up a long time ago and enjoys a good orgasm now and then. He'll survive."

"Babe, I think you've made your point, and I don't want to face off with him and Logan again. Once was enough."

I look at Rob and Sophie, "Stella is important to me, and I respect her. I explained this to you earlier, and Stella needed to address it herself. We're both aware that I live in LA, and she lives here. Right now, we're enjoying our time together and will discuss the future as needed. Privately. Now…how about that beer?"

"For the record, I'm fine with you and my little sister being together. You're very important to Sophie, and I trust her judgment as much as I trust my little sister. Just promise me, Stella, for the love of God, do not ever talk to me again about you having sex. I'd like to stay ignorant and not know those details. Okay?"

"I promise. I will not share any of my dirty, sweaty, sex talk with you ever again, big brother."

"Jesus, Jax…come in here with me and get Stella a glass of wine. Girls, handle the puppies for a minute."

Chapter Thirty-Five

Stella

Jax and I are at the studio early helping Sara set up her singing bowls and gong. She is one of my new sound therapy healers, and this is our first session with her. I visited another studio where she had a session so I could experience her technique, but since Tillie highly recommended her, I didn't question her experience or knowledge at all. I just wanted to meet her before bringing her to my studio so that we wouldn't be strangers.

To say that Sara was surprised to see Mr. Hollywood in my studio is putting it mildly. Jax jumped right in to help and to make her feel more comfortable around him. He's been asking her all about the gong since this is also his first sound therapy session, and she's answering all his questions with grace.

I have no clue how many people are going to show, but I already have over thirty registered. It's going to be body-to-body in my largest studio. I'm going to need to either cap the registration off at a certain point or offer them more often. I need to see how this one goes. Evander is doing the next sound therapy in two weeks.

I look to the front of the studio and the big pieces are in place. Sara quietly sidles over to me, "Stella, you could have given me a heads up that your boyfriend is Jax Turner! Mr. Hollywood Hottie."

"Aw, I'm sorry. He's not that special, so I didn't think to say anything. He's just a normal guy. I promise."

"I know that now, but it was a bit of a shock at first. He's so nice, though, and his questions were cute. He was asking about the gong and how in the world I had managed to cart it around since I was so little. Even if he is just *a normal guy* like you say, he is very charming. You are one lucky girl."

"I am lucky. We grew up together here in Lake Harmony, and we've gotten to know each other as adults during the time he's been home. Things moved in a new direction, and we're enjoying each other right now."

"He told me all about the accident and how much you've helped him. I'm so happy he had someone like you and your knowledge to help him heal. He kept saying he wouldn't be this happy for many reasons if you weren't in his life. See…so charming and he's not so hard on the eyes, you know?"

"Oh, I know. It's going to be hard when he goes back to LA, but we're focusing on the right now. Are you all set, or do you need anything else from me? I'm going to head up front and unlock the door. We've got a big group coming in. Mostly family and friends, so they may be a bit in your face. They're excited and have no boundaries. I suppose I should warn you that Sophie Knight is also a townie and my brother's girlfriend."

"Lake Harmony is awesome! Don't worry about me. I love it when I have a session that's filled with people who want to experience something new and get some healing out of it even if they are movie stars. You go do what you need to, and I'll finish up my staging."

I let Jax know that I'm going to unlock the front and wait for everyone to arrive, and he puts our yoga mats on the floor in front of Sara and begins talking to her again. I love that he respects all this and believes in different ways of healing. That's important to me, and his understanding means a lot.

As I get to the front, I already see Logan outside with his sound therapy accessories. I unlock the door and let him in.

"Stella bug! I'm so ready for this session. Who's here? Is it someone fabulous?" Logan asks. He's wearing his joggers and a t-shirt that barely stretches over his big frame. His tattooed sleeves are on full display, and he's sporting what I can only tell is a buzz-shaved mohawk.

"Hey, Logan, I think you're going to be very happy today. Sara is here and brought her singing bowls and a gong."

"A GONG? YES, BABY," he says while rubbing his hands together. "I'm going to hurry and set up my space and introduce myself to Miss Sara. I got here early to save my spot. See you in there."

Some of my family members slowly make their way into my shop. "Hey, Hillary, Garrett…thank you for coming for another sound session."

My big brother gives me a bear hug, "Hi, Stella. I should be thanking you. You know what these do to my beautiful wife."

Hillary comes up next to him, "You got it, G. They get my engines fired up, baby! Let's go get a front spot this time. Stella said the vibrations are strongest closer to the front."

"Hey, Hill….Sara also brought her gong tonight. Can you do me a favor and let me know which vibrations you prefer? And if they cause anything *different* with you?"

"Are you asking me to tell you which vibrations make me hornier, because, yes, I'm happy to report the stats afterward. Let's go, beefcake…momma needs her vajayjay recharged."

"Good God, I'm surrounded by my siblings and their sex talk," Rob says as he walks in with Sophie.

"Aw, baby, it's okay. Remember what we discussed at home? We're all adults, and we all have sex. It's okay to know that we're all healthy and exploring those things."

"No. I would rather stay ignorant of these facts. It's weird now. I know all the people doing the sex. I don't want to think about my siblings and my friends getting it on. It's almost as bad as thinking about my parents having sex."

"Your parents do have sex," comes from my father's mouth next, and Rob shakes his head and pulls Sophie into the studio and away from us mumbling about being sick.

"Dad, even though you didn't catch that entire conversation, that was one hundred percent awesome, and Rob is most likely ready to go throw up, so thank you." I lean in and kiss my dad's cheek.

"Hi, sweetheart. Mom is on the sidewalk talking to Jax's parents. She's inviting them over for the BBQ at our house later."

"That's nice of her."

"She figures since you two seem to be something of an item now, she wanted to make sure they knew they're extensions of our family now."

"Dad."

"You know your mother, and there's no stopping her. Where is Jax?"

"He's in the back getting our spots ready."

***

Everyone is here and the front is locked up again, so I make my way back to the studio.

"You ready, baby?" Jax asks.

"Yes, are you? Do you have any questions for me before Sara starts?"

"Sara's great. I'm excited about this. She filled me in, so I'm ready. Thank you for asking my parents to come. They were happy to be included and are back there with Aunt Gertie."

"Aw, you're welcome. Okay, let's get the session started."

I welcome everyone to the sound session and introduce Sara to the room before I go have a seat next to Jax.

Sara addresses the room, "Namaste, beautiful souls! Welcome to this sacred space. I'm thrilled to have each one of you here. Today, we embark on a journey of relaxation and healing through the beautiful vibrations of gongs and singing bowls.

In the next hour, you can expect to experience a profound sense of tranquility and inner harmony. The gong, a powerful and ancient instrument, will create waves of sound that can resonate deep within your being. Its rich tones are known for promoting relaxation, reducing stress, and facilitating a meditative state.

206

Singing bowls, with their resonant frequencies, will further enhance the therapeutic atmosphere. These bowls have been used for centuries to restore balance to the body, mind, and spirit. As the sound envelops you, allow yourself to let go of the tension and be present in this moment.

Throughout our time together, I encourage you to find a comfortable position, either sitting or lying down and simply surrender to the sounds around you. There's no right or wrong way to experience sound therapy; each of you will have a unique and personal journey.

Feel free to close your eyes, focus on your breath, and let the vibrations wash over you. If at any point you need a moment to yourself or have any questions, please don't hesitate to let me know.

Now, let's begin this transformative sound journey together. Allow the soothing sounds of the gong and singing bowls to guide you into a state of deep relaxation and rejuvenation. Thank you for being here, and may this experience bring you peace and serenity."

***

After the sound therapy session, Hillary informed me, and everyone, that the gong most definitely caused more stimulation in her vajayjay than the singing bowls but that both gave her an intense tingling in her nipples. Thankfully, everyone here is familiar with my sister-in-law and her blunt form of communication so it wasn't a shock to anyone.

Logan is in awe. Jax and I could hear him sobbing during the session and were aware of Sara going to him to give him comfort. Jax reached over and grabbed my hand at one point when I sensed he was also about to lose it.

"Sara, thank you so much for the wonderful session. The gong is always my favorite, along with the rain stick. I think you've made quite the impression on this group."

"Stella, it was an amazing session. The energy in this room was unbelievable. I got so much enjoyment out of it myself. Your sister-in-law, Hillary, is a hoot. We traded business cards, and she wants to connect sometime. I hope that's okay."

"Of course. Hillary is something, harmless and an awesome person to have in your corner."

Sara leans into me and whispers, "Um…what can you tell me about Logan?"

Ah…interesting. "Logan is a great guy. He's a local firefighter and Mr. Safety for the schools. He's a big bear hug kind of guy and one of my brother Rob's best friends. Oh, and single if that's what you wanted to know."

Sara blushes and looks down, "He is so sweet. I felt bad that he was sobbing, but he was so lost in the vibrations and letting the negative energy release."

"He may be a man-beast, but he is a gentle soul. Ah, speak of the devil." Logan walks up to us after he has collected his blanket, pillow, and all the accessories that he brought with him.

"Miss Sara, I want to thank you for this amazing day. I'm sorry if you were concerned about me, but your hands are responsible for helping me work through some lingering trauma I had. If it's okay with you, I'd like to stay and help you put your things away."

Sara blushes and nervously puts a loose strand of her hair behind her ear. "Thank you, Logan, I'd like that very much. The gong is a bit too much for me to carry, so I appreciate your help. Do you have time for me to thank you afterward and maybe get a late lunch?"

The two of them move towards her equipment and Jax puts his arm around me. "Thank you, babe. That was amazing. Is this the kind of stuff you've done all this time? I feel like I've been missing out on something. Do you have training in this, too?"

"No, I never learned how to do it because I'm selfish and would rather enjoy it myself than be the one delivering it. With Tillie in my life, I was fortunate enough to have her close and enjoy her sound therapy sessions. She tells me that no matter what she thinks she is going to do, the sounds take her on her journey and that's why each one is so different. If you'd ask Sara, I'd bet she would answer the same. She was great though. This was one of my best sessions, and the energy levels were amazing. Plus, I think everyone liked the addition of the gong. It will be fun to see the reaction to Evander when he comes in a couple of weeks."

"I'm sure he'll be great too, but I can tell you Logan won't be quite as impressed as he was today."

"He was a bit smitten. Sara asked me about him too."

"Oh, he was smitten all right. That tiny woman of barely five feet just took a huge man down to sobbing and being shy."

Chapter Thirty-Six

Jax

After the sound therapy, we went home to clean up and are now heading to the Stones for their Sunday BBQ. Stella is next to me with Blue on her lap. "Are you sure your parents will be okay with me bringing Blue?" I ask.

"Of course. Sophie and Rob will probably bring Betty, and it's good for the pups to socialize with my parents' dog, Molly. She's a black lab too."

"I like having him with me as much as possible while he's a puppy, but I don't want to impose."

"Jax, it will be fine. More than likely the neighbor's big Great Pyrenees, Ralphie, will be there or stop by. He has a thing for Molly, and my parents let him come and go as he pleases. We have enough property there that the pups can roam the yard and not get into trouble."

"As long as you're sure." I reach over and squeeze her hand and pet Blue's cute head.

"I am, so don't worry about it. Mom is excited that you and your parents are joining us."

"I feel pretty lucky about being invited to a Stone's Family BBQ. Sophie always tells me about the weekly cookouts and how awesome it is to have a weekly dinner with the family. Now, I get to experience it first-hand. My parents better be taking notes."

"Honey," I laugh, "Your parents will most likely be here whenever you're home. That's just how things work. The Stones invite friends, adopt you into their family, and then BAM you become one of us."

I put the car in park and looked over to her, "Bam, I'm one of you?" Stella stares into my eyes. I love it when she takes the time to pull me into her thoughts.

"Yeah, you may not be able to escape at this point."

"Babe," I lean over and gently kiss her lips, "There is absolutely no place I would rather be than part of your family."

Her breath catches and she continues to look into my eyes. Then, she leans back, winks at me, and says, "Be careful what you wish for, Jax. Ready to face the family?"

"Yep, let's do it." I get out of the car and walk around to open her door and help her out with Blue. "Do you want me to take him or grab the food we brought?"

"Go ahead and take him. I know you're dying to show off your baby. I'll grab the veggies and bring them to the kitchen."

***

Dinner was delicious with chicken, brats, and too many side dishes to even count. Now, I'm sitting in one of the Adirondack chairs with Stella on my lap talking to the rest of her siblings and their significant others. Sophie and Rob brought Betty, and the pups wore themselves out wrestling and being chased by Molly and Ralphie. We all agreed it was a good lesson for the pups to be schooled by two older dogs.

To the right of me, Garrett says, "What's next on your radar, Jax? Seems like you're recovering pretty well now from the accident. Your injuries don't seem to be keeping you down much anymore."

The group looks over and listens, "I just got an amazing script that my agent forwarded from the studio. I'm hoping that I start that in the next couple of months. It's the first of a trilogy about a detective in Chicago. I'm excited about it."

Hillary, who is sitting on the other side of Garrett leans forward, "OOH…do you need some pointers from my husband, THE SHERIFF?"

"I might. It's a suspenseful drama, and filming would keep me around for longer. It's been nice being home and getting to reconnect with all of you."

Bree smiles, "I loved having you around a bit more. I'm sorry about the reason that brought you here but not sorry for the reason that may be keeping you here."

Stella reacts to that comment by getting stiffer in my lap. I squeeze her hand and kiss her on the cheek. "The accident sucked. Not going to lie about that. And the days right after were brutal. Thankfully, Sophie and my mom came out and found Charlie. She was my home nurse and, among other things, managed to not knock my head off for being an asshole. She was the first good thing after my accident. Then I came back here and was lucky enough to have an amazing woman who worried about me and wanted me to heal inside and out. She pushed me and shared her own personal thoughts while being very patient with me." I smile and give Stella another kiss, noticing the pink of her blush. "Thankfully, after that horrible accident, I came out with Stella by my side, and yes, Bree, she is definitely a reason I'm still here."

Julia, Stella's oldest sister looks at us with concern, "I'm glad you're doing so much better, Jax, but are you making Lake Harmony home now full-time?" Jackson, her husband puts his hand on hers and squeezes knowing that is the elephant in the room.

Stella sits up taller in my lap, "Please, don't put pressure on him. We're enjoying getting to know each other and spending time together when we can. Jax has his home in LA, and yes, he's building that monster of a home next to Rob and Sophie, but for now, that remains home number two. He hopes to be here over the winter to shoot this film. So as far as the future is concerned," Stella smiles at me, "We're still figuring that out and enjoying the process. When we know, you'll know. How's that?" She pauses briefly glancing around the group and then directs her attention to Hillary, "So, Hillary, how long did the vibrations and stimulation last after the sound session today?"

Rob groans with frustration, gets up, and heads inside at the same time Hillary answers, "Oh, the vibrations and stimulation are still strong Stella-bug. I love all of you, but I cannot waste another moment sitting here." She stands and grabs Garrett's hand, "Come on, baby, let's go home and play while things are still sensitive."

Chapter Thirty-Seven

Stella

Jax and I are back at his rental and relaxing in the hot tub on the back deck looking at the stars. I always enjoy time with my parents and everyone. "How do you feel now that you've survived your first official Stone BBQ?" I ask Jax.

"It was awesome. Your parents have always been the cool parents in town. My parents got to know them a little better and Mom said your mom already invited them over for a parent-only dinner. Dad got invited to go fishing with my Uncle Peter and your dad next weekend. So, I'd say things went great. What about you?"

"I'm glad you enjoyed the day. Me…surprised that Julia was the one to bring up what's going on between us and your living situation but not surprised it came up. I figured it would have been one of my overly protective brothers that would bring it up, not Jules, to be honest."

"I don't want you to always feel put on the spot or that you have to protect me, Stell. I know you're being very patient with what comes next. Do you want to talk about it now?"

I snuggle closer into Jax in the hot tub, and he puts his arm around me. "Not really."

"Are you sure? We can open that door, but it doesn't mean we have to come up with all the answers. Maybe we should do that. I don't want you worrying about things. Do you want to hear what I think the future looks like?"

I tilt my head to look up at him, "I would like to hear your thoughts, and I'm happy to share mine with you too."

He pulls me onto his lap so that I'm straddling him. Of course, we don't have suits on, so this position brings me against his hardness. "Are you sure you can focus like this?"

He leans forward and kisses me, "I want to be able to look into your beautiful eyes and see your feelings. You don't hide your feelings well if I can look at you."

"Learning my secrets already?"

"Maybe, now…my main home is in LA. We've established that already. I am also building a home next door to Sophie and Rob. I'm doing this because I want to have my own four walls when I come home to Lake Harmony, and eventually, I may move here when I'm not on location filming somewhere."

"Okay, kind of what I figured, but maybe we need to focus on talking about the next six to twelve months?"

He leans forward and kisses me again, "Yeah, baby, let's talk about that. This," he kisses me again, "You and I--I like this. I don't want to lose this. How do you feel about us?"

My breath is stalled, but I need to answer him, "I don't want to lose this either. So how do we handle the distance?"

"I need to go home to LA and see my agent and manager in person now that I'm almost back to normal. I also want to visit with the guys, now that their music tour is over. I want to do something special for Charlie since she put her life on hold to get me healed enough to be human. The studio, if they take me on for the film, will also ask me to come in and do readings with other actors from the film. I can't do that from here. Those things will take me back to LA, and it could be a few weeks to a few months."

He stops talking and stares at me, running his thumb down my cheek, "I can't lose you, Stella. You have become very important to me. I'm falling for you, baby, so I guess what I'm asking is, can you be patient with me and help me figure out the next steps? The film will bring me back home for a few more months, and I plan on being here with you. Is there any chance that you can have someone in place at the studio so that when I'm away maybe you can come be with me in LA? I'd love to have you in my home and for you to meet my friends. What do you think? We give this a hard try and work through the distance when we have to. Technology has come a long way, and we can Facetime and call as often as possible."

"I can do that. I already have a part-time sub, but I know I can ask Griff to be my emergency person while I'm away, and I can find another part-timer to help with my regular classes."

"I'm happy to help support the cost of bringing in more people to help teach your classes while I have you in LA."

"Thank you, baby, but I can manage the cost of that right now. You just bring me there and handle that part, okay?"

"I can do that. So, do we think we have an immediate plan of action and that we can continue to see where this goes?"

"Yeah, I think that works for now, and I'm excited to see your place and be back in LA for a visit. I haven't been to LA in a couple of years. The energy is a little crazy, but it will be fun to be there with you."

"You say that now, but remember, being there with me means dodging the paps and all the fans."

"Aw, yes, because I decided to fall for one of America's Hotties. Lucky me," I say and roll my eyes at him.

"I'll give you lucky," he pulls me closer, and my center is now on top of his hardness. "Ride me, baby. Make yourself cum."

***

We walk inside naked holding hands and Jax pulls me towards the shower, "Come on, let's wash off and get ready for bed. You are staying here tonight."

He leads us into the bathroom, turns on the shower, and then pulls us both into the warm spray. He turns me to face him and frames my face with both his hands, "You are so beautiful. How did I get so lucky to find you?"

"Mmm, seems I've been here all along. You just had to come home and see me."

"Timing, it's all about the timing. Now, tilt your head back, so I can wash your hair for you. I want to take care of you tonight."

"You seem to forget that I was the one who just had a beautiful orgasm in the hot tub."

217

He smirks at me, "I want to take care of you tonight, now lean back please."

I lean back into the spray and then look up at Jax. He has shampoo in his hand and begins to lather my hair and massage my scalp. I moan as he massages me and runs his strong hands down my neck. "That feels nice. Thank you."

He leans forward and kisses me gently, "Lean back so I can rinse your hair, baby."

The warm water and soap suds wash down my body. He rinses my hair and I feel his finger trail down my neck and over my breast to my nipple. He leans down and sucks on the nipple and then moves to the other one and hums his pleasure. "Beautiful."

I straighten and watch as he puts conditioner in his hands, "We don't want your long locks to tangle, come here." He moves his strong hands down my hair, and I lean back into the warm water to rinse the conditioner out of my hair.

"I'm going to burn this image into my mind forever. The way your body looks right now, all wet and sudsy. Now I get to have some fun." He grabs the body wash and soaps up his hands, "Let's get your back washed first. Turn around for me."

I turn my back to him, and he begins by washing my shoulders and moves down my back. I feel his hands washing me gently as he moves down one leg and then the other. He asks me to turn around, but before I do, he leaves a kiss on my backside. Standing he lathers more soap in his hands and brings them gently to my shoulders, then my breasts, and to my stomach. His eyes never leave mine.

"Make sure you don't miss a spot," I say to him.

His eyes don't leave mine but his mouth grins at me, "Don't rush me enjoying taking care of you, but I promise, I won't miss a single inch of your beautiful body." He moves to my legs and goes slowly down one side to the other. Stopping to leave a kiss just above my center. He stands and I rinse off.

"That was wonderful, thank you." With a grin, I kiss him, "Now it's my turn." I pull him into me and spin around, so he is now the one closer to the spray, "Lean back, please."

He does, and I begin to wash his hair and massage his scalp. He closes his eyes, enjoying the care he's receiving. "Rinse, please." He does as I ask, and I begin putting conditioner in his thick dark hair. I move my hands down the back of his neck and run my fingers down his tight muscles. "You're supposed to be relaxed after the sound session. Why is your neck so tight?"

"Not sure, but your hands feel amazing, baby."

"Lean back and rinse, then turn so I can wash your back and try to release your neck a bit more."

"Okay." He rinses and turns dropping his head to his chest so I can lather his back and work on his neck.

"I hate that you are so tight still, Jax."

"Baby, your hands are magic."

"Shh, let me work on you a bit." I continue to put some pressure on his neck and run my hands down his back. I lather up my hands and move them over his ass. God this man's ass is beautiful. He is so strong and sculpted. Even with the setback of his injuries, he kept the hard angles and cuts of his muscles. I work my hands up and down both his legs and like him, I leave a kiss on this very kissable ass.

I stand up and ask him to turn. Once he's facing me, he looks into my eyes, "I love your hands on me."

"Well, you're going to enjoy this then." I tip up onto my toes and give him a gentle kiss. I lather up and work my hands across his strong shoulders and down that tapered stomach of his. I don't touch his cock quite yet. Although it's hard standing between us against his abs. Instead, I lather my hands and work his strong legs down one side and then the other, paying special attention to the knee that was injured. I work my hands around the scar, and before I move away, I leave another kiss. At this point, I have him where I want him. I look up at him and grin, "Better hold on to the wall, baby." Then I take him in my mouth down to the base. I come up and I lick all around the head of his hard cock and hear him inhale. His hand comes to my head, and he tangles it into my hair helping me move and setting me to the speed he wants. Of course, he keeps slowing me down, but I know how to take the lead and with my free hand, I reach up and wrap it around his balls. He tenses a moment and then allows me to take control. I can already taste him on my tongue. He won't last much longer as my finger pushes against the skin where I know it will trigger him to fall over the edge of the control he's fighting to hold onto. He groans and I feel the warmth enter my mouth and I swallow his release.

Once he catches his breath, he lifts me and his mouth finds mine. "You are amazing."

"I wanted you to relax. Feel better?"

"I feel amazing. Let me dry you off, then I'm wrapping you in my arms while we sleep. Come on, baby. Time for bed."

Chapter Thirty-Eight

Jax

I walked up to the house from the lake this morning feeling good. I swam for an hour in the lake before I went in for some weight training and mobility stretches with Keller. Blue is in his crate sleeping when I walk into the house. "Hey Blue, let's take you out quick before I jump in the shower."

He stretches his little body after waking and starts to bunny hop in his excitement that I'm back. "Come on, big guy, let's go potty outside." We head out, and he walks around the bushes smelling and peeing in numerous areas. "Good boy, Blue!" He squats down one more time to do some serious business, and I hear the phone ring. I'll have to call them back because Blue isn't quite ready to go inside yet.

"Good job, buddy. You've earned yourself a nice treat to chew on now. Come on, let's grab you a bone!"

Walking to the treats, I grab his bone and my cell off the counter. The call I missed was from my agent. I drop my wet swim trunks, throw them in the sink, and wrap the towel around my waist before I call him back.

"Hi, it's Jax. I just missed a call. Is he available to talk now?"

"Hello, Mr. Turner. Let me ring back to his office and see if he's still free. Hold on a minute, please."

I'm put on hold and a few moments later the call picks up. "Are you ready for some good news?" my agent asks.

"I'm always up for good news, hit me."

"You got the lead in the Chicago detective film. Congratulations, Jax! It's going to be a great project for you. They want to make all three films close together and release them a year apart. How do you feel about being in Chicago for a while?"

"I'd tell you that it sounds perfect right now. What other details do you have so far? I'm sure that there's a soft timeline being planned already."

"Yeah, knowing you wanted the lead, they've been reaching out to the other actors they hope to pair you up with. They need to make sure everyone is on board since this is a trilogy, and they want to do all three films back-to-back. The studio was hoping that you could be here by the end of next week. That gives you about two weeks for whatever you need to wrap up there. Will that work?"

"It should. My therapy sessions are just working on the mobility in my knee and wrists at this point. I think Keller can set me up with what to do at home. Same with my weight training. I know my limitations, and it would be good to be at home to use my pool for laps. Let me get some details on my end figured out, and you call me when you have some more concrete dates and times. Also, let me know what you hear about the others coming in to read with me."

"You got it, man. Again, congratulations. I think this is a win for you and will bump you back up after your injuries and the damn paps harassing you. I'll reach out to the rest of your management team and get them on board, too. I'll be in touch."

"Sounds good, thanks. It will be good to spin something positive for a change."

***

I called Keller to let him know we have two weeks to get an at-home routine figured out so I can continue the therapy needed to get me back in top shape. He's going to put together some different things, and now that those details are falling into place, my next stop is Stella. I'm parked in front of the studio and waiting as I watch a group of people leaving. She must have just had a class end. Once foot traffic slows down, I get out of my car and head in. Stella's standing behind her front reception area on the phone. As I walk in, she sends me a smile and holds a finger up, letting me know she wants me to wait. While she finishes up her call, I look around the room at the products that I know she makes and sells.

Her lean arms circle around my waist from behind, "Hey, this is a nice surprise. If you had been five minutes earlier you would have been surrounded by my last class."

I pull her in front of me, putting my arms around her, "I know. I was in the car waiting for your class to end before I came in. Do you have a short break, so we can talk a minute?"

"I do. I'm the only one here right now, so you have all my attention."

"Come sit with me for a minute." I guide her over to the cute bench built into the front window. She sits and turns to face me with her legs up in front of her and her chin resting on her knees. I can tell she's nervous.

"My agent called this morning after I got back from working with Keller. I got the movie."

Stella's smile takes over her face, and she leans over to kiss me, "That is awesome. I'm so happy for you."

"Yeah, I'm excited too. The only details I have so far are what we talked about before. I have the lead, and now the studio is reaching out to those they think would make a great cast around me. My agent said they want me back in LA in two weeks to meet and read with whoever is interested in the other roles."

"Two weeks," she says looking into my eyes. "At least, it's not immediately and it gives us time to figure some details out."

I pull her onto my lap. "I know, Stella. We have two weeks, then I have to head to LA. I don't have a timeframe for how long I will be there, but it gives us time to, hopefully, get a plan in place here so that you can come out for a little bit?"

Reality has arrived. That elephant in the room just came through our version of life like that big Kool-Aid man from the seventies. "This is your job, your life, so if we're going to work on this relationship, then I need to figure out a way to deal with you being gone at times, right?”

“Yeah, babe, but I’ll do whatever I can to make sure that we always have a plan in place to somehow be together. Even if that means I come to you when you can’t leave your studio. I’ll make this work. You’re too important to me not to make it work.”

“Same, Jax. As long as we do this together, anything is possible. Now, let’s celebrate this wonderful news. How about if we have some friends over for a nice dinner and maybe hit the hot tub this weekend? I can call Sophie, who will be happy you’ll be around longer, and of course, Griffin.”

I lean in and kiss her, “Sounds perfect. I’m going to swing by Mom’s house next, then head back home to Blue. See you later?”

“Yes. I’ll be there after my five o’clock class.”

I stand up and pull her into my arms, “See you later.” I lean down and give her a kiss when we hear the door open.

“Hey lovebirds, am I interrupting?” Sophie asks.

I turn with my arm still around Stella’s waist, “Yes. Come back later.”

Stella slaps my stomach, “Stop it. No, Sophie, you are not interrupting. Jax was just heading out, but while you’re here, do you and Rob want to come have dinner with us and celebrate tomorrow?”

“OH! What are we celebrating?”

“I got that film in Chicago,” I tell my best friend. “Stella and I were going to have you, Rob, and Griffin over for dinner and hot tub time to chill and celebrate.”

“YES,” she says while bouncing on her toes. “This means that you’ll be around longer. Oh my god, Jax. This is the best news EVER.”

Chapter Thirty-Nine

Stella

The puppies are gated on the deck while we sit in the hot tub with a cold drink. Dinner was courtesy of Maria and Antoni from Bella Roma's, and we are all stuffed.

Griffin rests his head on the back of the hot tub and groans, "Jesus, why did you let me eat that second helping of pasta? You are supposed to be my best friends and love me, not bring me harm."

I laugh and splash him, "Griff you are a grown-ass man, and I'm not going to police your food intake. Surprisingly, you aren't floating on top of the water with all your carb intake though."

Griffin being Griffin quickly stands up in the water and turns from side to side. He's wearing what I'd call a body glove small swim trunk in camo fabric. Pointing down at his defined stomach he says, "Do you see the bloating, Stella? Sophie? I'm serious you be-otches. You made me eat all that food and I'm bloating. I can barely move from all those carbohydrates tonight." He sits down with another groan and takes a huge gulp of his margarita.

Rob is laughing next to me, "Griff, what in the ever-loving kind of fucked-upness type of swim trunks are you wearing?"

I love that my brothers don't care that my best friend is gay and usually hits on them. Griffin stands back up, hands on his hips, and glares at Rob. "These just happen to be my most reserved swimwear, Robert. I didn't want to cast a shadow on either you or Jax, so I'm hiding my goods in my camo swim trunks."

Jax is laughing now too, "Griff, buddy…the camo isn't hiding things, man. I don't think I've ever seen in you so little clothing, but if this is reserved, I'm impressed. I also didn't know that you were so cut. Damn, why are you still single?"

Griff points at Jax, "THAT. RIGHT.THERE."

"What?" I ask Griffin.

Griffin says with a big smile as he sits back down, "Jax just showed all of you why, if he ever decides to swing to the other side, I have dibs. Thank you, sweetheart. I appreciate your compliment."

Griffin looks like a model off the cover of a Shape magazine, with bright blue eyes and dyed blonde hair. He always reminded me a little of a younger Justin Bieber. He is *single* if you don't count dating different people at the same time. He told me once that he's too picky to settle down with just one man right now. He needed to sample the offerings first for a while.

Sophie snuggles into Rob, "Hey Stell, I know we talked about the film and all, but how are you handling Jax going back to LA for a bit?"

"Jax and I talked about it, and depending on how long he needs to be there, I'll go out and see him when I can, and he'll come back here when he can. It won't be easy or fun when we're apart, but we talked and kind of have a plan."

Griff leans forward, "I'll cover the studio while you're out. Hill knows I promised to help you when I can, and I can come and go, but I won't be any help with your classes."

"I spoke to Sara, who is my sound therapy girl, and she has a friend who is a certified yoga instructor who lives close by. She just moved back to the area, and I'm going to try her out as another part-timer. She would be able to handle doing more when I would be away."

"Stell…um, I'm happy to help when Griff can't, and I think the town has gotten used to me, otherwise, I can wear a disguise. Just know, I'm here to help too. Rob and I are both here. We'll be going through the same thing as you guys when I decide to do another film, so we know what you're dealing with. Just don't be afraid to lean on us, okay?"

"Thank you, Soph. That means a lot to me," I answer.

"Me too guys, thanks," Jax says. "I guess Stella and I will figure out the details, but it means a lot to both of us to have you guys in our corner and ready to help."

Rob kisses Sophie and looks at me, "Stella, just ask okay? Don't try to handle it all. You've accomplished a lot, and we're so proud of you. Don't try to keep taking things on yourself. You have the three of us, not to mention the other thirty or so family and friends that would bust their butt to support you."

I wipe a tear away, "Thanks, big brother."

"Now, onto bigger issues. Jax, buddy. Your house will be done tomorrow. What's the plan?" Rob asks.

"Seriously? It's done?"

"Yeah, I have the final inspection tomorrow, and I should be handing you keys by the end of the day."

"I guess I need to go shopping then," Jax says looking at me, Sophie, and Griffin. "Who's up for some furniture and everything a house needs shopping this weekend?"

Griffin stands up in the water again and points his face and arms to the sky, "Thank you, Goddess, for all the joy you bring into my life."

Jax is laughing, "Ah, Griff…I take it you're good with the shopping?"

He sits back down all calm and leans forward. "You just tell me your colors, type of style, and the girls and I will make sure to fill your home with amazingness. Do we have carte blanche spending here or a budget? Oh, do you have an AmEx black card? This is going to need Hilly's White Board of Wisdom. Girls, we're going to need a plan; maybe a vision board. Oh my god. Girls, there is so much to do!"

Rob looks at Jax laughing, "Buddy, you have no idea what you just did."

"Oh no, I think my house will be completely furnished, accessorized, and done by Monday. Hey Griff, let's have coffee tomorrow. I can show you my style, and color choices, and you can dream up where we should go shopping. Does that work?"

"Jax, I love you. Come to Hilly's shop in the morning. I'll get us goodies from Ellen, and girls, if you're free, you can come."

"Thanks," I say sarcastically to my best friend. "I have a class, but I know Jax is in good hands with you, Griff. Soph, if you're free though, can you assist so Griff doesn't get carried away."

Jax just smiles and relaxes against me. "I do have a collection of art in LA. I'm going to want to ship some of it here. Especially the more modern pieces. I think they'll look better in my contemporary house here than in my LA house."

"Seriously," Griff asks Jax with his eyes all big. "You collect art too? My goodness, I couldn't love you more."

Chapter Forty

Jax

Shopping Day Griffin-style means we have a list of designated locations all around the Chicago area. I wear jeans and a T-shirt, a baseball hat, and my dark aviator sunglasses. Sophie is in her pregnant disguise, and Griffin is dressed in his best. Stella is the only one who looks relaxed. They know my style type for the house, and we are off. Griffin has even called ahead to schedule time with a designer at each of our stops. This was probably a good idea considering we are furnishing a five thousand square foot house.

"Now team, going in, the designers all have their to-do checklist. Are we all good to go? They know the style Jax prefers is modern but earthy. Strange but it works. Are you ready to go in and bust out bedrooms, living area, viewing room, den, kitchen, and dining tables?"

"Jax, are you sure you want to buy all new for this place and not just ship your furniture from LA here," Sophie asks.

"Sophie, I love you buddy, but this is my second home. It also needs to be furnished. You know it's not about the cost. I'm glad I have you guys here with me to help. My LA house was done completely by a designer. It works, but this house has my input, and I'm excited. I want it to be comfortable and inviting. I have a big crew here in Lake Harmony that I will have to host, eventually. There are a lot of you guys at home."

"Okay, I just wanted to make sure. LET'S DO THIS."

***

We're back in Lake Harmony, sitting at a table at Cooper's Corner for dinner. "Jesus, Griff, you are amazing. Do you realize how much money you could make doing this shit for people in LA?"

"I don't want to do this for a living," Griff tells me. "Today was a blast and exhausting, sweetie. But I did this for you and Stella. I wanted to make sure my friends had a home that was welcoming and made them feel good to be in it. Mission accomplished?"

"Absolutely, you managed to furnish…," I start counting off on my fingers, "Four bedrooms, my den, the living room with a huge sectional and side chairs, a kitchen table, bar stools for the island, a beautiful dining room, three amazing couches for the viewing room, and awesome outdoor furniture that will host at least a dozen or more people. I can't believe it, but you have a real gift. Not to mention all the accessories that are needed in a new house."

"Aw, sweetie, it was fun. Thank you for letting me have my way all day."

"No, you listened to what I like, and you got it right."

"I loved that you always asked Stella bug what she thought. That was sweet," Griff adds.

I look at Stella and wink, "That's because I hope one day that will be her home too." She blushes and stares into my eyes trying to get a read on me.

"So romantic," Sophie says.

Before Stella can respond, Rob comes up to our table, "Hey guys, how'd it go today? You buy out all the stores in the Chicagoland area?"

"Just about, but the house is good to go. I may have to hire someone to be here when it's all delivered if I'm gone, but it's done. Griffin is amazing. Rob, do you ever need to stage your model homes?"

"Yeah, we always have the models or special homes staged. Why, what's up?"

"Next time, hire Griffin to do it. He's amazing, man."

"Really," Rob looks over at Griff. "Would you be interested?"

"If you ask nicely," Griffin says with a smirk.

"Cool, I hate having to do that shit. You're hired Griff. Next time it's all you. What'd you find for the viewing room? I know you put a lot of thought in there with the staggered floors."

"Oh, sweetie, I found Jax the most luscious soft, deep couches for each level. They each seat six people comfortably. They will be amazing."

"I'm looking forward to that room. Viewing parties will be fun, although not my films. That'd be too weird."

"Aw, and here I thought we could all sit around and watch one of you and Sophie in a rom-com. Although I'm not sure if that would be awkward watching my woman with you, or hilarious knowing that there is some real acting between the two of you to pull off something romantic," Rob says.

"Oh god, Jax, we need to promise each other right now that there will never be a watch party of the two of us in anything romantic," Sophie says.

"Promise buddy. Not happening. Ever."

Everyone laughs, and Cooper, our friend, and owner of the restaurant, comes over to our table. "Hey gang, how is everyone doing today? What's with the costume, Soph?"

"We all went furniture shopping for Jax's new house today. To avoid more spectacle than usual I put this on."

"Did it work?"

"Well, they didn't recognize me, but Jax stood out. So that's promising."

"What can I get you guys tonight?"

"Dinner is on me tonight," I say. "How about beer, wings, fries, onion rings, loaded nachos? Anything else guys?"

"Sounds good. I'm trying out some new sliders. Want to sample for me?" Cooper asks.

"I won't say no to that," Rob says.

"I'll bring those out, too. I have buffalo chicken and Cubans."

"Coop, those sound amazing. Thanks."

Chapter Forty-One

Jax

For the last two weeks, Stella and I have both done whatever we could to make sure she was able to go to LA with me. Chartering a plane was the easiest solution for this trip. Since Stella could only stay with me for five days, she was okay taking a regular flight back home. Of course, I bumped her up to first class, which she said wasn't necessary.

We have a lot of things scheduled while she's here with me. I'm meeting briefly with my agent while she goes to a studio in LA where Tillie is doing a special weekend with her community. Stella was happy to hear that Tillie was also in town, and she would be able to see her. Then, I have big plans to introduce her to Mattie and the guys. She doesn't know that yet, but I know Stella won't think anything special about it, which is going to be epic.

We land at a small private airport, and after unloading, see the private car I hired for the drive back to my place. "Welcome to LA," the driver says to us as he opens the door.

"Thank you," Stella replies, getting in the car with Blue.

"Straight home, Mr. Turner?" he asks.

"Yes. Thank you."

We drive through LA toward my home in the hills. Stella occasionally glances out the window, but otherwise, she's content to hold my hand with Blue in her lap.

"Jax, how are feeling being back in LA? Are you doing okay or are you having any negative feelings?" she asks with concern, her nervous hand still petting the puppy.

I glance over at her and see the worry in her eyes. "Baby, I'm good. I'm here with you. I honestly don't think I'll feel anything until you head back home Sunday and alone. Right now, I'm happy you're here with me. I get to show you my life in LA. The good, the bad, and where I call home. I'm very excited about having you here in my bed. I may not wash the sheets after you leave."

"Aw, I can sleep in one of your shirts, and then when I go you can wear it and smell me. Would that help," she says with a twinkle in her eye.

"Yes, I think you should do that for me. You wouldn't want me to be here all alone and completely miserable."

"You are ridiculous. At least you have Blue to love you."

"I know, but you adore me."

"That I do, babe."

***

After arriving at my home, we take Blue outside to do his business, unpack all his toys and bed that we shipped here, and finally crawl onto the couch and snuggle.

Stella says, "Your home is beautiful, but I'm going to like the other one better. You put more of your personal touch in the one at home."

"I did. I wanted it to be mine, with things that I picked out, things you would like. I was serious when I said I hoped one day you would call it home, too," I tell her.

"One step at a time, okay. Let's navigate this separation and we can come back to that later. Okay?"

"Baby, no rush. If you aren't telling me no, I can wait. We do have some timing to work through, but we will. I have no doubt we can figure it out together. I know it's not late, but with travel and time differences, you up for dinner and then bed?"

"That sounds perfect. I'm wiped out from doing nothing today, but I guess I was anxious about flying with Blue and seeing where you called home. It's nice, though. Impressive, Mr. Hollywood."

"Stop. It's a nice place, but it isn't warm and cozy like your place or the rental. I hope my new house will have that cozy vibe."

"I promise I'll make it warm and cozy for you. Never fear, babe. What's for dinner?"

"Go out or order in?"

"Please order in. I don't want to share you quite yet."

"What do you feel like?"

"Whatever gets here in under an hour. Anything. I'm going to go shower. You make the call, then come find me in the shower."

"That sounds like a great idea. You know where to go. Meet you there shortly." She stands, and I smack her butt.

"Hey, Mister."

"Dibs on washing your body."

She heads upstairs to the master suite mumbling about me being ridiculous, and it puts a big smile on my face.

***

Later, we lay in bed wrapped up around each other and talked about the next few days.

"Tomorrow, I'm going in to see my team," I say. "I haven't seen them in person since the accident. They said they wanted eyes on me and not over a screen. We're going to go over the contract for the films and talk schedule. Looks like I'm stuck here for at least four weeks. If I can make it home sometimes, I will."

"It'll be okay, Jax. This is just a temporary absence, and most likely, the first of many. Let's just take it as it comes. If we continue to communicate and be available to each other when we can, things will work out. I'm willing to put the time and effort in for you."

"Yeah, you are?" I turn her into me and kiss her. "I'm willing to put time and anything else to have you in my arms and my bed. Stella, I love having you here in my bed. In my place, surrounded by my things. When I come back to Lake Harmony, my house should be furnished, and I can move out of the rental. Move in with me, babe."

She turns her eyes to mine and whispers, "Jax." Her eyes study me.

"When we CAN be together, I want you with me in my bed at night. Blue wants you with us too. Don't make a cute puppy sad."

"Blue will be sad? I think his daddy is the sad puppy here. I have been in your bed for weeks buddy."

"That's where you need to be. Just think about it. You have time before I get back. I won't pressure you, but it would be easier for you to move in with me instead of packing a bag every couple of days."

"You're serious?" she asks.

I want to roll my eyes but instead squeeze her tight, "Very Serious. As serious as a wizard who lost his wand."

Stella snorts, "Ridiculous. I promise to think about it."

"That's all I ask. Thanks, babe. Now that we have you moving in with me settled, when do you go meet Tillie?"

"Tomorrow afternoon. I'm meeting her at the retreat she's part of. It's not far from here. Do you have a car I can use?"

"Babe, I'll call a car service for you. I don't want you to deal with LA traffic. That way you have the car all day."

"Okay, thank you. I appreciate that."

"Would you be up for me taking you to dinner tomorrow night?"

"I can be back in time to get ready."

"I'm not worried about that…what I'm asking is if you are sure you want to handle the public and the paps."

"Honey, this is part of your world. If I have you in my life, I have to be ready to accept everything that comes with you. I can manage it fine."

"Okay, baby. Then I'll take you out to one of my favorite places. If it's too much, we leave. Once we get inside, they won't bother us. Usually, someone leaks they see me somewhere, and by the time I leave, it's all cameras and flashes."

"Stop worrying. Let's show LA that Jax Turner, America's Hottie is back and healed and out on the town with a mystery woman."

The smile on my face is busting my cheeks.

Chapter Forty-Two

Stella

Tillie told me to come prepared to do some workshops and healing sessions, so I'm wearing my typical yoga attire with a kimono type of shift over it. My hair is down, and my bag is hanging over my shoulder with the gifts I brought her from the personal products I make. Jax came through with a car service that got me here while I enjoyed my peppermint tea in the car. He even took Blue with him today to the meeting with his management team, so he wouldn't be home alone. That man and his dog. He said if anyone harassed him, he would say Blue is his emotional support dog. He is ridiculous, but he is my Mr. Ridiculous, and I know I'm the lucky one.

As I make my way into the retreat and the front desk, my senses already pick up the incense thick in the air and the quiet. My energy and mood immediately shift and move me into a natural state of calm.

"Hello, may I help you?" the retreat person asks.

"Yes, I'm here to see my friend, Tillie. She's a sound healer participating in the retreat."

"Oh, yes. You must be Stella Stone. Welcome to our retreat center. We're delighted to have you here. Tillie asked that we bring you up to her room when you arrive. Can I get you anything to drink?"

"No, thank you. I had tea on my ride here," I tell her.

"Then, please follow me."

I walk alongside the woman bringing me to Tillie. She stops and knocks on a door, and a moment later, my wonderful mentor opens the door with a smile. "Stella! You're here." She pulls me into a big hug.

"Enjoy your visit, ladies," the retreat person says, then turns to leave us to ourselves.

"Tillie, it's so wonderful to see you again," I say and give her a big hug.

"Come in, come in." I follow Tillie into her pretty space, and we sit down on her couch. "You look lovely."

"I'm here to do yoga or whatever you need me to do."

"That's not exactly what I said. YOU look lovely. Happy. Glowing. In love?" Tillie asks.

"Wow, Tillie! Do you have a magic mirror," I giggle.

"Alright, sweetheart, how have you been? I see you're here in LA with Jax. Things are going well with him then?"

"Things are amazing. Is it awful to wait for the other shoe to drop? He's amazing. A great communicator, and he understands me. He sees me Tillie and appreciates what and who I am. But will it be enough for him?"

"Are you asking because of who he is, or because of who you are, honey?" she asks me.

"I think I'm asking because he has LA and all that comes with being someone from Hollywood. I have my studio, my belief system, and how I live my life. How do I compete with all of Hollywood and the stars and bling that come with it?"

Tillie takes my hand into hers, "Oh darling, has it ever occurred to you that you are exactly what Jax needs in his life?"

"How? How can I be enough?"

"You and who you are bring both calm and energy into his life. He needs you in his life to bring him balance. He has been living the LA lifestyle for a long time. He said he wanted more, but couldn't find it here. Being home healing all these months, maybe he found what he's been missing in you?"

"He asked me to move in with him," I say with a nervous exhale.

Tillie sits back, and pats my hand, "Did he now? Interesting. Did you give him an answer?"

"No. I told him I would think about it."

"Alright. So, he's back in LA for work and he wants to show you this side of his life."

"Yes, he wants to take me out tonight and warned me we may be dealing with fans or paparazzi. I told him I would be fine."

"And you will be dear because he will make sure of it. Stella, I would never advise you wrong. Listen to your heart and settle your mind. Get your balance today during sessions. You're here as my guest. Do whatever workshops you find amusing. I have a sound session at the end of the day. It may be a good end to your visit. We can have a cup of tea afterward while you wait for your car. How does that sound?"

"Sounds perfect. I'm so glad I'm here with you today."

***

I'm completely relaxed and feel like I can charge ahead with whatever chaos this dinner out in LA brings. I got home before Jax and was able to check in with Griffin and Sophie on the ride home. My studio is fine, and Sophie told me to go out and have fun. Show those stupid paps that my man is healed, hot, and showing me off.

I'm almost ready to get dressed, and as I am applying lotion to my legs, Jax and Blue come into the room. Dog beats man, and I reach down to love on the puppy. Jax comes up behind me and wraps his arms around me.

"Hey, baby, how was your visit with Tillie?"

I turn in his arms and wrap mine around his waist, "It was a nice day, and I am very relaxed. How was your day with your team?"

"It turned into a session of playing with Blue. Everyone is in love with him, and we spent a little bit of time going over contracts and next steps. It was good. I'm definitely here through the end of the month, which sucks since you're leaving Sunday, but I made it clear that I would ask them to limit my availability with the studio until I need to be on set. They listened but wanted to make sure it didn't come across as me needing more time to heal. My PR person was happy to hear that we're going out tonight and will probably be seen. Will you be okay with pictures that will

239

most likely pop up on social media? We don't have to tell them who you are, but they usually find a way to figure it out."

"Honey, I'm ready to go show you off. Let's go have a nice dinner, enjoy our time out in LA, and if we get attention, then we go with the flow."

"Wow, is this how retreats always leave you? If so, I may want to participate too."

"Tillie says hello, and she can't wait to meet you."

"Aw, that makes me feel good. So, she approves of me with you?"

"Yes, she does. She thinks I'm good for you."

"That you are, baby. I need to jump in the shower. How much longer do you need?"

"I just need to throw on my dress and shoes. Go ahead and take your shower and get ready. I'll feed Blue his dinner and let him out before we leave."

Jax leans in with a deep kiss and a smack on my butt, "I'll hurry."

***

Wow! LA is hopping tonight. We take Jax's new Audi, which he replaced while he was in Lake Harmony, to the swanky restaurant and pull up in front of the valet parking attendant. Jax comes around the car to help me out and a few flashes hit us.

He takes my hand in his, "Come on, babe," and we go inside the restaurant. He leans into me, "Sorry. They must be camped out here tonight to see who arrives."

I look into his eyes, "It's okay. Let's enjoy ourselves."

"It's you. They are out there now, along with all eyes on you in here, wondering who this sexy and beautiful woman is with me tonight."

I grin at him, "I think I like that kind of attention."

He shakes his head, "How did I get so lucky?"

The hostess doesn't have to ask who we are, and we're quickly taken to our table in the back. Jax keeps his hand on my lower back until we slide into our booth.

"Thank you for coming in to enjoy your meal with us this evening. Your server will be right at your table to bring you warm bread and get your drink orders. If there is anything else I can do for you, Mr. Turner, please let me know. My name is Angela, and I am the manager here tonight."

"Thank you, Angela, I appreciate you getting our table tonight. This is a special dinner with someone very special."

"Of course. Please let me know if I can do anything. Here comes your server, Thomas. Enjoy your evening."

"This place is amazing," I say. We are at an LA hotspot that Jax said is one of his favorite places. No wonder they knew who he was. The atmosphere is lovely. We are in a whimsical Western Mediterranean-style restaurant but with major LA vibes. Dark, rich colors are throughout on the seating and walls, creating a romantic feel with a lot of real plants to bring in a touch of nature. The smells coming from the kitchen have my mouth drooling.

"Good evening, my name is Thomas. May I get you started with a cocktail?"

"Hello, Thomas, do you have any that you recommend? I'm open to trying anything," I say.

"Do you lean toward light or dark liquor?"

"I'm usually a vodka or tequila drinker."

"How do you feel about carrot juice?"

"Love it."

"Then I would suggest the tequila and carrot cocktail made with fresh lime."

"Perfect."

Thomas turns to Jax, "And for you Mr. Turner?"

"Stella, they have unusual drinks, and I'm only going to have one tonight. Do you want me to order something different, and you can try it too?"

"Why, Mr. Turner, are you trying to get me liquored up tonight?"

"Absolutely not. I would prefer you to be awake when we get home. What should I order, babe?"

"May I suggest the Vodka and Basil cocktail made with a touch of sherry and lime juice? It would complement the Tequila Carrot," Thomas says.

"Thank you, Thomas. That sounds delicious."

"Before I leave, let me go over some of our specials tonight."

***

Dinner was delicious. We each ordered something different and shared. A few times at the beginning of the night, I noticed people looking over at us, but by the time I had half my drink down and the conversation with Jax was flowing, I forgot all about being in LA with my personal movie star. The staff and manager made sure that our dinner was not interrupted, and we both appreciated that immensely.

"Stella, before we go, let's talk about our next steps," Jax says. "One, I can ask the valet to bring the car around as close to the back door as possible, and we attempt to sneak away. Two, we leave the way we came in, deal with the paparazzi, have pictures taken, and get in my car and leave. You pick, I can arrange either."

I take his hand in mine on top of the table, "You said that your team was happy we are out and showing the world that you, Jax Turner, are all healed up and back to being a shining star, right?" He nods his head at me. "Then, I will take door number two, which is holding your hand, walking out the front door, looking fabulous, I might add, most likely get our pictures taken, and then get into your car, take you home, let our boy outside to do his business, and then take you to bed and have my way with you."

"You are amazing. Ready?"

I nod, and we leave the restaurant and immediately get bombarded by a group of paparazzi. The flashes are going off and Jax has his arm around me and pulled into his side. The valet is already bringing the car.

"Jax, who is this pretty woman on your arm tonight?"
"Jax, how are your injuries from your accident?"
"Are you healed and ready for your next role?"

242

"How do you feel about Max Thorne taking your roles?"

Finally, after that one, Jax pauses, squeezes me, and faces the paparazzi who asked that question. "As everyone knows I was in a car accident this summer that I did not cause. My car was totaled, and I had some injuries to my leg and arms. I've been hard at work healing and doing whatever the doctors ordered. Max Thorne was able to step into the role I was about to film because he was available, and the studio and other actors didn't waste time or money waiting for me. As you see, I'm out with someone special tonight and healthy. Thank you for your concern, I appreciate it."

With that, the car is delivered and Jax helps me into the seat, kissing me first. More flashbulbs go off before the door closes. He comes around and gets in the car. "You okay, baby?"

"I think you handled that like the star you are. Now get me home and naked."

Chapter Forty-Three

Jax

We wake up to a multitude of text messages and voicemails. "What the hell is going on?" Stella asks all sleepy. "Why are both our phones sounding like drums?"

"Morning, beautiful," I kiss her. "I'm guessing it's everyone telling us they saw our date last night. I'll grab my phone first." I reached over for my phone, and the first message from my PR rep had a link. I open it, "Yep. Nice picture of us outside the restaurant and an article. I'm sure there are more versions of this one, but my team thought it was all very positive. Doesn't look like they named you, other than being a shrouded mystery."

Stella rolls and takes my phone, "Let me see this nonsense." She starts laughing and hands the phone back.

"What? It's not bad," I say. I look at another text, and it's another link, another article. "Oh, here's another one, listen…"

Hollywood Heartthrob Jax Turner Spotted at Swanky LA Hotspot with Mysterious Beauty!

Lights, Camera, Action! Hollywood sensation Jax Turner, known for his charismatic presence on the silver screen, stirred up a buzz in Tinseltown as he was caught dining at a high-profile Los Angeles hotspot last night. The A-list heartthrob seemed to be relishing both the culinary delights and the company of a mysterious woman, setting tongues wagging and cameras flashing.

Clad in a sleek designer suit that accentuated his chiseled physique, Turner oozed star power as he made his way into the upscale restaurant, keeping the paparazzi on their toes. With his trademark grin and those piercing blue eyes, it was hard not to be captivated by the leading man.

The real talk of the town, however, was the stunning companion by Jax's side. Our sources reveal that the mystery woman, whose identity remains shrouded in secrecy, turned heads with her elegance and charm. Dressed in a fashion-forward ensemble, she held her own in the glamorous world of Hollywood.

Jax Turner, recently rumored to be in the running for a highly anticipated blockbuster, appeared to be in the best of health, sending fans into a frenzy as they eagerly anticipate his next big screen appearance. His physique hinted at rigorous training sessions, adding fuel to the speculation that he might be gearing up for an action-packed role.

As the evening unfolded, the duo engaged in animated conversations, occasionally sharing laughter and stolen glances that left onlookers wondering about the nature of their relationship. Are we witnessing the birth of a new Hollywood power couple, or is this simply a platonic rendezvous between two industry insiders? Only time will tell.

In the midst of all the speculation, one thing is clear – Jax Turner is ready for his close-up, and the city of angels can't get enough of its favorite leading man. Stay tuned as we keep our eyes peeled for the next chapter in Jax Turner's star-studded saga!

"Well, they have the most important thing right, and that is my stunning companion stole the night away."

"Silly, but I think it was good for you to handle that the way we did. Do we need to dig out of all these texts and messages, or can you find me some tea first?"

"Come on, baby, let's get you some breakfast and get Blue outside. Then, we can go through our phones together. Maybe we can handle most of it with a group text to the gang? I'm sure most of it comes from them."

"You're probably right. Tea, baby…I need some."

***

We sit around the table in the kitchen laughing and reading through the messages together. My team is very happy with the result, but I've already let them know I won't let it become a habit to use my personal life or Stella to clear any doubts in the media.

"Oh boy, Stella, we have plans for lunch now," I say.

"I didn't think we had any plans today."

"Mattie just sent a text, and he says if he doesn't meet you today, he will be heartbroken and never speak to me again."

"Mattie? One of the boys from the band?" Stella asks.

I laugh and pull her onto my lap. "As much as I want to make you put a name to a face with my friends in Brick Row, the famous band, I love that you still have no clue, so I won't."

"Just don't let me embarrass myself. I know their music, but I guess knowing more than the song and lyrics doesn't matter to me. Just like you're Mr. Hollywood--yeah…don't care."

"Gotcha. So, lunch at Mattie's, where I expect the band, kids, and significant others will be. You cool with that?"

"Yep, what should we bring?"

"He said nothing, but we can take beer and wine."

"Perfect."

***

We arrive at Mattie's, and as expected, all the cars are here. "Yep, looks like everyone is here. Are you still, okay? Not nervous?"

"Why should I be nervous? These are your friends."

I smile. She's awesome. "Let's go."

I barely come around the car to get Stella and Blue when I hear, "There he is! My long-lost brother from another mother. Good God, it's good to see you man. Also, nice that I never have to assist with bathroom trips again."

Mattie gives me a big bear hug. "I missed you, man!"

"Aw Mattie, I missed you too. Good to see you." I pat his back waiting for this lingering hug to come to an end.

He pushes me away abruptly and walks over to Stella with a big smile and his arms out, "Here you are. Miss Stella.

247

Just as beautiful as my man Jax said. Come here little lady and let me give you a big hug.”

Mattie moves in without pause and wraps Stella in his arms. “Nice to meet you.” She says while being smothered.

Mattie continues to hug her, “I don’t know how to thank you for helping my friend. He was so…ugly…and you made him pretty again. Please, whatever he does, do not ever go away. We need you in his life.”

“Okay, buddy…don’t freak out my girlfriend, please.”

Stella’s eyes find mine and hold, and I see her blush. Mattie releases her then sees Blue.

“Oh my sweetness, Jax, you bring Stella, and is this Mr. Blue?” Then he picks Blue up and walks towards the house waving to follow him as we hear him baby talk, *“Aren’t you the prettiest boy? You are going to love meeting my little Lizzy and Mason.”*

I put my arm around Stella, “You, okay? Mattie can be…a lot sometimes.”

“He’s great. Reminds me of Logan, but girlfriend? That’s new. It caught me off guard, I guess.”

I wrap my arms around her, “Ah…so, that’s what gave you the pretty blush. You are my girlfriend. Are you ready to meet the rest of them?”

“Yes, I am. Let’s go enjoy time with your friends. If they are all like Mattie this should be fun.”

“You will fit right in. They aren’t too much different than hanging with everyone at home.”

We head inside and Mattie’s wife meets us at the door. “Jax, I’m so glad to see you up and healthy. Who would have thought the last time we saw each other you would end up in that damn accident. I feel guilty for keeping you here so late that day when I knew you wanted to get home and be off the street before everyone started partying.”

I pull Bonnie into my arms, “Bon, it’s not your fault. It’s the fault of the idiot who came barreling toward me around a curve and lost control. I’m all fixed up.”

She pulls out of my arms and wipes a tear, “Gosh, I’m sorry for being rude. Stella, I’m Bonnie, Mattie’s wife.

Welcome to our home. I watched the debacle of my husband outside. He's missed Jax and was so worried about him while they were in the last month of touring. He's so happy you're both here today. Was that a puppy you brought? You are taking it home with you when you leave right?"

"Oh, he won't leave Blue here. No worries. That's Jax's baby. Where Jax goes, Blue follows. Bonnie, we brought some beer and wine. Can I help you put it away while Jax goes to play with his friends?"

"Oh, I like her. Please keep her, Jax."

"Jesus, you sound just like your husband. Go. Go be women and talk about me. I know you can't help yourself, Bon."

"Come on Stella. Let's go gossip."

I walk toward the back where I'm guessing my dog is along with the rest of the guys. I walk into the room and stop when I hear clapping. "What now?"

Josh stands and heads my way, "We're just happy to see you on both feet without crutches, casts, or bruises and looking sharp."

"You guys are stupid. Knock it off."

"Okay, okay enough of the shit. Where's Stella?" Josh asks.

"Bonnie stole her, and they're in the kitchen getting drinks."

Mattie, still holding Blue and getting a face full of kisses says, "She sure is a looker. She's good for you."

"What's the story," Jeff asks.

"The story is I've known this nerdy geek since we were in elementary school. He was this sports-nerd-theater guy, and I was the hippie little girl laying in the grass watching the clouds make pretty shapes. We both grew up, Jax gets hurt, I could help so I did and well…he isn't the nerdy geek anymore," Stella says, hands me a beer, and sits on my lap.

"Oh yes, I REALLY like her," Bonnie says.

"So, I hear you guys are all in a band together?"

The guys all laugh, their heads back, and Mattie points his finger at Stella, "You darling, are good for the soul. Please keep her."

I wrap my arms around Stella. "She isn't going anywhere. I've asked her to move in with me, but she's still thinking about it."

"He's a lot to handle, you know," she says and winks at the guys. Yeah, I think they have all fallen a little for her, too.

Chapter Forty-Four

Stella

Leaving Jax and Blue this morning broke my heart. I took a car service to the airport because I didn't want to say goodbye to either of them in front of a crowd or make a scene that would most likely become public knowledge. Instead, I made a scene in his driveway, even though I fought with all my strength to leave without breaking up. Jax was torn up just as much as I was, but this isn't forever. It's only for now. He has things to wrap up in LA with his new film, then he'll be back in Lake Harmony for a long time while working on the three films for the trilogy. We can handle this. It's only a few weeks until he's home.

I take my phone from my purse and send Jax a quick text message.

Stella: On the plane and we're about to taxi to the runway. I miss you already.

Jax: Baby, I miss you too. Call me when you land. I will worry until I know you are safe on the ground.

Stella: I will. Go snuggle with Blue and watch something happy on TV

Jax: Mattie is coming over with his family. I called him when you left and he said I sounded ridiculously sad and that was terrible. He's bringing the kids and pizza for lunch. They want to make sure Blue is okay with you leaving and I think he wants to check on me

Stella: He's a good friend. Poor Blue. Is he okay?

Jax: He cried for you and maybe I did a little bit too when I couldn't see you anymore from the drive

Stella: I know *Sad smiley emoji* We can do this. It's not going to be that long we're apart

Jax: Feels like fucking forever

Stella: Don't be so dramatic

Jax: I'm an actor- can't help it. FOR.EV.ER until I have you in my arms
Stella: We are going to take off, I need to get offline. Let you know as soon as I land. Say hi to Mattie and the kids and give Blue some extra love and kisses from me
Jax: Okay baby, talk soon

"Excuse me, would you like a drink before we prepare to close the doors and get in the air," the flight attendant asks me with a smile.

I try to wipe the tears quickly and give her a forced smile, "Is it possible to get a hot tea?"

"Yes, I can make that for you. Straight or with a kick? You look like you may need a little extra."

"I may need an extra kick later, but for now the tea is fine while I collect my thoughts. Thank you."

"You got it," she says with a wink and walks to the galley.

Sometimes I feel like Tillie knows exactly what I need before I need it. She gave me some new crystals, which I pull out of my bag and hold in my hand while I find my sound therapy app for meditation. My tea is delivered quickly with another concerned smile, and I thank the flight attendant again before putting in my earbuds, turning on my app, and leaning back with my eyes closed. I have my crystals in one hand and the warm tea in the other while I focus on the sounds and my breathing. Slowly, the pain around my heart releases, and a calmness begins to wash over me.

***

I step outside of arrivals with my bags and see Rob and Sophie standing by their car. Sophie, in her pregnant disguise, takes off at a run for me and nearly knocks me off my feet as she throws her arms around me. "You're home, and I'm here." She leans back and looks at me concerned, "It's going to be okay. Trust me. I've done this separation, and I know your heart is sad. Let's get you home, okay."

I try to hold in the tears and sadness that is consuming me, and I give her a weak smile back as a tear falls down my cheek, "Okay."

Rob takes my luggage from me, concern on his face knowing my heart is in LA, "Come on, Stella, let's get you home."

Sophie sits in the back with me and puts her arms around me as I let the tears fall. Quietly, she says to me, "He's miserable, too, sweetheart. Mattie took the kids there to keep his mind occupied. He asked us to do the same. Do you want to go home, or do you want to come home with us for a little bit?"

"I'll come home with you guys if that's okay. Otherwise, I'll just sit at home the rest of the day and be miserable. Jax and I are going to Facetime, but not until I go to bed. I need to stay busy until then, or I'll break, Soph."

My brother watches us as best he can from the rearview mirror, "Soph, it will be okay. Come hang out with us for the day, play with Betty, and we'll get you home in time for your call. Do you want to give him a text or call so he knows you are safely on your way to Lake Harmony?"

"Yeah, let me call him really quick." I take my phone from my purse and call him. "Hey, babe."

"Rob and Sophie get you?"

"Yeah, we're in the car heading home. I'm going to hang out with them and Betty for the afternoon. I'll be home in time to call you later. Is Mattie still there?"

"No, they just left, but Blue had a blast playing with the kids. They were working with him on tricks. I think he has *give paw* down now. If not, he's a good con for treats."

That forces a little chuckle, "Aw, he's a good boy. I miss him."

"He misses you too, babe. Before we upset each other again, I'm going to let you go until later. I'm working through the script again. Tomorrow is a read-through with a couple of people who are slotted for the other roles. I want to distract myself with the script until I can see your beautiful face later."

"Sounds good. I'll call when I'm home."

"Great! Say hi to Sophie and Rob for me and give Betty some love from me and Blue."

"I will. Well, bye. Talk soon."

"Bye, honey."

I put my phone away and turn to Sophie, "This sucks. How did you leave Rob and go back to LA?"

"Because I went back to LA to sell or pack my shit so that I could hurry back here to be with the man I love."

"Aw, baby. That's so sweet," my brother says from the driver's seat.

"Because it's true honey. I did everything in my power to hurry back here as fast as I could. Now, Stella, this may seem horrible, but it's not forever. He will have the film here, then the other two, so he's going to be here for a while. Plus, things went smoothly at the studio with you stepping away for five days, right?"

"Yeah, my part-timers handled classes perfectly, and Griff was there in case of any emergencies. It went well."

"So, you know if you need to travel in the future that it's possible. Jax has the means to travel to you if needed. There's Facetime, texting, and *sexting*," she whispers, and we hear Rob groan so obviously he heard her.

This brings a real smile to my face, and I squeeze my friend. "Thank you. We've been together for the last couple of weeks, so this is just a new norm for now. You're right, it's temporary. I just need to keep myself busy, and if I'm sad I can reach out to him or to any of the people in my life to keep me busy."

"Exactly. Plus, while you were in LA, our house was finished, and starting tomorrow, I get to pack. If you ever need a distraction, there is always packing to keep you busy."

"Wow, when do you guys plan to move into the new place?"

We're going to have my stuff that is still in storage delivered first. That's happening this week. I figured once we have my things from LA sorted into the new house, then we can move the stuff from our current house in. Griffin has been awesome, and after the amazing work he did helping Jax with his place, Rob and I asked him if he would be willing to help us combine all our stuff and mix it nicely into the new house. He accepted the project, and I feel like I can breathe easier knowing I don't have to do it all myself. Mom, my brother, and my sister are all coming down the following weekend to help with the second move."

"You guys are going to be so busy. If you want me to take Betty out of the chaos during moving days just let me know."

"Oh, that would be perfect. Rob, we didn't even think of poor Betty in this mess."

"Stella, that would be great. I figured I could drop her off at Mom and Dad's, but sometimes she drives poor Molly and Ralphie nuts. Plus, you can snuggle up with her and get some puppy love."

"You got it," I say.

***

I spent the day with Rob and Sophie helping plan the move and just snuggling up with Betty. She's a sweet puppy and calmer than Blue.

After I got home, I walked down to the studio. I still stay closed on Sundays, unless there's a sound session, but nothing was on the calendar for today. The studio is clean, and the products I make are stocked on the shelves. I check the schedule for the next day, so I can prepare for my classes. Feeling settled and confident everything is ready for the new week, I go back upstairs to shower before calling Jax.

When I walk into the apartment, Griffin is in the kitchen, "Hey, Griff. Thanks for watching the studio for me."

"Aw, Stella bug, you know it was no bother. Now come here and give me a big hug because I missed you."

I walk into his arms and get a big squeeze from him, "How're you doing, bestie?" he asks gently.

While still in his hug, I say, "Rob and Sophie kept me very distracted all day. Now, I'm going to shower then call him. I'm doing okay right now, but that could change after we talk."

He leans forward and kisses my forehead, "If you need me afterward, come on in my room and snuggle down. I don't want you to be sad. We will be okay until he gets back."

"Aw, Griff, do you miss him too?"

"Sweetheart, I know that you're in love with him. He's in love with you. By extension of the best friend code, I love him too. So of course, I miss him."

"I'll let him know."

"That's sweet, Stella bug, but I already texted him like three times since you left to go to LA that I'm miserable without him here and that he needs to make LA his extra pad and here home."

"Did he reply to those texts?"

"Of course he replied. I'm his favorite person here outside of you and Sophie."

"We are so lucky we have him, Griff. This is going to suck being apart. Promise to keep me from falling into a gutter of despair?"

"Oh, sweetie, I got you. Don't worry, but if we need some sad time, we can allow ourselves time to be sad. We just limit those times with a lot of distractions. Our shows, ice cream, momma's lemon squares. You know…all the things."

"All the things. Love you, buddy."

"Love you, too. Now go shower and Facetime that hunky man of yours. If you happen to take a screenshot, please feel free to forward it to me."

"Okay." I get another kiss on the forehead before Griffin releases me from his hug then he walks to the couch and grabs the remote for the TV.

"Go!"

Laughing, I head to the shower and prepare for the quickest one possible so I can get to my room and get Jax on the phone.

Chapter Forty-Five

Jax

Thankfully, my week has been packed with meetings for the film. The studio has the main characters cast, and I wasn't aware, but they had some of them cast before me. We're set to begin filming in just over a month. I'm doing everything I can to wrap up my time here in LA, so I can get back home to Stella. Home to Stella. Fuck, I hate being across the damn country from her. Making time for each other has been tough. She starts classes before I'm even awake, and by the time she's home, I'm still dealing with the studio or my team. It's late for her to wait for me sometimes, so the majority of our communication is through text messaging. At least, I have my eyes on her through Griffin and Sophie, and they assure me that she's handling me being away okay so far.

Tonight, I have dinner plans with Charlie and her husband. I wanted to reach out to her and take them both out for a nice meal, but she didn't want to deal with the paparazzi, so they're coming to my house. Charlie wasn't only my nurse; she became my friend in LA. I never got the chance to meet her husband, so I'm looking forward to this.

"Blue, you need to be a good boy tonight. Feel free to be your charming self, because a good friend is coming for dinner."

Blue is sitting in front of me with the stuffed elephant Stella bought him. His big eyes looking at me listening. His head bobs up and he tilts his head. "Aw buddy, I know you miss her. I do too."

The doorbell rings, Blue barks and follows me to the door. The food from a local hot spot that I like has been delivered. It's Italian food, not as good as Bella Roma's, but close. I tip the delivery person and take the food into the kitchen to stay warm.

The doorbell rings again. "Okay Blue. Our company is here. Time to show them what you're made of." I walk to the front door and open it to see my friend and her husband there. "CHARLIE!" I pulled her into a big bear hug. "Oh my god, it's so good to see you!"

She pats my back and laughs, "Jax, it's good to see you, too. Now, let me go, so I can introduce you to my husband."

"Oh shoot, sorry." I let her go and face him, "Sorry to steal your wife, but she has become important to me. I'm Jax."

"It's nice to meet you, Jax. I'm Ray. You're special to Charlie, too. I thought she was going to tear someone's head off with all the gossip floating around about you when you went back home."

"Please, come on in," I say, "and let me get you both a drink."

Charlie squats down by Blue, "Who is this little cutie?"

Puffing my chest out like a proud daddy, I say, "This is Blue. My little boy. Stella got him for me."

"Well, hello, little Blue. You are adorable." Charlie stands and looks at me with her eyebrow raised, "Stella? I think we have some catching up to do, mister."

"You have no idea, Charlie!"

***

After dinner, Charlie, her husband, Ray, and I are sitting in my living room relaxing with a drink. "Jax, I can't tell you how happy I am to see you healthy," Charlie says to me.

"I have you to thank for that."

"Not just me, Jax. You put the work in to get strong and heal. Not all my patients I work with get through the mental aspect of it as fast as you managed. How are you doing here in LA alone? You've had a lot of support around you since the accident."

"Not going to lie. Being here without Stella sucks, Charlie."

Ray asks, "How long have you been together?"

"Ray, it's a funny story really. I've known Stella my whole life. We grew up in the same town, went to the same school, were in the same grade, and if you'd ask her, I was the sporty nerd, and she was the girl with her head in the clouds. We were never in the same friend circles. I reconnected with her a little bit when Sophie, my best friend, fell for her brother earlier this year. Then, being home with my injuries, she felt sorry for me at first and came by. She works with spiritual healing and gave me some tools to help my healing along. We got to know each other better and fell for each other."

"You look happy Jax," Charlie says.

"I'm in love with her, but this distance is rough."

"How long are you in LA?" Ray asks.

"Not completely sure. I've been doing some work here with the studio and my team preparing for a new film series that I got the lead in. I'm hoping that wraps up soon, but I'm probably stuck here for a while yet."

Charlie smiles at me, "Then you'll relocate to home to be with her?"

"Not sure," I say. "I mean this is my home base."

Charlie cocks her head, "Jax, you just told us it isn't easy being apart, what's keeping you here once work is wrapped up? Do you have to stay in LA?"

"Well, no. I mean I can always fly out here if I have to go into the studio," I admit.

"How is the house you're building at home? Is it still under construction?" she asks.

"No, it's done, and we just furnished it and are waiting for the stuff to be delivered."

Charlie grabs my hand, "Honey, what is your heart telling you? Where will you be happiest?"

"With Stella."

"And where is Stella?"

"At home in Lake Harmony with her family and business."

"Then, make Lake Harmony your home base. Be with her. You can keep a place in LA if you're here often enough, but if your heart is there, and that is her home base, what the heck is keeping you here?"

"I don't know…You're right! I need to be with Stella."

"Then, there's your answer. Move home, be with the girl you love. I knew it the minute I saw that picture of you two. She is beautiful Jax. Go home, be happy."

I sigh, "There's a lot I need to do. It's times like this that I wish I had a personal assistant. I don't have time to waste, and I need to get some of this house shipped back home."

Ray and Charlie look at each other and have a silent conversation in front of me. *Huh…what's this all about.* Charlie turns back to me and says, "We may have a solution and someone you can trust."

"Okay…"

Charlie continues, "Our daughter, Shelby. She just lost her job, and she's a maniac when it comes to organization. She's desperate to find something to generate income. Would you like to talk to her and see if she can help you organize whatever you need shipped home?"

"That would be perfect. Are you sure she'd be interested?"

"We could give her a call right now if you want. She ugh…doesn't know we know you, though. You know, patient confidentiality and all that, so she may have a fan girl moment. Don't hold it against her, okay?"

I laugh, "No worries. I just need someone I can trust, and I don't have time to sort through background checks and all that goes along with bringing someone into my home. She'd be okay with signing an NDA, right? I do that with anyone coming into my personal space."

"She has experience with high end clients, so I don't think she'll care. Let's give her a call and see if she can help you out."

Charlie digs her phone out of her purse and makes the call. "Hi, Shelby. I'm sitting here with a friend who needs a personal assistant-type helper to move some of his things from LA to Chicago. I told him that you're organized, are in-between jobs right now, and kind of desperate for work. He's just as desperate to get things handled but too busy with his own work to find someone himself. He's in the LA industry, and you'd have to sign an NDA, but I told him that would be fine. Uh huh…uh huh…Jax Turner. Yes, I am serious. No, I'm not pulling a prank on you. Hold on, Shelby." Charlie says to me, frustrated, "She thinks I'm lying. Are you okay putting this call on speaker?"

"Of course, go ahead." I bite my lip to avoid laughing.

Charlie puts her phone on speaker, "Okay honey, I have you on speaker. Dad and I had dinner here with Jax, and he mentioned he could use the help."

"Hi, Shelby. This is Jax Turner."

"Right. Hi, Jax Turner. Is Sophie Knight also there having dinner with you and my parents?" she asks sarcastically.

"Ah no, Soph is in Lake Harmony with Rob at home. Listen, I know this is weird, but I know your mom because when I got in my accident she came to help me, and she was my awesome nurse. I'm back in LA for meetings with the studio and my team for my next movie project and need to ship some art and personal items to my new place in Lake Harmony. Your parents thought you'd be able to help so I wouldn't have to worry about finding someone I trust. So, what do you think?"

"*Oh, my fucking God. Mom, are you shitting me! This is honest to God Jax Turner?!!*"

"Yep, it's the real Jax Turner, Shelby," Ray says. "Nice mouth, honey."

"*Shit, shit, shit,*" she whispers, then, "Mr. Turner, I'm so sorry. Please ignore the first half of this call. I had no idea Mom worked with you. She isn't allowed to share who her patients are, but this is making a little more sense now. I can help you. I've worked for other *private* people before. I am organized and I can assist with whatever you need. I'm available now because I'm unemployed. Just let me know details, and I'm good to go."

"Thanks, Shelby. I appreciate it a lot. I'll get your number from Charlie, and I'll call you later to set up a time for you to come over here and see what I need done. Does that work?"

"Yes, Mr. Turner. I'll be waiting for your call."

"Oh, and Shelby."

"Yes, Mr. Turner?"

"Please call me Jax. I promise I'm not a stiff jerk. We are almost family considering your mom had to take care of me like an infant," I say with a chuckle.

"You got it, Jax. Mom and Dad, thank you for the referral and maybe next time give a girl a little warning before you put me on the phone with Jax Turner. *Jesus*."

"Thanks, honey. Dad and I will talk to you later. Thanks for helping Jax out."

"Yeppers."

I rub my hands together and laugh, "Who's up for dessert?"

Chapter Forty-Six

Stella

Sophie and I are at the park because I told her that I needed some grounding today, and we decided to do some stretching and meditation outside near the lake. Now, we're just sitting here on our yoga mats staring at the water.

"Hey friend, you're lost in your thoughts again," Sophie says.

"Sorry, I feel better. Thank you for coming out here with me today. I needed to feel connected to the earth. My body wasn't feeling very grounded today when I woke up."

"It's been a week. That may have something to do with it too. Are you sleeping okay at night?"

I turn and sit crossed legged in front of Sophie. "I miss him so damn much, Soph. I hate being apart, and it has only been a week! How will I ever survive him being in LA full time?"

"Has he not decided to make Lake Harmony home?" Sophie asks.

"No, he hasn't said anything. Nothing related to his living situation, and I'm too chicken to ask. Plus, I don't want to put pressure on him. It needs to be his decision to make this home."

"I know he's miserable there without you. He told me he hates sleeping alone. He even allowed Blue to come up on the bed. Which, good luck with that later."

"Yeah, he told me the same. At least he has Blue. I have to resort to Griffin."

We both started laughing. "I love him, but he likes to sleep in next to nothing and the couple times he checks on me, god forbid I'm crying because he'll come in my room and tell me to scoot over and then snuggles in with me."

Sophie and I continue to laugh, "He's nut!"

"Oh yes, he is, but he is a loveable nut. Thank goodness you have him, Stella. He made my stuff from LA look amazing in the new house. He's going to help us merge all our things together to make it look like a home and not a resale shop." Sophie stretches her arms over her head, "Do you feel better now? Grounded?"

"Yes, thank you for meeting me here. I'm going to just enjoy this a little bit longer but go on and head home. I know you have the movers set to come tomorrow. I'll come grab Betty early in the morning and bring you some coffee and treats from Ellen's Bistro."

"Oh, I would love you forever considering our coffee pot is packed! Thanks, Stella. See you in the morning."

"Bye, Soph."

I turn to face the water and get lost in my thoughts again. I close my eyes and try to recapture the ease I had before when I hear someone talking to me.

"Stella, I'm sorry to interrupt but I wanted to check on you."

I open my eyes and see Carter. *Hmm*?

"Carter, I'm okay."

"You have tears on your cheeks. Are you sure?"

"Oh," I reach up with my hands and wipe my wet cheeks. "I guess I didn't realize I was crying. I was trying to find some grounding today. Life's been a bit rough lately."

"You know everything will work out the way it's meant to."

I tilt my head to look at him, really look at him. "I hope you're right. Do you know something that I don't?"

Carter smiles at me, "Maybe. You *see* me don't you."

"All the time Carter," I say with a grin. *Ah, he knows, I know.*

"Thank you for keeping my secret."

"You are good for Lake Harmony. Always helping when things become serious. I appreciate knowing you've always got our back around here. Don't you want to go, though?"

"Stella, there's no place I'd rather be than here. Just remember that sometimes we need to go through the motions to get to where we're meant to be. You'll see. It's all coming together."

"Thank you, Carter."

With that, he turns away and when I look back for him, he is gone.

Chapter Forty-Seven

Jax

"Shelby! You are amazing," I yell as I walk through the house.

"Jesus, Jax! You scared the hell out of me. I didn't hear you get home. I was on the phone arguing with the shipping company that's going to move all your art pieces."

"Is everything okay?" I ask.

"Yes. I found them through an art gallery I worked with before. The gallery people said they're the best around to get your big pieces moved without damage. It's just that they were trying to increase the cost because you own some huge pieces of art!"

"I know. It's my guilty pleasure. I don't care what it's going to cost me if they can get the art to Lake Harmony. What else is up?"

"I packed whatever else you felt needed to go. I still think you should take more of your personal items. When you leave, it should look like a rental, void of personal items. You told me you're not sure if you're keeping this place. So, why do you want to leave those things? Do you want to come back to LA without Stella to do this crap again?" Shelby asks.

"Ah, no. You're right. Let's do another walk through and pull whatever else should go. I'm not sure if I want to sell this place yet, but I do want to leave it to be sold as-is with furniture, just in case. What's left here?"

"You have the kitchen stuff, linens, things in your office, and the popcorn maker and candy in the theater room."

"Hmm, let's donate the linens, pack up the rest except for the candy. I'm going to take that over to Mattie's later for his kids."

"Nothing like the friend that brings mass amounts of candy filled with sugar over to little kids."

"Right," I laugh. "They will love it, and it will get eaten."

"I'll get that handled starting tomorrow. I'm going to head out now. I have plans for dinner with Mom and Dad."

"Say hi to them from me."

"Will do."

"Hey, Shelby. Have you found another job yet?"

"Not yet but helping you has cushioned my bank account for a little longer, so I appreciate you giving me this job."

"You've been amazing, and I haven't had to worry about a thing knowing you had it handled. I had no clue how to get the art shipped home. I may have a lead for you, but I'll know more later."

"That'd be great. Keep me posted."

***

Dinner tonight was at Mattie's with the rest of the guys. They were having a band meeting and then called me to come over and eat with them. It also gave me the opportunity to deliver the candy.

"How's the lovely Stella?" Mattie asks.

"I think she's pretending she's not missing me as much as I fucking miss her. I think she's trying to act like she can handle being apart so I don't feel guilty."

"Ah, so maybe the better question, is how are you?" Jeff asks. He's the only other one in the band that's married.

"Fucking lonely. I even have Blue in bed with me at night. It's almost impossible for me to sleep without having Stella wrapped tight around me. She sleeps like she's climbing me like a tree, and I miss it."

"I get it, man," Jeff continues. "That's why, when it's possible, my wife comes along for the tours. When do you head back?"

"Soon, I hope. The studio timeline has me here for three more damn weeks, but I'm hoping we can make it sooner. We've read the scripts, the cast is in place and solid, now they need to let us be until we're needed on location."

"You said this is a trilogy, that should have you back home for most of next year then, at least," Mattie says.

"I think so, but it won't matter too much."

"No? Why's that?" Josh asks. "Oh shit, I'm losing my wingman for good, aren't I?"

I sit back and smile, "Yeah guys, looks like my heart is calling me home."

"No shit? The beautiful Stella has your heart in her hands," Mattie says. "BONNIE," he yells, "Baby?"

Bonnie comes into the room, "What's up, honey?"

"Jax is moving home. You called it."

Bonnie turns to look at me, "I love her for you."

"I love her for me too."

"Aww," Bonnie's eyes fill. "Promise to come visit us."

"I promise to see you every time I'm in LA, even if these losers are nowhere to be found. There's also enough room in my new house for you to come visit me. Bring the kids, and we'll go out to the lake. Stella would love to have you at her studio."

Bonnie looks over at Mattie, "Honey, get that on the calendar. Let's hope you can get away as a nobody just like Jax."

"Um…huh?" I ask Bonnie and Mattie.

They laugh at me. "Oh my god, that sounded hilarious," Mattie says. "What my beautiful wife meant was you always tell us you aren't anything special at home and don't get harassed. Now Sophie lives there, and they leave her alone, so I'm hoping I can also be a nobody if we visit and be left alone."

"Worst case, Sophie does disguises."

"Cool. We're in…guys?"

"I think if you all come, we need to stay close to the house, but Soph is my neighbor, and her and Rob have a huge place, too. Then, there's always the love shack."

"THE LOVE SHACK? Can I have that location?" Josh asks.

"Sure, buddy. All yours. Before I go, I wanted to ask you. Are you still looking for someone to handle keeping things organized for the band? If so, I have the perfect person for you."

Chapter Forty-Eight

Stella

It's been two weeks since I left Jax in LA. The girls are worried about me and scheduled a dinner at Julia's. I'm sitting on her porch now surrounded by my sister, her best friends, and Sophie.

"We're just worried about you, that's all Stella," Julia says.

"I know, it's not like we broke up or anything bad. I just miss him. He'll be back in a couple more weeks."

Bree takes a sip of her lemonade, "It's sweet that, after all this time, the two of you found each other. It was meant to be. Neighbors, not seeing each other as anyone special. Growing up and as adults finding true love."

"Bree, are you drafting a book about us?"

"No, but it would make such a lovely book, wouldn't it? Girl next door, the boy next door. OH. Who fell first? Him? You?"

"Yo--Bree, cool it for a second," Hillary says. "Don't get all crazy now. Stella, what's the current situation? I know he has the big house next to Sophie and Rob, and I heard you guys went and bought furniture. Is that in yet?"

"No, it's supposed to be delivered at the end of the month sometime. I haven't heard an update. I'll have to ask Griffin. He's handling all the purchases and delivery for Jax."

"So, when Jax comes back, he's still in the Love Shack?" Hillary asks.

"Well, he still has things there. Right now, he's got it rented out through this month. He's hoping to be in his new house by then. If not, he was going to stay with Sophie or me."

Sophie laughs, "Girlfriend, he has no intention of staying with me and Rob. He said he doesn't want to hear us having sex next door to him."

"Damn, Sophie," Hillary shouts. "He'll be able to hear you from next door? What kind of sexy times are you and my brother-in-law having?"

"Hill, I meant next door bedroom. Jesus, I'm not that loud!"

"Does he muffle your screams? Garrett does that with me. He told me otherwise there are times he thinks the neighbors would call the station thinking I'm dying."

"And…time to change the subject. As much as I'm happy you and Garrett AND you and Rob found each other, I don't want to discuss my siblings having sex," Julia says and looks at Hillary, "We've talked about this Hill."

Hillary rolls her eyes at Julia, "Girl, who is it you came to for pointers on spicing up your sex life?" She points at Bree and herself, "Yeah, us."

"Let's get back on track here. Stella, so Jax comes back here and moves into his new house, and you continue to stay there with him," Julia asks. "I mean it's pretty much understood you two became inseparable the last couple months."

"He asked me to move in with him."

Silence. Eyes are bouncing around the table at me, at each other. Sophie's eyes get as small as slits because her smile exploded and caused her cheeks to go up. "Seriously!"

Julia calmly asks, "So you are moving in together?"

"Oh, are you going to shack up together for good?" Hillary adds doing a little shimmy dance.

"I love this love story. You two are so perfect for each other," Bree says to me and squeezes my shoulder.

"I told him I needed to think about it."

Hillary puts her hands on her hips, "And have you?"

I nod, "Kind of. It depends. I want to say yes. I hate being apart, and it will be bad enough when he's on set doing films when I can't have him close, so I decided that, yes, I think I'm going to move in with him."

Sophie is holding me and bouncing up and down, "I am so happy. We are going to be neighbors! He must be so excited."

"I haven't told him yet."

"Why the hell not?" Hillary yells.

"Because I was waiting to see if he decides to call Lake Harmony home first. I can't move in with him if LA is still his home base. That would be dumb. Why should I give up my apartment and living with Griff if Jax decides that he needs to stay in LA? I'd be all alone in his big house without him. That doesn't make sense."

Julia comes around now and hugs me. She pulls away and looks at me, "Stella, that is a good decision, and I admire you for making it. I know it wasn't easy, but I agree. He needs to figure out if this is home or not first. I'm here for you no matter what, okay sweetheart? We all are. Do you love him?"

"With all of my heart," I answer, and the tears fill my eyes.

"I think he loves you too." She wipes away my tears. "Sometimes, men need to see what they've lost or could lose to get that fire burning under their ass. I think he's making some decisions while he is out there in LA. Stay patient, see what happens, but you have a lot of us that are here for you."

"Thank you, Jules. I just miss him so much."

"I know, Stellie. I know."

Chapter Forty-Nine

Jax

It's been a long day with everyone doing another table read for the film. The screenwriter, director, producers, department heads, cast, crew, and any other members involved all gathered to hear the script read aloud. It gave us the opportunity to fine tune the storyline, sharpen some of the dialogue, and take key notes before shooting begins. It's exhausting, but we established that this is the last week we need to be in LA. Then, we have another week or two before we need to head towards our filming location in Chicago. They are building a police station and offices inside an old building to create an authentic vibe for the film.

All I want to do is shower, see Blue, and check in with Stella. This is the third week we've been apart, and I hate it. When I walk into my house, Shelby's still moving about the kitchen. "Hey, Shelby."

"Hey, looks like you've had a long day. I took care of Blue today while I was here and left him roaming. I figured there really wasn't much left he could get into since the shipment went out yesterday."

I stand in my living room looking around, "It looks empty in here. Worse than before."

"It's not like you had a lot of personal items staggered about but yeah, now it has zero personality. Good thing you won't be calling this home much longer. Did you get an update on the timeline today?"

"Yeah, finally! We should be wrapped up here in LA by Friday. Then, I'm taking Blue and going home."

"I'm sure you are ready to get back. The shipment should arrive Saturday in Lake Harmony. Will you be back for that, or do you have someone handling it?"

"I'm going to call a buddy. I'm hoping that I'll be home for it, but I have a house full of furniture being delivered Friday and he's already handling that for me. He won't mind helping with the art. He's probably going to be the one helping hang it anyway. Did you hear from Mattie and the guys yet?"

Shelby is standing in front of me a little nervous, fiddling with her hands clutched in front of her. "I did, and Jax I want to thank you. I've been looking for something new, and Mattie gave me some idea of what the band needs help with. I'm going to meet with all of them later in the week. He wanted to give me time to bring some ideas to the meeting."

"Shelby, you've been a great help to me, and I think you'll fit in well with them. They're a cool group of guys and totally down to earth. They don't want to deal with handling the schedules and all that goes with tours and studio times. They want to focus on the music and time with their family and friends."

"I'm excited to meet them, and I think I have some ideas that will be beneficial. Bonnie called me and said it would be a group dinner, then they'd have a meeting just the band and I."

"Bonnie is great, and one of my closest friends. You can handle this. I know you will be a great addition to the band."

Shelby blushes, "Thanks, Jax. I'm going to go. There is nothing left here to pack or put away except for your clothes and personal items. You'll kind of be living out of a suitcase this week. I left Blue's toys and bed because I want him to feel comfortable while he's still here."

"Thank you so much, Shelby. I have one more ask of you. I know the organization and shipping stuff is done, but are you free to hang with Blue this week? I can't take him to the studio this week. Too many people, too much going on. I'm cool with you being here or taking him with you during the day. Whatever you can manage."

"Sure. I can plan on being here during the day with him, so he doesn't get lonely. Maybe we can go to the park and walk around. I'm going to my Mom's for lunch this week, but I can take him with me. Does that work?"

"That'd be awesome. Thanks."

I raced through a shower and settled to relax on the couch before I called Stella. She should be home and getting ready for bed.

Jax: Hey baby, I'm home and ready for our call. Give me a heads-up when you have time to talk
Stella: Going to shower and put cream on-give me 5?
Jax: Shower and then Facetime. I'll watch you cream up *Winking emoji*
Stella: *laughing * winking emoji*

My phone rings with a Facetime message from Stella. "Hey, baby, I miss you," I say.

"Hi. I miss you, too. How was your day at the table read?"

"Crazy busy. We had a good day though. A lot of bodies in the room listening to the read-through. Changes were made, but they work better. I still have meetings with the designers for my wardrobe and all of that. I think I'm going to get some cool tattoos for this role."

"Oh gosh, that's funny. I didn't even think about all of that."

"Yeah, and they're thinking about me having a trimmed beard. How do you feel about a bearded man?"

"Hmm…could feel nice," Stella says.

"Ah, I see you go straight to what I want to do with my potential scruff."

"What else is happening? Are you happy with everyone they cast for this one? Is the vibe good?"

"I am. The actress that's going to be my partner is perfect. You know Felicity Marshall, right?"

"Oh…she's that beautiful black actress that had the mohawk in that one movie, right?"

"Yep, she's the one. We have awesome chemistry, and the producer saw us at lunch just talking about whatever and laughing, so now he wants to bring that mood into our partnership. That we understand each other and can kinda finish each other's sentences. He wants to showcase that we've moved up the ranks together and have a long-established friendship, lots of trust."

"Sounds to me like things are coming together perfectly."

"Yeah, but not sure how much longer I'm stuck here. I want to come back to Lake Harmony. I miss you," I say.

"Jax, it will go fast. I miss you, too, but we knew you'd be out there for a couple of weeks, and we can do this. Now, how's Blue?"

"He's great. Since I need to be at the studio most of the week, Shelby, who's been helping me organize things a little around here, is going to take care of him so he isn't alone. It's been so great having her around to help me, and I think I found her a job with the band. The guys have been wanting to bring someone on to handle the schedules and logistics, and she's smart."

"I'm so happy Charlie suggested her. You helped Shelby, she helped you, and now you helped find her a steady job that could be super cool. You are a good man, Jax Turner."

"You are a beautiful, smart, sexy woman, Stella Stone, and I miss having you in my arms."

Stella moves to the bed and crawls in, "I'm sorry I'm so tired tonight. I had a lot of classes today, and I'm just running around so much. Griffin said your furniture is scheduled to arrive at your new house on Friday. He and Sophie will be there to direct the movers, so the pieces end up in the right rooms. I'm sorry I can't be there, but my part-timers are both off for personal days. I have to run the studio and the classes. I already have Mom coming in to handle the front of the studio."

"Baby, you worry about your studio. Sophie and Griffin can manage the furniture. Sophie said her move was done. She and Rob just need to unpack some things and organize a little more. I can't believe we're going to be neighbors. I'm really looking forward to it."

I watch Stella hesitate and bite her lip, "It will be nice for both of you when you're in Lake Harmony."

I want to tell her I'm moving back full time, but I want to tell her in person. I'm going to push her now to gauge her reaction. "Have you thought any more about moving in with me?"

Stella exhales big, "Babe, I'm not sure I want to make that decision yet. I don't want to leave Griff hanging. Let's just see how things go while you're here working on the movie."

"Will you at least stay with me? I need you in my arms at night, Stell. Being away from you sucks."

"I know, baby, but it's only a little while longer." She yawns big and burrows down more in her bed.

"Stell, you look tired. Why don't I let you go to sleep. Dream about me, okay? Pretend I'm there, and you're wrapped around me tight. I miss you, baby."

"Miss you too. Night, babe."

Our call ends. I have one more thing to do today and that's touch base with Griffin.

Jax: Hey man, how's it going

Griffin: Good, you coming home soon? We miss you *kisses emoji*

Jax: Actually...yes but DO NOT TELL ANYONE

Jax: I need a favor, Griff.

Griffin: What can I do for you, sweetie????

Jax: Furniture delivery is on Friday still?

Griffin: Yes, Sophie is helping me guide things to their rightful place in your monstrosity of a home

Jax: Thank you! You're the best

Griffin: Yes, we know. What's the new favor???

Jax: I'll be home Friday night fingers crossed. The rest of my things from LA are en route to Lake Harmony. STELLA DOES NOT KNOW. Can you help with that delivery too? Should be Saturday. I'll hopefully be home, but I could use your help with placement.

Griffin: I'm all yours. Do you want me to sleep over on Friday so we can get you unpacked and ready for Stella Bug on Saturday?

Jax: That's the favor, yes. I need the kitchen, bath, and master functioning as soon as possible. Pick a spare room and get yourself situated too. No clue yet what time I'll get in with Blue, but I'm going to ask Stella to go to the house and check things when she's done working Saturday.

Griffin: She is GOING TO DIE. She misses you like crazy

Jax: The feeling is mutual. Thanks, Griff. I owe you!

Griffin: Cash, Check, or AmEx for the day is fine *winking emoji*

Jax: 10-4 *thumbs up emoji*

Chapter Fifty

Stella

Jax sent a crazy text earlier freaking out about the house and the furniture. Something about it isn't right, and he wants my opinion on how it looks now that it's in the house. I think he's exhausted from being in LA and working, and hasn't been taking enough time to rest. He's still healing, even though he argues with me that he's back to normal.

Griffin dropped a key off to the studio for me at the end of my day, so that I'd be able to get into Jax's house. I don't know why he's so nervous, but Griffin said he wasn't accepting anyone's word for it except mine, so here I am, on the way over there with house key and gate remote.

The gate opens allowing me to drive up the curvy road that goes left to Jax and right to Sophie. Sophie and Jax both designed the gated entrance so the houses are obstructed from the road. It's beautiful back here on the bluff. They each have a big chunk of acreage and a view overlooking the lake and Flynn Island. Jax's home is a modern contemporary style with a lot of windows and sharp lines throughout in natural tones. Rob and Sophie's house is a huge modern craftsman with covered porches, lots of molding and built-ins throughout.

I pull up to the house and park wondering why Griffin left all the damn lights on in the house. The electricity he's wasting right now is driving me crazy. I better get in there and walk through and start turning shit off. I walk to the front door and let myself in. The alarm isn't even set, *Griffin*! Jax has all his furniture here now so the alarm should definitely be on when he isn't home. I'm going to kill my best friend.

I start walking through the house and I smell food. Why is that smell so strong? Did he just eat before coming to drop off the key to me? I walk into the kitchen and, again, see that all the lights are on and the oven is on low. *What the hell?* I look, and there is still food in the over under foil.

Seriously, what is going on? I grab my phone, and as I'm texting Griffin to ask him what the hell, I hear puppy barks. I look up to see if Sophie is here with Betty, and instead, Blue comes barreling around the corner at me followed by a smirking Jax!

"What are you doing here?"

"I live here."

Frustrated I say, "I know that, Jax. But why aren't you in LA still?"

"I missed you too much, so I came home." He picks up Blue who is upset I am ignoring him. "Baby, aren't you going to give me a kiss?" He moves to me, and Blue gets his licks in before Jax puts him down and pulls me into his chest. "I didn't tell you I was coming home because I didn't want to get your hopes up just in case there were any delays."

"Do you need to go back to LA?"

"Not right now, no. I'm home. Where I need to be with you, baby."

"For how long?" I ask.

"Forever."

"What…what do you mean?"

"I'm done with LA. I'm moving home. Want to go take a walk around the house? I think you may notice a few things." He pulls me with him, and we go into the big family room, where I see his big modern landscape that used to hang in his LA house in the living room.

"How the heck did you get that here in one piece? It takes up the entire wall."

"I hired Shelby to get all my art and whatever was left in LA, and she shipped it here. Griffin was here all night and all day helping me get things together. What do you think?"

"Wait, Griff knew you were coming home?"

"Yeah, but only Griff. I wanted to surprise you."

"Well, you accomplished that. You sent everything here?"

He pulls me into his arms and kisses me softly, "Honey. I am home for good. Nothing is left in LA except furniture. I'm probably going to sell my place there. I can always get a smaller place or rent something if I need to stay there a while. There's always Mattie or one of the guys, too. I do not need a huge home in LA when I'm going to live here in Lake Harmony with you."

"You've decided." *I can't believe it. He decided to come home. Now I can share my decision.*

"Yes, I am home. This is it. You are it."

"Then I better keep this key," I say.

His smile grows big across his handsome face. "Yeah?"

I put my hand on his cheek, "Yeah. I wanted to tell you yes since you asked me, but I wasn't going to uproot myself on a temporary basis. If you were going to make the decision to be here full-time other than when you're filming, then I was going to say yes to moving in with you. I had to wait until you were sure, babe."

"I understand. Are you sure? Will Griff be okay living above the studio alone?"

"He already told me not to worry about it. When I was in LA, and I had Sara's friend working to help cover my classes, she said she was looking for a place. She moved here and is staying with her mom but wants to find a place soon. He asked if I would be okay with her taking my room over if I moved in with you. So, you see, you've been the holdout."

"I'm just happy that we both made the better decision, and you're moving in here. How about tomorrow?"

I laugh out loud, "We can start tomorrow, that's fine."

"Stella, I love you." He puts both his hands on my face. "You are my missing link, baby. I'm so happy that I finally opened my eyes and found you."

"I love you too, Jax. Now how about we turn off the oven, and you show me our bedroom."

Epilogue

Stella

Two Months Later

Jax and I are having an early dinner at Cooper's Corner since he didn't have to be in Chicago on the set today for Windy City Shadows, his current movie project. We're enjoying Coop's wings and fries with a pitcher of cold beer.

"You may need to keep the beard, baby. It's growing on me and--I like the texture of your soft beard on me."

"Baby, let me get through food before you get me all turned on again. We're only dressed and here right now because we needed food and to see outside our bedroom."

"I'm enjoying having you home today. You've been having crazy long days on set. I'm allowed to enjoy my man and his skills when he's home."

He stretches his arms out to both sides, "I'm all yours. Do with me whatever your heart desires."

Cooper comes over with another small plate, "Hey. How's the movie going? It must be keeping you busy because I haven't seen you guys in here lately."

Jax takes a sip of his beer, "I'm usually on set for twelve hours, and when I'm not filming, I'm looking over other scenes or dealing with some changes. I'm lucky to be off today."

"Yeah, people don't understand the work that goes into what you do. I'd have enough trouble just remembering all the lines."

"Coop," I look at him cautiously. He looks so tired, "How are you doing friend? You've had some crazy changes over the last couple of months. I'm here if you ever need some help."

Coop drags his hand down his face and through his hair, "I'm dealing. It's a lot. Honestly, I never thought I'd be in this situation. It wasn't on my to-do list you know. But Mel, well, Mel had other plans for me. Now with the help of practically everyone in this town, I'm surviving and figuring out how to deal with this new life. I'm okay though. We both are. It's just A LOT of changes and emotions we're both dealing with."

Jax looks at Cooper, "You're a good man, Coop. If there is anything you need just let us know."

"Thank you, guys. I just need some extra help around here. My focus now needs to be more on home and my priorities there. It will all work out, but I need to come up with a plan, because I can't keep asking for help all the time."

"Coop," I say. "You have always been there for all of us. Let us return the favor now, okay?"

"Stella, I wasn't raised to depend on people. For a long time, Mel and Garrett were about the only ones that I knew had my back. Like I said, I'm slowly getting my feet under me again. I'll figure it out. Well, wave the bat signal if you need anything else. I need to get back over to the bar. My regular bartender hasn't started his shift yet."

"Take care, Coop," I say as he walks away.

Jax looks at me with concern, "He looks beat."

"Yeah, everyone is worried about him, but he'll be okay."

***

Cooper

I get back to the bar, and while I'm wiping down the countertop, I see a woman at the bar alone. She seems exhausted, scanning the surroundings nervously, and it looks like she's wiping tears from her face. I casually walk over, "Hey, welcome to Cooper's Corner. Can I get you a menu or a drink?" She looks embarrassed but gives me a gentle smile.

"How are the burgers here?"

"I think they're amazing, and the onion rings are the best around town."

"That sounds delicious. I'll order both, and can I just have some ice water, please."

"Coming right up." I walk over to the kiosk to order her food and try to keep a careful eye on her. Something feels off. I'm not sure what it is, but I sense she's in trouble. Jesus, I don't have room in my life to take on other people's problems. I pour a big glass of water for her and take it over.

"Here you go. Are you new to town or just visiting?"

Hesitating a moment, she puts her hair behind her ear. She's stunning. Long auburn hair, freckles across her nose and cheeks, and brown eyes that are hidden by big glasses. She reminds me a little of a Katie Holmes type, the girl next door. Slim but fit, but after being closer to her she's obviously very tired and nervous.

"I'm just sort of passing through. My sister knows a guy who lives here through her husband. They were stationed together at one time. She thought it would be fun for me to stop and say hello."

"Who is it that lives here that you're looking for?" I asked her trying to see if it was me.

"His name is Garrett Stone."

"Who was he was stationed with? We did some serving together. Maybe I know him."

She looks even more nervous at this point, if that's possible. "My brother-in-law is Simon Gallagher."

"Hmm, the name doesn't ring a bell for me, but I was all over the place during my time in the service."

"Oh, that's nice. Um, is there a place in town to stay that isn't too expensive? I didn't really plan very well."

"Hmm…let me think about it for a minute. If you'll give me a second, I need to pour some drinks for a table, and I'll come right back. Your burger should be up soon."

"Okay, thank you."

I walk around the corner a bit to get out of her view and grab my phone. Something is off. I need to get Garrett over here.

Cooper: Hey man, a young woman is in here asking for you. Looks scared and nervous. Related to Simon Gallagher who served with you?
Garrett: Keep her there. On my way.
Cooper: See you soon.

Dear Reader,

Thank you for reading Stella and Jax's story-**Healing Forces**.
Want more of this hilarious group of friends? The series continues with Cooper and Calli's story **Rescued Hearts**, the sixth book in The Lake Harmony Series.

Not ready to leave Stella and Jax yet? To get an exclusive BONUS scene use the QR code!

If you want to start at the beginning and fall in love with Lake Harmony and all its characters read Julia and Jackson's story-
Five Dates.

Binge the rest of the series Free in Kindle Unlimited!

The Lake Harmony Series:
Five Dates (Julia & Jackson)
Sexy Secrets (Bree & Noah)
Covert Entanglements (Hillary & Garrett)
Star Obsessions (Rob & Sophie)

About the Author

Tanja Waltrip was born and raised in the 'burbs of Chicago and now resides in sunny Florida. Despite the tumultuous nature of chasing the sun, one thing has remained the same—her voracious reading habit. She always knew that she would one day turn this passion for the Contemporary Romance genre into her own writing pursuit.

Please sign up for my NEWSLETTER to receive news about upcoming releases and giveaways.

I love to interact with my readers, whether it's a plotline critique or a desire to see one of my characters live in infamy, so please don't hesitate to send me a message.
Tanjawaltrip.com

Book Links and other content:

www.ingramcontent.com/pod-product-compliance
Lightning Source LLC
Chambersburg PA
CBHW071454140726
47997CB00005B/1720